AMERICAN BITCH

a novel

Raúl Casso

Cover art by Alex Casso

© 2015 Raúl Casso

All Rights Reserved.

No part of this publication may be reproduced, stored in a retrieval system, or transmitted, in any form or by any means, electronic, mechanical, photocopying, recording, or otherwise, without the written permission of the author.

First published by Dog Ear Publishing
4011 Vincennes Rd
Indianapolis, IN 46268
www.dogearpublishing.net

dog ear
PUBLISHING

ISBN: 978-1-4575-3713-4

This book is printed on acid-free paper.

This book is a work of fiction. Places, events, and situations in this book are purely fictional and any resemblance to actual persons, living or dead, is coincidental.

Printed in the United States of America

Dedication

To my boys—
Raúl, Alexander, Andreas, Philip Gabriel,
and Sebastian

CHAPTER ONE
THE DISAPPEARANCE OF SADIE

Sadie disappeared on a Friday in mid-December. Lasting the better part of that afternoon, the entire evening, and stretching into the wee hours of Saturday morning, her disappearance might not have been such a big deal had she only left word as to where she was going and that she might be coming home a bit late. But she hadn't. So instead of casually shrugging the matter off, Jethro shouldered a foreboding that crept up in weight as the night wore on. There was something ugly about this little disappearing act of hers—rather like a small discomfort that nags just enough to have it looked at by a doctor, only for it to be diagnosed as something really serious; something malignant.

Though worried and annoyed, Jethro wasn't too surprised. For the last couple of years, Sadie's attitude had undergone a steady deterioration. And for the past several months, her behavior had become increasingly erratic, her moods unpredictable, the battles hotter. During the entire preceding summer, she'd been given to outbursts of anger, temper tantrums, and demonstrations of willfulness that kept Jethro on constant edge, wondering where it was all leading to. As the summer months took their turn, she seized on any excuse, however flimsy, to blow up, accuse Jethro of wrongdoing, and blame him for her mounting misery.

To Jethro, Sadie's antics did not seem contrived: her anger was genuine, indeed. But he wondered whether she was hormonally imbalanced, or maybe was struggling with the early onset of menopause, or was otherwise unwell. He could not figure out what was driving her mood swings. Regardless, he had grown weary of the spousal abuse she foisted onto him on a growing basis. How much would he have to tolerate? And now this, this disappearing act. How was he to deal with that?

Jethro tried to keep matters in perspective. Maybe this little disappearance was innocent. *You're freaking out; it's no big deal; calm down*, he kept telling himself. Yet, as he fretted away the time that night, pacing the floor and rechecking the clock, an unsolicited thought crossed his mind: the image of Lee Harvey Oswald on the second floor of the Texas Schoolbook Depository, only a scant minute after putting the Manlicher-Carcano to awful use on the sixth floor, having just run down the stairs, now standing innocently by the soda pop machine in the lunchroom on the second floor, holding a full bottle of Coca-Cola he had hastily bought instead of his habitual Dr. Pepper. Oswald never drank Coke, witnesses would later say; he always—invariably—drank Dr. Pepper. The miserly Oswald, in his hurried rush, in a simple, distracted moment, had pressed the wrong button, nothing more; a tiny mistake, but so out of character it betrayed a larger, untold ugliness lurking behind, awaiting discovery.

The bottom of Jethro's stomach dropped. This behavior was, like that bottle of Coke, out of character for Sadie. Over the course of their eleven year- marriage, and in spite of the quarreling, certain customs had evolved between them; customs that defined a code of conduct according to which they behaved towards each other in predictable ways. Perhaps, Jethro considered, such "marital customs" and predictable ways were what stifled the spark that kept a relationship, their relationship, alive and had caused Sadie to search elsewhere for excitement. Maybe that's where she had gone. Everyone loves to party; maybe she was just partying somewhere, that's all.

He kept repeating this to himself like a mantra, but it wasn't working. On top of verbal violence, she had now added AWOL. Matters would someday have to come to a head. And Jethro knew how it would go if matters did not change. He shuddered at the thought of divorce. The mere prospect scared the daylights out of him. He could not go there at this point, even just to think about it. There were still too many uncertainties; too many unresolved issues. He would have to wait and see how things developed.

His ire grew as the hours marched on. And so did his brooding. What was marriage if not a custom? Wasn't marriage a bundle of rights and obligations that each owed the other? Jethro stared out the window. No cars appeared in the darkness. *Maybe,* Jethro thought, *formal marriage, essential for comfortable life though it may be, is incompatible with romantic love.* On the other hand, marital customs provide at least a blanket of security, if not a sense of home. For many couples, such customs are all that is left of the love they once had, or rather, are what their love has become. *It is this customary way of life that more often than not binds two people together,* thought Jethro. *Custom may be stronger than love.*

"But apparently not strong enough to hold Sadie," he muttered. Nonetheless, he had come to rely on certain behavioral expectations, as did Sadie. And neither Jethro nor Sadie went about unaccounted for — not for any period of time. Jethro called Sadie repeatedly, but her cell-phone was mysteriously turned off — something else she had never done before that night.

Wherever she was, he knew she was safe. Had she been hurt, in trouble, or in an accident, the police would have already contacted him. Besides, whenever she went out, it was always to certain parts of the city, those most affluent, and therefore well patrolled by the local constabulary. But this departure from the norm was different. There was something willful and sinister about it; Jethro could feel it in his bones. Sadie's departure from expected behavior represented the proverbial bolt from the fence.

Earlier that week, on Sunday or Monday, Jethro and Sadie had fought in the style they had arrived at over the course of the preceding months. It was a style of fighting championed by Sadie, and one to which Jethro had not adapted, in spite of the rigorous training Sadie had put him through. The rows, increasingly common, always started in the same way, with Sadie accusing Jethro of some offense, sometimes adultery, followed by her demanding, vehemently, that he prove his innocence.

By the summer before her little disappearing act, Sadie's accusations had become unmitigated attacks and a constant feature on her weekly agenda. It would be a long time before Jethro would recognize any "formula" to Sadie's behavior, and then only after much exposure to her practice. In the meantime, he was kept busy negotiating with the ticking time bomb that his marriage was fast becoming. Often Jethro wondered why they were even together in the first place.

CHAPTER TWO

A BRIGHT SUNRISE AND A GATHERING STORM

Their star-crossed relationship had started with innocent chit-chat on a warm summer day, eleven years before. They had met at a health food restaurant in a large mid-western city where Jethro studied law and she worked as a fitness consultant. It was lunchtime, and they sat by happenstance at adjoining tables.

"Excuse me, is that the burrito supreme you're having?" asked Jethro, who was hungry for any excuse to talk to her, for she represented her gender well and had caught his eye. Of English extraction, although from California as Jethro was later to learn, Sadie had grey eyes and soft chestnut hair that glowed, and fell to just below her shoulders. She held her head high, atop a long, slender neck that rested on firm, not-too-broad shoulders that were themselves graced by a most delicate clavicle. Her skin was fair, and her prominent cheekbones added charming lines to either side of her face whenever she smiled. And smile she did often, for she was, generally, of cheerful disposition. About 26 years of age, she was physically fit, lean and trim, and beaming in robust health—a condition that only added to her gaiety and lightness of spirit. Although not classic in her beauty, she had a striking look all her own that turned the head of all but the blind.

"Yes, in fact, it is. What are you having?" returned a sunny Sadie.

Jethro could tell, as she looked at him, that she too was pleased with the looks of the dark stranger sitting at the table next to hers. Jethro, who was close to 29, appeared taller than he was, for he had excellent posture and he carried himself with pride. To Jethro applied the old adage that before one could be a fine gentleman, one had to first be a good animal. And what a good animal he was! Broad shouldered and solidly built, his entire body radiated health and vigor. His chest was thick and muscular, and his hands were large, with prominent veins like those of a sculptor, or perhaps a concert pianist. With hair that was dark, thick, and wavy, and complexion Latin, he dressed well to play his part of a handsome ladies' man.

"I'm having the veggie burger," he offered back. "Have you tried one? They're really good; do you come here often...?"

"All the time," she answered. "I love staying fit, and health food is part of my program! My name is Sadie, what's yours?"

Jethro introduced himself, and then added, "Sadie, that's a nice name. I don't think I've ever met a Sadie before."

"I doubt you have," she said with pride. "My parents were going to name me 'Sarah' because it means princess, and my daddy treats me like one. But they thought 'Sarah' was too common; so they named me 'Sadie,' which is more exotic."

"I see." Jethro heard none of this because he was mesmerized by her beauty.

"Yes," she continued unabated. " 'Sadie's a beautiful version of 'Sarah.' It's classy and classic, and it still means 'princess.' "

Jethro nodded as though his head were controlled by a puppeteer.

"Sadie is nice. It sounds kinda hip," he responded after snapping out of his hormonal intoxication long enough to realize that it was his turn to talk.

"Yes, that's what I say," gushed Sadie. "In fact, my parents lived in a commune when they had me."

"You don't say?" Jethro remarked, enthralled.

So much small talk was the start of it. Then an exchange of telephone numbers, the first date to be followed by more, lots of laughs, philosophical talk of the sort that flows best with wine, the first kiss, and, inevitably as such matters progress, the seal of the deal. There was no stopping them after that—they went at it with wild abandon. That they didn't suffer an accidental pregnancy was remarkable. *Certainly this must be love*, thought Jethro. *It is love, and she's the most beautiful girl in all the land.* He convinced himself of this, and he resolved not to ever let her go.

"Let's get married," he proposed one lazy afternoon in late summer as they lay in bed.

"I don't know, Jethro," she replied guardedly. "This is all happening so fast, and marriage frightens me."

"It's been happening fast because we are meant for each other, Sadie," Jethro advocated. "We belong together."

"I'm not..."

"And it's been fun," he pressed. "*Admit it.*"

"Yes, it has been fun, and thrilling, and I don't want it to ever stop," she conceded."But we're so *different*."

"How are we different?"

"Well..."

"Oh, you mean our differences in culture?" offered Jethro.

"Well, yeah. I mean, we do come from different worlds," she explained. "I'm from California, and of English extraction." She said this as she reclined against the headboard, her hands stroking her hair which fell to one side of her neck, her eyes soft and dreamy. "And...well," she continued haltingly, "your family came...well...from...*Mmmexico.*" At her mentioning the nation of Jethro's ancestry, her voice assumed a hushed intonation reserved for the utterance of profanity in polite company.

7

She drew slightly away from Jethro and her soft look hardened up just a bit, as though she had awakened from her reverie of merry England to the harsh realities of Old Mexico.

"Yes, but we love each other and so we're the same," he boldly retorted.

"Yes..."

"And our love will overcome any differences."

"I guess you're right," she conceded rather haltingly as she turned her face away from Jethro and at the wall facing the bed.

Her eyes glazed over as their focus shifted to somewhere far away, and then with a pleasant smile she again fixed her gaze on Jethro asking, "And what shall we do for a ring?"

Jethro took her question as an acceptance, and his heart leaped with joy.

"I already have one picked out," he announced.

"Oh, do you really?" Sadie squealed with excitement. "How *big* is it?"

"I haven't decided. Either two carats with a flaw, or one carat that's almost perfect. Which would you rather have, quantity or quality?"

Sadie bolted upright. "Unless the flaw is big enough for everyone to see it, I'd rather have the bigger diamond." She declared.

Jethro raised an eyebrow. "But don't you care about perfection?"

"I care what people think."

"So why not get a ring with a huge cubic zirconium?" he asked with a grin.

"What's that?"

"It's a man-made stone that looks just like a diamond," Jethro explained. "In fact, to tell them apart, they need to be weighed. We can get a huge cubic zirconium and no one will know the difference. Everyone will think it's a real diamond."

"Why don't we do that?" Sadie was really happy now. "That's what we'll do!"

Jethro sank back into the pillow and gazed up at the ceiling. "Ah, I don't think it's a good idea, Sadie," he advised. "People would wonder how we paid for it. Really big, flawless diamonds can cost a million. And we don't have that kind of money—*not yet*" He looked at her steadily as he stated this. "We're really just starting out, you know."

"Well then, I want the big diamond," pouted Sadie.

"Okay, I'll get you the big one."

"That's what my daddy would have done!" Sadie beamed with joy.

Jethro's persuasive manner was not limited to the right choice of words at the right moment. His actions spoke volumes about what he was willing to do to make Sadie happy. Any suggestion of any wish she had, he devoted himself doggedly to meeting. Anything she wanted that was within his reach he set himself out to provide. Her comfort was his comfort; her wish was his command.

With the arrival of their first autumn together came the flu season and Sadie fell victim to the infirmity. Jethro rarely left her bedside while she convalesced, and usually just stayed in it with her. It was only his strong constitution, along with a steady diet of vitamin D tablets that kept his body from sharing in her malady. The doctor prescribed antibiotics, and Jethro dashed off to the pharmacy to have the order filled but not before rubbing mentholatum on Sadie's chest, tucking her warmly in bed, and placing a cup of hot herb tea on the bed stand beside her.

The dosage of antibiotics was halved by doctor's orders, and Jethro, in order to spare Sadie of any labor no matter how small, emptied the bottle onto a platter and, while sitting by her bedside, took each pill one by one and cut them all in half so she wouldn't have to bother—just as her daddy would have done.

It was this type of doting that won Sadie over, and they were wed as soon as she recovered fully from the flu.

They married hurriedly over the course of a weekend and took up residence in a small apartment where Jethro had landed a law job—in the raucous Texas-Mexican border town of Laredo. Jethro knew the place well, having spent his childhood there.

Although Jethro was anxious about how Sadie would take to Laredo—a rough border town whose natural beauty lay hidden under a coarse exterior, he had confidence that she would handle the situation well, and simply took this for granted. He would continue to dote on her and provide for her every need, and he thought her to be of strong character, with plenty of energy to overcome the challenges of life on the border. He also knew that, given her fair complexion and striking good looks, she would stand out among the local populace—as would he for being the other half of the most dashing newlyweds in town. She would be welcomed and well received, he knew, and such a reception would serve to make her introduction to Laredo a most pleasant ride with a soft landing.

"We make the most handsome couple," he'd tell her often.

And what a handsome couple they made. Their physical beauty worked like a prestigious calling card, and they were greeted with open arms in all circles without their having so much as to open their mouths and say anything. Anywhere they went, they were greeted as Laredo's finest; Laredo's beautiful people. And they wore it well, dressing as they did in understated clothes of high quality. Broad shouldered and imperially slim, no one could fill a suit like Jethro, and, Sadie, in her simple skirts and dresses, wearing little jewelry and less makeup, sparkled in understated elegance and good taste. Only fancy breeding could lend her such grace, and only the flowing lines of her physically fit figure could awaken her simple style to such a brave vibration. It was not long before they were required guests at the most fashionable parties, where they enjoyed increasing popularity: Jethro as the up and coming lawyer who was gaining in reputation for solid courtroom work, and Sadie, for her cheerfulness of character and her radiant disposition. There was no question, in Jethro's mind, that with her at his side, his chances for success as a lawyer were much enhanced. And in this he was not mistaken.

As quickly as they rose in social prominence, so increased Jethro's success as a lawyer. His client base grew and they prospered. Two years did not pass before they acquired their first home—a quaint villa by the country club, overlooking the golf course. On warm weather evenings, Jethro and Sadie often lounged on their lawn furniture by the swimming pool—he nursing a cold beer, and she sipping on a Bloody Mary if not a *Margarita*. On many such evenings, Jethro smiled in self satisfaction, reveling in his success. *Everything is working out just as it should*, he'd congratulate himself. But he knew that the success they enjoyed was a shared venture. He well recognized that Sadie played a vital role in their good fortune, and that he won people's favor because he had Sadie at his side. This he believed without a doubt. It all added up: they were a popular couple, fast becoming prominent, and with their social appeal followed professional retainers. Jethro, reclining lazily on the garden lounge chair, eyed Sadie as she relaxed on hers. *She's my little good luck charm*, he'd reflect, *I have the responsibility, but she has the allure. Without her, I wouldn't be halfway where I am now.* Jethro swore he'd never let her go.

Their success as a couple did not stop on the social scene for Sadie took to homemaking with remarkable zeal. Working within their means, which were hampered financially to some degree due to the relative newness of Jethro's practice, Sadie nevertheless managed to decorate the interior of their home with much grace and finesse. To adorn the rooms and furnishings, she personally (if one overlooked her many telephone conferences with her mother) selected the drapery, wall paper, carpeting and all other accoutrements with an eye so keen on choice of colorings (and Sadie's eye and her mother's blended well) as to impress every visitor in their home with her talent for interior decoration with not a few asking for any suggestions she might offer for the improvement of the decor of their homes. To such appeals, Jethro lent encouragement by suggesting to Sadie that she might one day make a hobby out of such an endeavor, adding, "You never know where such a thing might lead." Sadie would only smile, affecting an air of modesty, and nodding politely to her friends as the complements flowed. Jethro glowed inwardly knowing how well he had succeeded in choosing a mate. *The sky is open to us*, he assured himself. *The future is ours.*

Indeed, by all indications, Sadie was proving to be the perfect wife. The house was as pretty as a honeycomb, and their social popularity was ever growing as was Jethro's practice. Something else, however, was growing as well: Sadie's stature as a princess—Daddy's, Jethro's, and now, Laredo's. Her domain was the home and social scene, where, increasingly she ruled as would a monarch. Jethro, in the face of her taking charge domestically, let go of the reins little by little, and acceded to her growing demands as queen of the palace. As for the traditional role of a housewife, however, she never bothered: Jethro did the cooking, and the cleaning, and grocery shopping, and, generally, the less glamorous of domestic chores. As her prominence grew, Jethro's shrank. Although still a glittering couple, their roles evolved to reflect the changing character of their personal relationship.

As though becoming increasingly appreciative of her integral role in their mutual success, and in particular, Jethro's as a lawyer, she gradually imposed her will, and claimed the recognition she thought herself to deserve, at first, and then, eventually, the reverence she demanded. At home, while alone, Jethro deferred to her; and, at social events he found himself standing at her side, or slightly behind, increasingly quiet as she came to dominate social intercourse and he assumed a supporting role. He'd calmly take his post, as would a dutiful prince, in dignified pose, confident of his rule in the legal domain, ever attentive to her highness' needs, while she'd go on with her amiable pleasantries. He knew, however, that he needed her: she was the talisman for his success—their life together glowed as no one else's did, and together they'd scale the heights of fame and fortune. Personal sacrifice was part of the price, and Jethro was simply willing to pay it.

The years passed quickly, but not always happily. Gradually, the realities of marriage set in as their union evolved from its passionate early stages where they couldn't be without each other into a much cooler social contract that required them to be together, and which was governed by a code of civility that could sometimes be rather brittle in practice. With the passage of time, they arrived at a stage in their relationship where favoring each other was not what set the tone of their shared existence. Instead, it became, increasingly, the observation of the rights and obligations that flowed from the marriage license. Gone was an open door that kept each on their best behavior while they fell in love. It was locked shut now, to be reopened only by the key of divorce—a key they had never reached for during all the years before the thought of it now, for each had more fortitude of character than would allow for that. Or so they liked to believe. Jethro could fairly say that he and Sadie had enjoyed a majority of happy times in their early years, when their union still glowed with the heated ardor that first brought them together. And once time had mellowed those passions, a mutual understanding and acceptance now reigned, allowing them to coexist in relative peace, albeit with an uneven distribution of domestic chores and duties.

Jethro, while still very much enamored of his spouse, had to use his discipline in order to continue accommodating the demands that her status as princess of the palace required. Often he arrived home tired from work, looking forward to sinking into the easy chair in the study with a cold beer and just relaxing after a long day. Instead, he had to continue working, this time in his evening job as house-husband. He'd get to work with the cooking, for Sadie was lost in the kitchen. Afterwards he'd wash the dishes for she hated doing that and he hated piles of unwashed plates in the sink. But then, after all was said and done, they'd retire to the bedroom for an evening's lovemaking. It was with satisfaction that Jethro would close his eyes to sleep. *I'll always have her* he'd assure himself before drifting off to pleasant dreams while thinking of the house on the hill they'd one day surely have.

They never got around to having children. Although Jethro had wanted to, Sadie always pushed the subject off with one excuse or another: if it wasn't the bikini she wanted to wear at the beach in the summer, it was the ski slopes that would not allow for a fall if she were pregnant. Whatever the reason, she had always to wait until after the upcoming season. And one by one the seasons passed into years and the memories of their early days grew further and further away. Still, they had birthed a life together, and although not as merry as it once was, both enjoyed a sense of home and security. Indeed, Jethro felt, their home and marriage was who they were, and what once had been a roller-coaster ride of passion was now a steady, predictable drive on cruise control — perfect for the long haul, or so Jethro liked to believe.

That was certainly what Jethro had thought up until that mid-December, anyway, and wished it had remained so. But aside from evolution as a royal personage, Sadie had also grown cold and sour, and increasingly estranged, with senseless outbursts of temper like distant claps of thunder, announcing the approach of an epic tempest. As their marriage clocked the years, the road they travelled together grew rockier with Sadie's mood increasingly violent. And, it became clear to Jethro, Sadie had two types of heated outbursts. One was the normal, angry tantrum where she'd scream, bitch, and cuss until she had sufficiently vented. Such displays of weak temper happened often enough. There was another type of fit altogether different, and far more severe in order of magnitude. This second type of angry display, Jethro believed, issued straight from hell and assumed a white-hot intensity so extreme, that when confronted by it, Jethro could only look fixedly at her, with eyes wide open, until thoughts of asylums or exorcisms compelled him to look away. And there was no fighting back on such occasions: she would scream and threaten so violently, spewing out vulgarities like pea soup, that to challenge Sadie while in the throes of such an episode would be to flirt with a potentially lethal danger.

Sadie first demonstrated this category five fit of anger about five years into the marriage, upon her return from a trip to California to visit her family. She seemed fine on the telephone the Saturday before her return, but when she arrived on Sunday, she suddenly burst into a thunderstorm of anger so extreme, with an intensity Jethro had never seen her display before, that he could not respond, but only stare at her in fearful astonishment: her main complaints being that she hated her life, and, moreover, she hated him. Were it not for the extreme intensity to her anger, Jethro would have dismissed the outburst as another dose of mere bitching. Instead, Jethro wondered whether she needed therapy.

That first mega outburst subsided, and things returned to normal. Jethro assumed his work habit, and did not mention the episode again. *I wonder what happened in California*, he would later ask himself as matters progressed. About six months passed before that thing from hell again stopped by for a visit:

the same category-five-fit-of-anger, with a character all its own, something markedly different from even a most spirited marital row. After that episode, the Cat 5 came back in less than six months; and then less than that, until finally, it came home to stay. Woe for Jethro! Gone were the normal fights between husband and wife, replaced now by a demonic beast looking to find its maximum mode of expression. Jethro could only brace himself for the gathering storm which finally burst forward with a furious rain of verbal violence one hot August evening five months before Sadie's December truancy.

By then, Jethro had built up a profitable private practice. He now shared a firm with a handful of lawyers on an upper floor in one of Laredo's only two low-rise buildings. Although he considered his fellow lawyers as "partners" and his firm a firm, Jethro knew that he and his partners were really just a band of confederates sharing overhead. Each lawyer had his own individual practice, with Jethro devoting much of his to toiling away in dingy courtrooms about the region, representing criminal defendants who either hired him for grudging but needed pay, or were put upon him by court appointment for a standard fee which helped, at least, to pay the utility bills. But he had his civil clients as well, and from these Jethro enjoyed respectable fees, allowing Sadie and him to live comfortably as far as dressing well, driving late model European cars, vacationing, and being accepted in fashionable social circles would allow.

In the summer, five months before Sadie's December disappearance, he had been trying a case in the nearby community of Zapata, Texas, about fifty miles south of Laredo. Early each morning Jethro would wake up and commute to the little hamlet that was Zapata. There he would dedicate himself to the direct and cross-examination of witnesses, and to arguing the law and its application. At the close of business in late afternoon or early evening, he'd journey back home, where, after a small dinner, he would hit the books long into the night in preparation for the next day of the continuing trial. This forced schedule lasted for the better part of a month.

Throughout that busy time Sadie maintained an ice-cold regard toward Jethro. She'd walk around the house and avoid looking at him. And, if she had to pass close by him to get to wherever she was going, she would do so with her lips pursed tightly together, as though holding back a mouthful of vinegar, the muscles on the sides of her jaw tightly clenched and showing in bold relief. What offense he had committed to earn such displeasure was unclear to Jethro. Apparently, Sadie had simply grown to hate him. Her icy attitude haunted him, and he frequently cringed in anticipation of yet another dose of Sadie's invective, which was always lurking behind her stony demeanor, ready to emerge suddenly like a monster in a cheap Hollywood movie.

So there was Jethro at the dinner table, studying for the next day's proceedings, when Sadie lobbed her harassing grenade.

"I know what you're up to," she hissed. "You're having an affair in that raunchy little town you're pretending to have a trial in, you bastard!"

Jethro, momentarily stunned into muteness, could offer no immediate response, which seemed to confirm, in Sadie's mind, the accuracy of her accusation.

"I knoooww," she growled. "That's where you have been going every day for the past month, and your 'homework' doesn't fool me; you sit there every night as though you're working, but I know what you are really up to, you fucking bastard!" And then, with all the seriousness of unshakeable belief, she added in a hard, level tone delivered between clenched teeth, "You think I'm stupid; you think I don't know what's going on. I'll tell you what's going on: you have another family over there! That's right, you thought I didn't know. What's the bitch's name, and how many brats has the whore given you?"

Jethro looked twice at her, studying her features for any indication of playacting, but no, she wasn't kidding. She looked like a lunatic, glaring at him with fury-filled eyes while maintaining, amid shouts, a completely preposterous notion.

Flabbergasted by the magnitude of the accusation, Jethro finally offered meekly, "Why don't you come with me tomorrow and watch me try the case I'm in? You can see for yourself what I'm up to."

"Fuck you!" Sadie shrieked. She then withdrew into her bedroom, and the stony silence resumed.

CHAPTER THREE

A WOMAN'S PERFUME

The next day, during a courtroom recess, Jethro called Sadie from the hallway of the courthouse. Sadie had not spoken to him since the tirade the night before, and even though it was only the next day, Jethro was fed up with wondering how long the silent treatment would last.

"Hi, it's me, I'm on break. How are you, what are you up to?"

"How am I supposed to be?" She sounded as though wounded, but before the conversation could progress any further, a chattering throng of people passed along the hallway where Jethro was standing.

"Who is that," Sadie yelled, her voice crescendoing in rage. "Who is there with you, huh? Is that your other fucking wife? It's her, isn't it, you bastard!"

"No, no, wait, Sa—"Jethro protested, but before he could utter another half-word Sadie slammed the phone shut, leaving Jethro standing there in the hallway with the phone still pressed to his ear. *Could she be doing this on purpose?* Jethro wondered, *or is she delusional?* Although she had refused his invitation to watch the trial, and therefore didn't seem too interested in the truth, she had nevertheless accused him with an anger that would have been more appropriate had she actually caught Jethro with another woman in *flagrante delicto*.

Just then, the court's clerk called out into the hallway, "The judge wants to see all the lawyers in chambers…". Peering over towards Jethro, who had not moved with the phone still to his ear, she barked, "That means you too, Jethro, let's go; the Judge doesn't like to be kept waiting."

Much later that evening, Jethro drove home from another long day. The judge had grown decidedly grumpy, and became impatient and testy in his dealings with the lawyers. To add to the oppressive atmosphere, and the judge's displeasure, the many lawyers just wouldn't shut up. And to think that he, Jethro, had been one of them.

Jethro felt spent. Relaxing with a cold beer would be nice, he thought, as he turned onto his street, but he was apprehensive as to how he would be received so he didn't set his hopes too high on a comfortable *brewski* in the armchair. *But surely Sadie won't carry this matter any further, ridiculous as it is*, he thought.

He entered the house with caution and went straight to the bedroom walk-in closet. He removed his coat, and as he was working it onto a hanger, Sadie appeared at the entrance of the closet and stood there looking at him as though she were in a trance. *Her mood appears stable enough*, reflected Jethro, though noting that her face was strangely lacking in expression, as though she were about to do something deliberate.

Jethro moved toward her to give her a proper greeting, and she smiled pleasantly at him, but as he came close, the expression on her face instantly changed as if she had put on a theatrical mask. Her eyes darkened and, drawing away from him in a seeming state of alarm, in a shrill voice she accused Jethro of smelling like another women's perfume. Her face, turning a bright red, twisted as her eyes turned wild, with thick veins now bulging at her slender neck. Only her failing to froth at the mouth kept Jethro from considering seriously whether he was witnessing an acute case of rabies.

"Who—was—with—you?" she yelled. "Who were you with?"

"I...I...I—-" stammered Jethro.

"You fucking bastard, I can smell her perfume, so don't you lie to me, you piece of shit, *pendejo*, bastard!"

"I...I haven't been with anyone. What are you talking about? Why—-"

"I knew it all aloooooong, you fucking baaastaaaard!"

Thus Sadie tumbled headlong into an all-out emotional meltdown, while Jethro remained so baffled he could not effectively respond to her accusations, much less fight back. Pathetically, his personal defense consisted of his standing there like a spectator, wide-eyed with his mouth half open as the fireworks raged on, slowly shaking his head in stunned disbelief.

CHAPTER FOUR

MARITAL PATTERNS

Eventually, Jethro discerned a pattern to Sadie's behavior during the summer and into the fall—a cyclical pattern that traveled from weekday to weekend.

Mondays were always observed in silence, as Jethro and Sadie were not quite reconciled from the increasingly routine weekend disputes. By Tuesday, however, Sadie usually gave Jethro a subdued smile at the dinner table, a gesture Jethro would readily respond to however guardedly. Wednesdays were played out in good spirits, marked by happy, wine-washed suppers. Thursdays were even better, with the ambiance positive enough to allow Jethro to relax into thinking that maybe things might get back to normal. By that autumn, however, a by-then-better-trained Jethro knew the good Thursday mood would not last long.

On Thursdays, Sadie would go out with her friends for a night on the town. Usually on such evenings she'd return rather late, and always with a wide grin and bloodshot eyes. Jethro didn't mind. She always kept her whereabouts known, and at least the mood would be pleasant. Sadie had her fun, and Jethro rested; that was the deal. But on Friday evenings Sadie would invariably turn gloomy, and, as though on cue, she would accuse Jethro of some wrongful behavior, sometimes of having an affair. Other times she would complain about the house, the finances, or life in general. Then, the specter of conflict would resume its ugly presence for the balance of the weekend.

The increasingly predictable Friday-night dispute led to Sadie's Saturday sullenness until she left on prolonged jaunts with her friends. Saturday mornings were reserved for Sadie's workouts. Saturday nights were devoted to "girls' night out." Jethro, meanwhile, came to enjoy his Saturdays alone: he liked to relax, read, drink a few beers, and take a nap. But instead of appreciating Jethro's efforts to make matters easy for her, Sadie grew contemptuous of him. As her designs went unimpeded by a compliant Jethro, her boldness grew. Eventually, even one question from Jethro — one little peep — would result in an immediate outburst from Sadie, compelling Jethro to beseech her with a, "Yes dear, all right, you don't need to get angry."

Sundays became holidays for Sadie by unilateral decree, for she needed "her space." On Sundays, therefore, Sadie would dispatch Jethro to visit his mother so she could have her time alone. And Sadie needed her time alone. That much she made abundantly clear. Without her space she would become miserable, and, by default, so would Jethro.

"Why doesn't Sadie come along with you anymore when you come over for a visit?" Jethro's mother would ask. "I worry about you and her, Jethro. Is everything alright?"

"Everything's fine, mom." Jethro would brush her off. "She's just tired."

It was easy enough for Jethro to avoid issues with his mother. His mother didn't insist on prying. Jethro meanwhile, would grow silent and stare out the window. *All these years I've tried to give her a life that made her happy: I let her shop all she wanted, do whatever she wanted, and if she didn't want to do anything, then do nothing. I did all the cooking, I brought home the paycheck...I let her live on a permanent vacation, and now this...I spoiled her...I enabled her to become a little brat monster. It's all my fault— and her daddy's, too.*

That this pattern occurred every week, true to form, convinced Jethro that her moodiness was a matter of expediency, and that this was no early onset of menopause or some hormonal imbalance setting the humors aflame. No, Jethro realized that the disputes were deliberate. In the throes of it, though, as it was happening, his recognition of the pattern remained latent, and he was kept off balance by his need to maintain peace.

Gradually, with the march of time, Jethro's willingness to combat his wife's behavior reached peak erosion. It became clear to him that no behavior on his part provoked Sadie's outrage, for he studiously avoided any action that could cause problems; nor did he ever deliberately provoke any dispute. But his forbearance served only to embolden Sadie, as would a schoolyard bully be spurred on by the meekness of his carefully selected victim. Jethro assured himself that his docility was due to his concerns for his home, his moral sense of commitment to his marriage, and, last but not least, the success of his practice and the promise of financial prosperity. *Yes, that's what keeps me at bay,* he told himself. Beyond that, though, and for reasons he could barely explain, he felt paralyzed into inaction. As though his emotional engine seized up and froze, he could not move: he could not confront, demand, nor defend. Simply put, he became a regular pushover; the proverbial doormat she trampled on.

And, as if the anguish brought on by his own emasculation were not enough, Jethro punished himself further with self blame by admitting that by treating her like a little princess just like her daddy did, served only to build the chit he was now dealing with, and to reduce him to the low domestic status he was now subjected to. And, it was getting worse, and worse. *It's all my fault; I'm getting what I deserve.*

Yet he could not bring himself to simply break up with the troublesome woman his wife had become, be rid of her, and get on with a peaceful life alone—and he wasn't sure whether that made him a coward. Was he a coward for not standing up to her? Or would he be a coward for not sticking it out when the going got tough? *I'll find out which is which if this keeps going on as it is*, he knew. In the meantime, the question of whether he was a coward for not standing up to her was the question the circumstances put to him. Sadie's increasing willfulness rendered any attempt by him to assert control as an absurd gesture, pathetic in its hollowness, causing Jethro to undergo his own evolution in character. While negotiating the increasingly rocky road Sadie was making him take a tour on, Jethro had shed certain notions along the way like so much useless baggage.

Among the first notion to go was the idea that he was the head of the household, a status naturally conferred upon him by virtue of his being "the man." Following closely behind was the idea that as the man of the house, he had the authority to override the will of a woman, namely, that of Sadie, his lawfully wedded wife. In the reality now upon him, however, he was the head only of the household that existed in his mind, and he had authority to override the will of a woman just as he could override the weather.

Jethro continued staring out the window, brooding. It was a dark night, but he could see where his marriage was going.

CHAPTER FIVE
SADIE'S NEW FRIEND

About six months or so before she disappeared on that Friday night in mid-December, Sadie had begun taking exercise classes at a local fitness club to add variety to her Saturday morning outings. One of them was a spinning class conducted in a room full of stationary bicycles. This class was attended by a group of cyclists who, as part of their fitness regime, went on bike rides out in the country almost every weekend. It was not long before Sadie joined the group for the long-distance rides — excursions that soon became quite happy for Sadie and a source of increased misery for Jethro.

Among the cyclist group's members was a certain groovy photographer. At first Jethro paid little, if any, attention to him. Precipitously, however, the groovy photographer crept into Jethro's awareness as Sadie began speaking of this person with so many cameras, occasionally at first, and then increasingly as a glorious new friend. Gradually, Jethro became jealous of what he noticed to be Sadie's marked enthusiasm over this paragon. He had no indication of anything actually happening between Sadie and the cyclist-photographer, but his instincts warned him nevertheless. Jethro's mind, on the other hand, clamored with reasons to dismiss his growing concern. *You're just projecting your own fears and insecurities onto the situation.*

As sensible as he tried to be, however, Jethro's fears continued to nag at him. And he soon had reasons to be fearful. One day in the middle of October Jethro came home to find Sadie sitting on the bedroom floor, marveling at a digital camera she had just purchased. How suddenly, noticed Jethro, Sadie had developed a keen interest in photography; how fast she had taken to a new hobby. And what a fancy—read expensive—camera she had bought. Jethro went about his business as though he had noticed nothing, but notice he had, and forget he did not. His fear of the implications kept him from asking what the camera was all about; and Sadie offered no unsolicited explanation. She simply sat there with a bemused look on her face, fiddling with the camera's many buttons and dials.

Not long after that, Sadie's behavior toward Jethro took a severe turn: she began demanding that he get out of the house. Such a demand was not altogether new, for she had done so before on a few occasions during a particularly heated argument. These had been but blows of desperation, however, easily deflected, and never productive of any lasting harm. Now, though, not only was she willing to order Jethro out of the house more readily, and more frequently, but there was that added quality to her demeanor—that intensity Jethro had first experienced after her visit to California a couple of summers before. And there was something else. Along with her increasingly shrill demands, Sadie added a new phraseology, the origins of which puzzled Jethro.

A discernable pattern of attack began to emerge. Sadie would start by proclaiming, in glowing terms, how much fun her new group of cycling friends were, how free in spirit, and how, for the first time, she'd found company she really liked. At the start of such talk, Jethro would brace himself for what he knew was coming. After thus laying her basic groundwork, Sadie would proceed with her "trump card." Her glowing reverie about her newfound friends would quickly turn to a scowl as her focus zeroed in on Jethro. She'd start accosting Jethro about how miserable he made her, and then follow up with an announcement that she wanted a separation and wanted Jethro to get out of the house—with that added intensity, of course. It was as though Sadie's new friends — this bicycle club – acted as a support group that empowered her, perhaps. And then there was that new language, ominous comments about how she had found "new strength" in her "fight for freedom" from "the oppression of her role as housewife," with all its attendant chores, resulting in a subjugation of her character. And for this, of course, she blamed Jethro who, she now claimed, had relegated her to that demeaning role "by mere virtue of her gender and the brutal imposition of his."

Jethro recalled that she'd never liked to work, not really, but was nevertheless impressed with the intensity of Sadie's anger and her outcry for freedom. With mounting anxiety he began to question the nature of Sadie's involvement with the groovy photographer. He did not have long to ponder, though, for a new development arose having to do, ostensibly, with Sadie's schooling.

For as long as Jethro and Sadie were married, Sadie had always attended school, taking part-time classes at community colleges. Her academic goals were loosely defined; eventually, she thought to earn a degree in *something*. But mostly her class-taking continued as an ongoing pastime, offering her distraction, amusement, interesting subjects to pursue for as long as a semester lasted, and a standard excuse among many in her arsenal for not wanting to have children. Now, along with her nascent interest in photography, she suddenly became actively involved with the local college by helping to arrange a photo contest that was to be held there, "as part of a school assignment," or so she told Jethro. The contest would culminate in a few months, she added, in a photo exhibition at a public festival in early spring.

Jethro was impressed. He was not aware of her taking any photography class at the local college, or whether the college even offered one. And if it did, he wondered how she could have gotten into one so late in the semester.

"Is your biking buddy also helping arrange this contest?" he just had to ask.

Sadie turned to him in a snap, then betrayed a moment of indecision: to hide or tell all. She decided to tell all in three syllables, "Yes he is," and then came the barb, "We're going to be doing a lot of things together, Jethro, but it's not what you think, I like him. He's my friend and that's that, and his name is Beneford, but I call him Benny."

"Beneford—what kind of a name is that?" asked Jethro. "You mean Benedict, don't you?"

Sadie sneered happily in return.

At the dinner table several evenings later, Sadie added to the picture growing in Jethro's mind about how this Benny was the nicest of gentlemen, and how different he was from anyone she had ever met. With feigned levity, Jethro asked whether that included him, to which she answered—after a dramatic pause, as though the realization had just struck her— "As a matter of fact, yes, it does."

Deflated, Jethro sagged at the table, and then began to smolder.

But Sadie did not notice Jethro's cowed demeanor and went on reflecting aloud about how Benny might be gay, or so she wondered, and about how his favorite color was lavender, and how he danced ballet. Then she asked aloud, rhetorically, "I wonder if he *is* gay?"

A fuming Jethro finally erupted in anger. "Why are you wondering at all about Benedict's sexuality if you're just friends?"

Sadie, quite unperturbed, stated, "I like him and I am going to see him, and if you don't like it, Jethro, too bad." And then she smugly added while turning a dreamy gaze to the table top as though reflecting on something wonderful, "And as I told you, his name is not Benedict; it's Beneford, but I call him Benny." She said this with a smile on her lips—smiling at someone she was looking at in her mind's eye.

Jethro seethed and then, closing his eyes, took three deep breaths through his nostrils exhaling slowly through his mouth in order to restore calm and control. *All right, get a grip*, he tried to reassure himself, *they're just friends. This is a casual thing, that's all, and if seeing some new friends is as bad as it gets, well, that's not so bad.*

Jethro needed to believe this.

CHAPTER SIX

THE DISAPPEARANCE REDUX

On that Friday in mid-December, when Sadie disappeared for those ominous hours, Jethro had gone about an uneventful work day, arriving in no rush at about 9:15 AM to greet his secretary, who waved hello while she was on the telephone. As Jethro took his coat off, he surveyed the pile of files on his desktop: client matters that needed tending. This he would do for the balance of the day, working steadily with good rhythm as he went through the files one by one, accomplishing the myriad tasks attendant to each from simple phone calls to correspondence, some legal research to the drafting of pleadings and demands, and, finally, preparation for contested hearings. Jethro could look back at years of such toil, and it was all a blur. *I could spend the rest of my life like this*, he considered with regret given the mounting domestic upheaval and in spite of lucrative reward, *whether I want to or not*. He stared out the window, over the city and at the horizon. *There must be more to life than this for me.*

For lunch, Jethro enjoyed a small sandwich *al desko;* it was easier like that sometimes, especially on a Friday, when leaving early just to be done with the work week was a goal. On that day, however, Jethro did not leave the office until six-thirty in the evening. From work, he went to the gym for his daily workout, which he often skipped on Fridays. But on that day, Jethro completed his entire schedule and did not get home until about 8 PM.

Sadie was not home when Jethro arrived, but this was not anything out of the ordinary. He uncorked a cold beer and took a generous swig while leaning against the kitchen counter.

The housekeeper, Lupita, walked into the kitchen. She was all dressed up as though she were going out. "Señor, Señora Sadie left the house this afternoon at about four, but she did not say where she was going." Jethro looked at her as though to say, "And…?" Lupita then added, "Señor, you know today is the day I leave for vacations. My sister is waiting for me at nine o'clock, but Señora Sadie hasn't called, so I don't know what to do. I need to speak with her before I leave."

"Yes, Lupita, I know that you leave today, and I know it's getting late. We need to just wait a little while. I am sure that Ms. Sadie will be here soon." Jethro polished off his beer.

As nine o'clock approached Lupita grew increasingly anxious about missing her appointment with her sister.

"Oh, Señor, it seems that something is wrong, Señora Sadie has never failed to be here, especially when she knows I have to go away." She remarked several times.

Jethro remained calm. He was not worried because if anything, Sadie had always been careful about her arrangements with Lupita. If ever there was a dependable practice that Sadie observed assiduously, this was one of them. He therefore had confidence that she would show up soon enough. He uncorked another brew and flopped into his armchair. Besides, earlier that day Sadie had mentioned to Jethro that she had many errands to run all afternoon because after seven-thirty or so, as she put it, "It's over" — meaning that with Lupita gone, so too would the general freedom from household drudge. Jethro took a gulp and thought, *Yeah sure, who's gonna have to take over the chore?* He knew Sadie would hardly bother for the sake of modern principles of domestic politics.

"Don't worry, Lupita, she'll show up at any moment now."

As the evening wore on, however, Jethro finally came around to recognizing how odd the delay was especially with Lupita carrying on with her worries and commenting on the strangeness of it all. Jethro called Sadie on her cell phone throughout the evening – nine – 9:45 – ten - 10:30, and still no answer. By 10:45, Jethro was genuinely concerned. Lupita now showed signs of worry irrespective of any rendezvous with her sister, for she had by then, cancelled her plans to meet her sister that evening, deciding instead to depart for her vacation the following morning. Lupita's worry had stopped being about whether she'd make her travel plans. Rather, the longtime housekeeper now wondered what may have happened to Sadie, who had never been so absent before.

Jethro's anger grew with his mounting fret. *What has gotten into her?* He wondered. At midnight he went off to bed and lay there troubled and uncomfortable until almost two, when he dozed off.

Snapping to consciousness, the telephone awoke Jethro with a start. The clock on the nightstand said 3:50 AM

"Where are you?" demanded Jethro. "Where have you been, why didn't you call?"

"I'm coming home now." With that Sadie hung up, leaving Jethro sitting upright in bed with the phone still to his ear.

What is going on here? Jethro wondered. A suspicion Jethro cared not to name now intruded in his mind. Something was dreadfully wrong.

CHAPTER SEVEN
SADIE THROWS DOWN THE GAUNTLET

Jethro lay on the bed with the lights on. He would pretend to have fallen asleep, he decided. But he wanted to see her eyes. He knew that if Sadie had been with her girlfriends they would have been doing what they invariably did whenever they got together, which was to drink plenty of wine and Margaritas and smoke a little weed. Sadie, who most enjoyed sipping Margaritas and smoking peace pipes with her tribe of rebel spouses, would certainly have bloodshot eyes. Or so Jethro hoped. He didn't stop to consider why her bloodshot eyes were so important to him that night. Another custom he had grown used to, perhaps, and that would assure him that in spite of the upheaval, all was well.

The electric garage door announced her arrival as it clanked its way open, and a moment later Jethro could hear Sadie walking into the house. A glance at the clock told him it was 4:10 AM. A book lay open beside him. He pulled the covers up halfway and closed his eyes as though asleep. Little did he reflect on the pathetic reversal of roles: it was now wife and househusband, and it was he who dutifully stayed home, quietly reading while his wife was out on the town.

Her footsteps, with a deliberate pace, came up the hallway, her high heels clapping loudly on the floor. No tiptoes, no attempt at quiet. The bedroom door burst open, and Sadie boldly strode in. Jethro affected nonchalance, but was immediately struck by the utter lack of humility on her part. Sadie swept into the room as though making a grand entrance into a ballroom. Not about to accept any scolding, her face was hard and stern, her lips tightly pursed. And her eyes were clear. *No redness there; not a good sign,* Jethro noted.

Sadie made for the bathroom, pausing long enough to throw her keys onto the couch by the bed and to glare at Jethro as though he were the one who had disappeared. Without saying a word, she locked the bathroom door behind her. Almost immediately, the spray of the shower splashed in Jethro's ear.

Is she showering to wash away the traces? Jethro flew out of bed, throwing the blankets wide like a matador's *capote*, and, gathering the will to remain calm, knocked softly on the bathroom door.

"What?" she barked.

"I want to come in," answered Jethro in a moderated tone of voice so as to avoid a challenge.

"No," she answered sharply.

"I need to," protested Jethro.

"Oh please, go use the spare bathroom," she replied with insolence.

It was obvious to Jethro that she could not have cared less about his concerns, his feigned need to make water, let alone his anger. So after debating for a moment whether to kick the door in but deciding such action would be ill-advised, he crept back into bed like a dog with its tail between its legs. He lay there staring blankly at the ceiling for what seemed a long while, impatient as he was for an accounting.

Thoughts swirled around in his head. "Goddamn, what a bitch!" he muttered. "I oughta just slap the shit out of her." On second thought, however, he knew that that wouldn't work. *But just what should I do?* He kept asking himself. *Hell, I don't even know what she did...*

Eventually, Sadie emerged from the sanctuary of her toilet. Jethro could hold his outrage no longer. "Where were you?" he demanded. "I was worried about you."

"I was out, and it's none of your business where I was."

The gloves were off. No statement of hers could have been more precise, more deliberate, more provocative.

Jethro sat up in bed, not knowing quite how to respond to the challenge. How could he put this rebellion down? He didn't have long to think, however, because she continued her assault.

"I want you to get out," she yelled. "Go sleep on the couch in the living room. I want you out of here. Get out! It's over between us!"

Her face turned crimson. Thick veins bulged about her neck as she stood at the edge of the bed, her eyes wide and wild, her mouth gaping as she poured out her invective like so much vomit. *She looks insane*, thought Jethro, as on she went.

"What's the matter with you?" he demanded.

"It's over between us; I want nothing to do with you!" she yelled.

"Why didn't you call, Sadie?" insisted Jethro as if he had not heard her. "Who were you with?"

This was all Jethro could manage to get out before she screamed, "No one, anyone, nobody, anybody!"

"Were you with a guy?"

"No!"

"Then where were you?"

"None of your business; now get out!"

"Hey, hold on just a minute," pleaded Jethro. "I was worried."

"Well I'm here now," came her sarcastic reply. "So stop your worrying, okay? I'm safe and sound. Now leave me alone, I mean it. Get the fuck out – *now*!"

Jethro withstood the verbal pummeling, but didn't budge. After Sadie's spleen had fully vented, the couple retired for what remained of the night. Jethro had to pretend he was asleep. Filled with anxiety, he just lay there, gazing at the ceiling once Sadie began to softly snore. He had to consciously resist grabbing her and shaking her until she lost her senses or else told him where she had been. *She must have done something; something is wrong.* Jethro's inward dialogue kept repeating this until at last he fell into a troubled sleep.

CHAPTER 8

CANCELLED PLANS

It was Sadie's custom, especially on a Saturday, to rise bright and early, usually by seven, regardless of how late she had turned in. The next morning, however, she stayed in bed until almost eleven. *She must be cowering*, thought an emboldened Jethro. *She's stalling for time. She knows the trouble she's in and the confrontation she's gonna get when she "wakes up."* Jethro found it difficult to wait. Lupita didn't wait, though. Dispensing with her need to talk to Sadie before leaving for her holiday, the housekeeper had fled in haste so as to avoid the domestic fireworks that were sure to follow.

Jethro was anxious for some resolution he hoped would spell closure. A primal fear gnawed him into compulsion. While Sadie continued with her beauty sleep, he went into the bathroom in search of evidence.

Half wanting to remain in blissful ignorance, he checked her clothes for telltale traces of love. Her intimate apparel, thankfully, were clueless. Then Jethro encountered another sign that brought him comfort: there, at the bottom of the toilet, lay a soiled tampon. Jethro sighed with relief. With so much on her mind last night, Sadie must have forgotten to flush. *Lucky for me*, he considered, because that ugly object resting underwater at the bottom of the toilet quieted his fears. *She's PMSing, so no sex.* He felt some consolation. But why was she still in bed? Did she have a moral hangover?

When Sadie finally arose, Jethro tried to talk to her, but she simply went about her business and ignored him.

It was supposed to have been a normal Saturday. There were certain plans that Jethro and Sadie had agreed to earlier in the week. Jethro had arranged to go out to the country with some friends for a bit of barbeque and beer. He had even placed an order for assorted cuts of meat with a local butcher. With the developments of the night before, however, Jethro wasn't going anywhere.

Sadie had planned to travel to San Antonio that afternoon. About 150 miles north of Laredo, San Antonio was ten times the size of Laredo, and had lots of nice stores and fancy restaurants. Sadie had wanted to do some holiday shopping.

Midday rolled around. Jethro was in the study, seated in the armchair and gazing out the window into outer space, when Sadie appeared and broke his brooding by snapping, "When are you leaving for your barbeque?"

Jethro looked at her questioningly and responded with calmness. "I don't know." She did an about face and retreated to her room.

About ten minutes passed. Sadie emerged and demanded of Jethro once again, "When are you leaving?"

"I haven't decided; I might leave this afternoon. Why?"

Sadie did not answer.

Perhaps another ten minutes passed when Sadie again emerged from her bedroom and went right up to Jethro, obviously anxious about something. This time, she issued a command. "Jethro, you're gonna have to get going with your plans because I want you to leave the house before I do."

"What do you mean I have to leave the house before you do? Why?"

"Because I want to make sure that the house is securely locked up."

"What are you talking about? I know how to lock up the house, you know that. What's the matter with you?" Jethro stared at her questioningly. "When are you leaving for San Antonio?"

"I don't know; I'm thinking about exercising first."

"Exercise?" Jethro was beside himself. "You never exercise midday; you always exercise in the mornings. And what's this concern about the security of the house? Anyway, there's no need to worry. I may just stay home today." Jethro had shifted tactics just to test her; from his point of view, she made no sense. She wheeled around and stormed back to the bedroom and into the bathroom, where Jethro heard her turn the shower on.

A while later, now just after noon, Jethro went into the bathroom to find Sadie dressed in biking gear, leaning over the sink and into the mirror, carefully putting on makeup. A baffled Jethro, his forehead stitched in perplexity, asked, "Where are you going?"

"I'm going on a long bike ride, and I don't know when I will be back," was her curt reply.

"A long bike ride? I thought you were going to San Antonio. Are you going on this bike ride with a group?"

"No, I'm not." She snapped.

"Who are you going with?" asked Jethro now truly apprehensive of what answer she might give. She then dealt the blow Jethro had feared.

Speaking slowly and deliberately, Sadie said, "I am going on a long bike ride with Benny."

"J-j-just you a-a-and *him*?"

"That's right. Look, it's over between us, Jethro; you might as well face it."

Jethro was too shocked to fight. He felt small and weak against the now emboldened Sadie who was openly and flagrantly violating their almost twelve-year-old marital relationship. Collapsing against the bathroom door frame, he asked meekly, "Why are you doing this?"

And that's when Jethro noticed "The Gesture."

CHAPTER NINE

THE GESTURE

One of Sadie's personal proclivities was to mimic people's gestures, although not just anybody's and not just any gesture. Sadie was not an impressionist or a comedian. Rather, she would mimic the particular mannerisms or demeanor of an especial friend who, at the time that the friendship flourished, had a particularly strong influence on her. Of course, such a friend would be someone whom Sadie liked and admired. In addition, however, and more importantly, it would be someone whom Sadie *followed*. Take, for example, Sadie's friendship with Shirley, a person with whom Sadie had started socializing a few years before.

An heiress to a considerable family fortune, Shirley was thrice divorced, lived in a mansion, and loved to gossip. Indeed, it could be said of Shirley that she was the most accomplished gossipmonger in the border town of Laredo. Generally, Shirley devoted all her thoughts and discourse to the topic of people, but only about those belonging to her select circle of friends, which now included Sadie, and, on the rare occasion's he'd been compelled to go along, a reluctant Jethro as well. Sadie, however, became a regular attendee at Shirley's soirees, which were held in Shirley's plush living room. There Shirley held court, surrounded by more than a few female denizens of Laredo's upper classes, who reclined on plump couches in the style of ancient Rome, drinking red wine or Margaritas, while Shirley directed the topic of conversation from one person as a subject to another. As irony would have it, Shirley might have been the best topic for the rumor mill given her history of failed relationships, including the three formal ones she had left in her wake. She seemed to have trouble getting along with men—venomous as she was, she much preferred the company of her ophidian females.

No one was spared Shirley's vicious slandering, unless, of course, one was present at the party. Nothing would be said of anyone in attendance, and one would not expect it, for that would be far too confrontational. Direct confrontations, after all, are not sport for slander. Rather, proper character assassination requires a stabbing in the back, something at which Shirley was quite expert.

Rumors of a sexual nature were Shirley's specialty. Indeed, Shirley seemed to have been in every prominent person's bedroom at the naked moment, given the impressive number of intimate details she claimed to know about people's lives behind closed doors. She simply loved to share juicy details with her eager listeners, although no one salivated more than her. And she was not homophobic. In her select circle traveled a number of notable gays. Among them was her flamboyant hairdresser, who dabbled in astrology and became her spiritual advisor; her travel agent, who arranged for all her excursions and kept her well informed as to where the "Joneses" were going for their vacation so that she could be sure to go somewhere more exotic and thus secure superior bragging rights; and, of course, there was her interior decorator, who afforded her so much taste and kept her fabulous home in style. Such characters would not, however, be spared Shirley's forked tongue, for she also spread rumors of gay relationships and those of her close friends in particular: rumors replete with steamy details, such as who played the sheep in the homosexual union.

"Gay men play roles, too, you know," she'd go on. "Some are girls and some play the man. Take Carlos, for example, he's a girl. And so's Rene—he's a girl, too."

"I didn't know Rene was gay!" responded one enthusiastic attendee. "And he's a girl? I didn't know. What about Alberto, he's always with him?"

"That's right," continued Shirley while nodding knowingly, "Not only is Rene gay, but he's always the girl in the relationship when they do it. Alberto does both. He likes to be a girl, too, but he's willing to play the part of the man for all the other girls." This last remark producing titters and giggles among the fashionable ladies gathered in Shirley's living room, while she glowed with self-satisfaction.

It was with this Shirley character that Sadie started hanging around. And, by "hang around," nothing casual or sporadic is thereby meant. No weekly luncheon or occasional chat and trip to the movies. This "hanging around," once Sadie put herself to it, consisted of numerous daily phone calls, morning, noon, and night; a steady stream of emails; and multiple daily visits as she'd ferry back and forth from her house to Shirley's. "Hanging around," in this context, meant that Sadie's relationship with the selected friendship came to so dominate her social life as to define it for as long as the friendship lasted. Indeed, Sadie's devotion in such cases was nothing short of sycophantic.

As for gestures, Shirley had a habit of dropping her lower lip and exposing her lower teeth whenever she sought to make a point in conversation. As she spoke, and arrived in her talk at the conclusion of a thought to which she wanted to draw particular emphasis, she'd bare her lower teeth in this manner, and jut them out at the listener. This little mannerism was her personal exclamation mark. And, because Shirley considered almost everything she said to be of considerable importance, she dropped her lower lip and jutted her lower teeth quite often during any discourse, often several times a sentence.

Apparently, Sadie considered Shirley's gesture to be quite effective because, as Sadie went on absorbing this friendship, she took on that little mannerism, too. In practice, this meant that as Jethro would be talking to Sadie on any given evening, he found himself being treated to a perfect imitation of Shirley's peculiar gesture. And, if the talk became testy, Sadie would mimic Shirley's gesture with increasing emphasis — just as Shirley would.

Such adoring friendships were episodic for Sadie, seldom lasting very long, and soon Sadie moved on to Carla.

An insufferable feminist, Carla believed sexual intercourse to be an antifeminist institution. The male sex, she maintained, represented a degeneration and deformity of the female, '…the product of a damaged gene,' she would say. As she had with Shirley, Sadie became obsessed with Carla, absorbing her into her life like a sponge absorbs water. Soon, Sadie's every day was punctuated throughout with calls, visits, and emails to and from Carla.

On one memorable afternoon, at least for Jethro, Carla was visiting Sadie. The two sat on a couch in the den, enjoying mid-afternoon refreshments. Jethro wandered into the kitchen to fetch a cold brew from the fridge and overheard Carla preaching to an engrossed Sadie who sat there nodding and signaling her consent by peppering Carla's speech throughout with, 'You're so right,' and 'That's so true.' Carla's rambling, or what little Jethro heard of it, went as follows:

"All men are rapists—that's all they are, and I mean, with modern scientific advances, I mean, like artificial insemination and cloning and all, I mean, man will soon become an obsolete life form. You can already go to any sperm bank and specify what kind of sperm you want. I mean, if you want to have a man around for pleasure, that's fine, but, of course, we as women don't need them at all anymore. I mean, let's face it, the only purpose that men have is to copulate with females and propagate the species, and that's a task for which science has rendered them all but redundant. I mean, all we need to do is keep a handful of donors on a sperm farm for that purpose. Just give them pizza and beer and they'll be happy. The belief that married-couple families are superior is probably the most pervasive prejudice in the western world. I mean, if you think about it, the nuclear family is a paradigm that just doesn't work anymore. All the nuclear family is, is a hotbed of violence and depravity. We women need to establish our own community so we can fight collectively. Men deserve our violence..."

"You're so right," applauded Sadie throughout the harangue. "That's so true."

"Yes! Violence!" Carla went on, her voice up a few decibels. "That's what they deserve. You see, if you happen to be tied to one, like you are right now."

"Uh huh..." Sadie acquiesced.

"It's not enough to just get rid of them when the time comes; you have to destroy them; you have to grind them into the ground; you have to strip them of everything they cling to for the sake of their inflated little male egos and that pathetic, gratuitous respect and deference that they have only because society has been *soooo* weak and all *toooo* willing to give them control. We need to fight; we need to kick them right in that little flap of ugly flesh they have hanging there between their legs like a little marble bag; we need to cut if right off of them!"

Jethro listened to as much of Carla's speech as he could stomach. *A royal feminazi*, he thought. At the same time, however, he recognized her appeal. Carla was a genius of pure beauty, no less than any man's dream. *But why her? Why would a ballbuster such as that have to be so damn beautiful?* Jethro wondered. That Sadie sat there listening so intently and agreeing with Carla's sulphuric acid made Jethro wonder where Sadie's brain was. *Strange*, he thought. He had never known Carla to have had a relationship with a man. He wondered how much of

Carla's harangue Sadie really bought into. He didn't think how much of it she might actually put into practice.

Like Shirley, Carla had her own signature in body English. Whenever Carla emphasized a point (something she felt the need to do often), or whenever she waxed enthusiastically about whatever she was going on about (and she loved her own talk), she had a way of jutting her lower jaw, while at the same time affecting a hint of a smile, consisting of her moving only the corners of her mouth by pointing them in opposite directions. This gesture she would finish with a slight chuckle, or rather a small, double-syllable giggle. And so, when Sadie dispensed with Shirley, or vice-versa, and took on Carla with like intensity, Sadie was soon punctuating her speech by jutting her jaw and mimicking that same Carla giggle. Again Jethro was impressed with how accurately Sadie copied her friend's behavioral accents. He wondered to what extent his wife was consciously aware of her chameleon-like behavior.

Such reminiscing about Shirley and Carla crossed through Jethro's mind in the time it takes to change a thought while Sadie stood there in her biking outfit, absorbed with the application of her rouge, leaning into the mirror as she brushed copious amounts of blush on her cheeks. Except for eyeliner, Jethro could not recall her ever putting on so much makeup, and so carefully, and certainly not to go exercise. *You'd think she were about to go on stage. A long bike ride, indeed,* he thought with repulsion. *She's putting on enough makeup to grow a crop.*

As Jethro pled with her—"For heaven's sake, Sadie, what are you doing?"—she answered by making a face; a certain gesture. Jethro almost didn't notice it at first, so engrossed was he in the heat of the moment, but then she did it again, and this time Jethro paused and took careful note.

The gesture consisted of her lifting her eyebrows up a certain way — both eyebrows, in unison, along with a slight shoulder shrug, and at the same time, she pursed her lips into a tight smile that seemed to say, "Oh well," all of this accompanied by a shallow and rather jerky shake of the head – a slight trembling, almost. Jethro, detecting this gesture, could make no connection: this wasn't Shirley or Carla, but someone else.

At first, the gesture angered Jethro only because it seemed to say, "Too bad" or "That's tough," as though Sadie were thumbing her nose at him. But as the dispute went on, and the more Jethro focused on the gesture as Sadie demonstrated it with increasing pervasiveness, he could neither dismiss it nor comprehend it. *Where did this gesture come from*, he wondered. *It's something new, something alien. From where did she pick it up – or, rather, from whom?*

As Jethro pondered, off Sadie embarked on that "long bike ride" with Benny. With any desire for a barbeque long gone, Jethro remained behind to stew in his brooding.

CHAPTER TEN
JETHRO DRAWS A CONNECTION

To say that Jethro was deeply upset would be to put it mildly. If human affairs were governed solely by biological impulses, Jethro would have given Sadie a sock on the jaw and Benny a one-two, followed by a swift kick to the balls. Feelings aside, however, Jethro knew he had to keep his cool; he had to use his brains to see his way through this widening dilemma.

He went into the garage to Sadie's car. It was locked. Sadie had taken the keys with her. Jethro peered inside, and there on the front seat were booklets featuring the art of photography and what appeared to be the instructional manual for the new digital camera Sadie had recently purchased.

It had been about two months since Sadie had joined that bicycle group, and it wasn't long after that when she suddenly developed that keen interest in photography. At the time, Jethro had not put two and two together. He had taken little notice that Benny, a member of the bicycle group, was also a freelance photographer working for Laredo's only print organ. Now, however, with Sadie's disappearance of the night before, today's revolting bike excursion with Benny, and those camera manuals there on the car seat, Jethro could clearly see. "Photos…what bullshit," he muttered. There, in plain view on the front seat of her car, lay the answer to the question of Sadie's whereabouts the night before.

It was now obvious to Jethro why Sadie had played the game of "who leaves the house first" until her hand was forced when she ran out of cards. "She had a fucking date," said Jethro to himself. "What a bitch. Who are these people? Damn, had I gone to that barbeque, I would never have known a thing, and they would have continued their little sneaking-around game. Laughing at me behind my back. Yeah, well, they can continue having their fun," vowed Jethro through clenched teeth. "I'm gonna get 'em; one way or another I'm gonna make them fucking pay for this!"

Moreover, recognizing the situation now before him for what it plainly was, Jethro knew where it would end, though he shuddered in fear at the thought; and, he knew, as a lawyer, that he would need to somehow document their criminal conversation for his own sake and protection. *If this thing blows up*, Jethro assured himself, *the last thing I want is holy deadlock*. He knew he needed time.

Sadie came back from her bike ride late that same afternoon, only to encounter Jethro, black in humor, waiting and ready to pounce. He confronted her as she was stowing her bike in the garage.

"I know who you were with last night, Sadie; you were with Benny, that fucking usurper!"

She handled the accusation calmly, affecting a smile, however nervously. "How did you find out?"

There, she admits it; I've busted her, thought Jethro. He demanded, amid shouts, to know where they'd been, or rather, where she, his wife, had gone with another man, but it was back to "None of your business."

"Why the deception if you're really just friends? Why the hiding with no calls, why the preposterous stonewalling?"

"Jethro, you don't know anything, and—"

"What the fuck are you talking about?"

"—and you're incapable of understanding anything. You can't handle it!"

"Understand what, Sadie— that you were out alone with another man until four in the morning? I understand that perfectly!"

"Oh, do you? Do you know what kind of a man he is? No, you don't; you think all men are macho pigs like you, Jethro, that's all you understand."

"Kind of man? I'll tell you what kind of man he is; he's a piece of shit causing trouble in other people's homes, sneaking around with married women behind the backs of husbands—mine in particular; meanwhile, he's hiding in the woodwork while the problems he's causing are happening right here in my home. I'll tell you what kind of man he is: he's a worthless opportunist and a coward. He's a piece of shit, Sadie!"

Sadie gave Jethro a sly smile that put the man in his place—a look that said, "I'm the one who accepted his invitation, Jethro, and you don't know what he's got." And then, she did the unthinkable—she winked at Jethro, and placing a hand on one bouncing hip she stood there grinning at him.

Jethro fumed on the verge of homicide. Such was the extent of his rage that he did not notice himself begin to shudder and clench his fists tightly at his side. With eyes that narrowed like those of a snake, he advanced toward her in a steady, determined gait which itself picked up a hint of speed the closer he came to her. There seemed no stopping the assault, except by Sadie's rush of panic. The mocking grin vanished as her eyes widened at the terrifying prospect of an enraged man turned animal, fully capable and on the verge of committing an act of violence against her—and he was coming right at her like a *toro* provoked into a charge. Seeing that she was about to get thrashed, Sadie fled screaming, "*Ahhhhhh...*"

Jethro seemed to wake up as she shrieked and found himself standing alone in the garage as though he had arrived there while in a trance. Realizing that he had momentarily lost his mind in a fit of anger, he stood there, his chest heaving, his eyes looking at the floor but not seeing. *My god, what did I almost do? This could really turn into a bad situation*, he was saying to himself when he was further brought to his senses by the sound of Sadie speaking excitedly to someone on the telephone. Sadie had called her friend Carla to tell of her woes. Jethro could only stand there as he heard her declare, "It's really bad, really bad. Yes, he's crazy, and he's abusing me."

Jethro listened in dismay. "Abuse; says who?" he muttered. *You're damn right I yelled at her; she's lucky I didn't beat the hell out of her*. But he could not correct the report Sadie had fed Carla, who, Jethro was sure, was lapping it up with much enthusiasm.

The pent-up anger and frustration he had just given expression to rushed back again in full measure, along with his desire to wring her slender neck like that of a chicken. But there could be no more warfare, and nothing could be resolved by force, Jethro knew. He had no desire to continue with any bickering. He plodded into the study and flopped into the easy chair. Leaving the lights off, he stared vacantly out the window. After a while, he wandered into the bedroom and crawled into bed. His wife was already in it, with her back to him, seemingly asleep for she was quiet and still. Rolling onto his side facing the wall, Jethro sandwiched his head into his pillow.

I'm gonna get them back, and get them back good. But outright confrontations won't work. Violent confrontations can backfire on me; they'll make me out to be the bad guy. No, I'll have to be far more subtle than that. I'm going to have to find a way to have my revenge without their knowing it until it's too late for them to do anything about it.

But how?

CHAPTER 11
THE LEAVING

The next morning, Sunday, Sadie arose early, readied herself, and went to San Antonio with Carla for the day. *Now* she was going to San Antonio, even if only to get the hell out of the house and away from Jethro. And of course Carla would accompany her, considered Jethro, for they now had much to talk about, and maybe plan. Sadie needed the positive reinforcement that Carla's vitriol would have to offer, and Carla needed to be fully informed: a scandal of soap opera proportions was in the making, and Carla was not about to miss out on any of it. Besides, Carla was happy to have an opportunity to gloat about her theories by listening carefully to Sadie, and then saying something like, "You see, what did I tell you? Didn't I tell you?" at appropriate intervals, followed by that little giggle of hers.

To Jethro's surprise, as Sadie was leaving, she hugged and kissed him. *What the hell was that for*, he wondered. *What, is that supposed to butter me up and make me melt?* But then she stood in front of him and said, "Jethro, I want you out of the house." With that, she was off for a day of shopping.

"I guess not." Jethro concluded.

What could that hug have meant? Was she acting out of habit before leaving on a daytrip? That perfunctory hug gave him a strange sense of hope to which he readily clung. Maybe they could get through it all, even though Sadie said nothing about any reconciliation. Although she had said that she wanted him out, there was no aggression, no anger, no cutting edge, and they had kissed, after all…so Jethro kept thinking, *Maybe we can turn this around, and maybe we can work things out, maybe … maybe.* Jethro felt like a yo-yo and thought he was being played like one. *Maybe that was what the hug and kiss were for-to keep me off balance and guessing.* Jethro paused to consider this, but not for long before a tidal wave of anger washed over him, and his instincts gnawed at him as he reflected on what appeared to be going on. *There is something between her and that Benny guy that she is hiding, I just know it. And, that gay stuff she talked about was bullshit. No, she has feelings for him, or is developing them. Maybe she doesn't know how he feels for her, so she keeps me off guard with a little hug and kiss—to keep me hanging in there, just in case. On the other hand, she's got the hots for this guy and she wants me far enough away to explore those feelings—that's why she wants me out — out of her bed, out of her life, even out of the bathroom.* Jethro paused on this last thought. Her locking the bathroom door behind her signaled she wanted no intimacy with Jethro whatsoever. *What am I thinking? These thoughts won't stop; I'm going to go crazy!*

Jethro needed distraction; he needed comfort, and for Jethro, that meant dining alone at a dark, cozy Chinese restaurant and eating a bowl of Chinese fried rice. Yes, Chinese fried rice—that was the only comfort food Jethro knew. Unfortunately for him, however, there were no Chinese restaurants in Laredo that were dark and cozy, so he settled for Hung Wong, the only Chinese restaurant of any merit in town. It was brightly lit. Its walls featured various oriental designs, all traced in neon—a pagoda, an imperial dragon, a blossom of some sort, and what appeared to be a phoenix in flight. And, on the ceiling for customers who bothered to look up, giant Chinese and American flags joined at one corner to signal solidarity and friendship—a national, neon handshake. As Jethro gazed at the neon flags stuck to the ceiling, he considered America's relationship with China. *Yeah right, a friendship at the market: they make everything we buy.* Jethro turned away from the flags. The lights made his eyes hurt.

Jethro tucked himself into a familiar corner booth and contemplated the green bottle of Chinese beer that the Mexican waitress served up. It was certainly cold enough, as was the frosted mug he poured it into. Soon, the same waitress placed before him a mound of barbequed pork fried rice. The barbeque pork had a reddish color, and tasted rather sweet. In a word, delicious. With feigned gusto Jethro stabbed his fork into the pile of happy rice and, shoveling it into his mouth, began chewing it methodically like a horse masticating a mouthful of alfalfa. This he washed down with the cold beer. *How very comforting*, he told himself as though he needed convincing. But there would be no ensuing comfort, however, for Jethro could not eat in peace given the anger that seethed inside of him. And when not engulfed in anger, he felt he was on the verge of emotional collapse, wallowing in self pity, and feeling impotent against a wayward wife who was bent on self-satisfaction as an end that justified any means, and at Jethro's expense. Overwhelmed by it all, Jethro's brain would simply not stop over-analyzing every detail as though trying to read tea leaves for hidden messages.

Above all, Sadie's last words kept ringing in his head: "Get out. Get out. Get out." He decided he would. He would leave this wretched woman and be done with her. Yes, that was the answer. There would be no more fighting; no more pleading; no more trying to preserve the household. No shameless begging. Enough was enough. "I would rather live alone in a bark hut in the woods than in a nice home with a contentious woman," said Jethro aloud.

He resolved to be gone from the home before Sadie returned that evening. His personal sense of honor simply required it. It was time to put his foot down. As opposed to continued bickering, there would now be consequences. *That'll do it,* Jethro assured himself. *She'll return to an empty home and the grim reality she has made for herself; I'll show her!* He finished the beer in a single gulp, but left his plate of comfort food half full: what appetite he may have had was eclipsed by his newfound resolve, and his wanting to get on with the business at hand.

    Boldly he strode out of the restaurant with his stomach half empty and drove home with a purpose.

CHAPTER 12

JETHRO INTERCEPTS AN EMAIL

Jethro set himself to filling the trunk of his car with his clothes and a number of items he thought he might need or simply wanted to have with him. He would not leave right away, however. He decided he would drive away just as she returned from San Antonio later that night. He wanted to make a statement. He needed Sadie to *see* him leave. Then he would march off to a hotel and not return unless she begged him. He would show firmness; he would show resolve; and he would act like a man with dignity and self respect. *She'll be sorry when she realizes what she has done, and what she's lost*, he kept telling himself.

Packing his clothes did not take nearly as much time as Jethro thought it would, and he found himself sitting around, imagining his dramatic exit. Secretly, he hoped she would run out after him and beg him not to go. *Once she sees me actually leaving*, Jethro assured himself, *she'll come to her senses*.

With the car all packed up, Jethro went into the study and sat before the computer. It was either that or settle down in front of the television and flip channels with the remote. Jethro much preferred surfing the internet, which had the same effect as daydreaming. It was into cyberspace that he now lost himself until he was snapped from his reverie at about 11:15 PM by the ringing of the telephone.

Jethro let it ring a few times, half thinking he would not answer, but then he grabbed the receiver on impulse. It was Sadie. Emboldened by his newfound resolve, he hung up on her. *I'm not even gonna to talk to her*, he assured himself. She called back, and this time he took the call.

She sounded calm, and subdued. She even seemed reconciliatory.

"How are you, Jethro, I'm actually worried about you. Look I don't know what's come over me; I don't know what I am doing. We need to talk. I'm in Cotulla, so I'll be home soon."

Jethro thought, *Well, maybe she's sorry and she should be. Several hours driving on the highway must have done her some good. She's had time to engage in some cognitive thinking, and maybe that Carla talked some sense into her.* He rolled his eyes as he considered this last thought. Still, he replied curtly, "I don't know, Sadie." With that, Jethro drew a deep breath and hung up.

As soon as Jethro put the phone down, he kicked himself for being proud. He regretted not having responded to her overture with warmth, acceptance, forgiveness, and a reassurance that he'd be there to work things out, and that he would stick it out with her through thick or thin, just as they always had; together they could make it through any difficulties, including their present dilemma. Snapshots from memory played through Jethro's mind, and instantly he was transported thousands of miles away, to the other side of the world where they had had an adventure a few years before.

Ever since the beginning of their marriage, Jethro and Sadie had dreamed of visiting the pyramids of Giza and the enigmatic Sphinx. They often spoke of it with shared delight— a dream so exciting yet seemingly out of reach. Cairo, Egypt seemed so far away, not only in length of travel, but also in terms of cultural differences as to be forbidding. They might as well plan on going to Mars. But they kept dreaming about it together until finally, early one spring they made their talk real, bought airline tickets, and off to that antique land they went.

And visit the pyramids they did, as would any tourist. They wandered about them, on them to the extent allowed, and toured the inside of the Great Pyramid with its damp, narrow passageways to the inner tomb it contained. They rode ill-tempered camels on the Sahara, and visited perfume and papyrus shops where they were treated to hot tea by the shop owners. They visited mosques and the museum of antiquities, wandered the myriad stalls of the bazaar, and took an evening boat ride on the Nile. What they also did, however, was misjudge the culture and how they might fit in.

For clothes, Sadie packed pastel-colored blouses that when worn in America, demonstrated an appreciation for understated style, but when worn on the nighttime streets of Cairo were outrageously scandalous and provocative. Free flowing hair, exposed shoulders and arms, and too much neckline with a hint of cleavage was far too challenging to a culture where woman covered everything but their hands and faces with an approved *shalwar kameez*, a full-length *jilbab*, or a traditional *burkah*. But Jethro and Sadie were far too spontaneous to have considered that. Instead, they ventured out for walks in the Cairo nighttime, only to endure the heavy stares of groups of men huddled about, for there were no women to be seen on the streets on any typical Cairo night. While Sadie seemed oblivious to the fixed gazes, or perhaps basked in them, Jethro felt menaced by the many hungry eyes riveted on his wife, then on him, and then back on his wife again, like a gang of predators on prey. Every street corner seemed to offer such a collection of young men, and all stopped whatever conversation they were having in order to openly ogle at Jethro and Sadie walking arm in arm as though on Broadway, in New York City. Jethro sensed danger as the groups of men broke up, with several individuals now following casually behind them.

As Sadie talked nonchalantly about how hot the day had been atop those angry camels at the foot of the pyramids, Jethro guided their walk toward a subway terminal, and down the stairs they went. Quickly they boarded a subway train, Jethro intending only to get away from the threat he felt, while Sadie went along amused by the abrupt change of scenery and the adventure—for they did not know to where the train was taking them. With the air whirring past as the train picked up speed, they were carried mindlessly away, to what far reaches of Cairo they did not care.

But they should have cared. They wound up in some distant neighborhood that was even more forbidding than the downtown region of Cairo. They emerged from the underbelly of the metropolis onto a vacant but narrow street. Across the street from the subway entrance there sat a *sheesha* bar, full of men puffing on waterpipes through one of multiple hoses attached to the brass or glass bodies of the hookas containing a water basin for cooling and purifying the tobacco smoke. At the instant Jethro and Sadie emerged from underground, all the men having hookah stopped at once and stared intently at the spectacle of Sadie's breasts. Jethro would later swear that many of those men were openly salivating. While an oblivious Sadie asked what the matter was, Jethro pulled her back downstairs into the subway.

They stood before the subway map, but all was in Arabic. Jethro knew they were lost. He also knew that the subway could take then on an endless merry-go-round to nowhere. So, with determination, it was back up the stairs and onto the street.

The men at the sheesha bar again stopped in unison and put a fixed stare on Jethro and Sadie, but Jethro pushed past them all and directed their course up the street toward what appeared to be a busy intersection. Cats seemed to swarm everywhere, and they'd slink out of sight as soon as Jethro and Sadie approached them.

"Do you think they are related to the cats the pharaohs worshipped?" asked Sadie, seemingly unaware of Jethro's immediate concerns. Jethro, charmed by her aloofness, thought her all the more beautiful. It seemed to him that rather than being unaware of any danger, she was confident in that nothing would happen to them.

"I'm sure they are, Sadie. They never left Egypt after all," he answered with panache.

At the corner they encountered the same scene—groups of men who readily turned their stares at them, and wayward cats lounging about as though they couldn't care less about anything.

There on the far side of the intersection stood a lonely taxi. Jethro pulled Sadie toward it and signaled the driver for a ride. The driver appeared to have been taking a nap. Speaking no Arabic, however, Jethro stood before him, mute, as the taxi driver, appearing not too appreciative of the interruption, eyed Jethro impatiently, and then stared at Sadie with eye-opening astonishment.

But Sadie was quick to the rescue, for she remembered the name of the bazaar and commanded, *"El Khalilli."*

As though by magic, the driver straightened up in his seat, turned the car on, and quoted the fare.

"Twenny-fi bob."

Jethro and Sadie climbed in and were soon on their way through dark neighborhoods towards the lights of downtown Cairo and the ancient bazaar where they could blend in more easily.

They were safe after all, and Sadie looked at Jethro with a reassuring smile that said, "I told you so."

Once at El Khalilli, they made for the heart of it and were soon lost amongst the crowds of locals mixed with plenty of tourists. They were hungry, so they stopped at one of the many shish kabob stands. There they ordered barbequed quail on spits, then chewed into the tiny breasts of the little birds, laughing openly with each other. What a marvelous adventure it was. They had been lost in Cairo, with menacing gangs about them, and they had escaped to safety—never losing their style. That's what they were about. That was the essence of their relationship. And as they celebrated their triumph, Jethro, with a now-detached mind, quietly observed her, and her sunny smile…there was her vibrant grin, always at the ready, and the sparkling grey eyes to match.

Now, in the emptiness of his den, Jethro pictured her as she had always been, there, next to him. He recalled their quiet moments together when the world seemed right just because they were together, and how fortunate he had thought himself to have found such a woman among so many in the world; a woman seemingly made just for him. No matter how hard the struggles, her lightness of spirit always made matters easier to deal with. Yes, theirs had been a happy, peaceful home. Jethro shuddered at the thought of losing it, or that it might already be gone. There could never be a replacement, he knew. Even now he could hear the sound of her soft voice as she called to him from another room. No place could ever sound the same once those golden tones had rung.

He now questioned his resolve, sitting there staring at the computer screen. *Should I leave or should I stay?* But as soon as he thought of her asking forgiveness, memories of all the insults clobbered him, and waves of anger engulfed him. *I'll just see what she says when she gets home*, thought a now-vacillating Jethro.

Jethro expected Sadie to arrive at about midnight; Cotulla was only about forty-five minutes from Laredo. Growing increasingly anxious with every passing minute, he kept browsing on the computer, mindlessly, and with difficulty in maintaining his calm. But he simmered down a bit and sat there, staring blankly at the computer screen, brooding, when, at 12:04 AM, up popped an email from Benny to Sadie!

Jethro bolted upright in the chair, blinking in disbelief. He opened the email, though it was not addressed to him. *Whose privacy is being intruded upon here, anyway?* His inner voice insisted. The email was short. It said something about some photos that Sadie had emailed Benny and their not making it through. The email asked Sadie to try sending them again. Jethro's right eye began to twitch involuntarily. Benny's email continued: "Give me a call if I don't see you in spinning class." The temperature of Jethro's blood was now considerably warmer; on he read: "Oh, by the way, I'm not working on Wednesday. Why don't we do lunch?"

Jethro's blood now boiled, and red was all he saw. But for his lack of criminal propensities, he would have contemplated his choice of weapon. Civilized as he was, however, instead he immediately emailed Benny a reply:

"Listen, you asshole, you'd better stay away from my wife — and I mean it."

Jethro clicked the send button, and then deleted every trace of the emails so Sadie would not see them, at least not yet, not that night. Jethro knew that she would learn of them eventually, but he also knew that there would be a fight as soon as she arrived. He wanted no additional fuel for the fire, such as his "invading her privacy" by opening her correspondence from Benny.

Just then, as though by appointment, Sadie drove up the driveway. Jethro looked out the window to see the headlights of her car; his blood had not yet cooled— at all. There was no time to simmer down. He flew out of the house to confront her, shouting at her as he did, just as she was climbing out of her Chevrolet Suburban.

Sadie appeared stunned by the confrontation. She had no doubt expected a moping Jethro, but not a wild animal such as this, storming out of the house as though it, or he, were on fire.

Quickly Jethro hustled her inside the house. There he yelled at her, accusing her of infidelity. Pleadingly, she argued back, "He's just a friend," but Jethro was having none of it. He thought of her lies, and of her hiding, and he shot the facts at her like aimed bullets, certain to hit home. Some did. Others were defiantly deflected by her new mantra: "None of your business."

Jethro stayed the night, the fight having drawn on late enough to leave Sadie too tired to push him out of the house, and Jethro too tired to leave. But the confrontation had left a huge, gaping wound in the corpus of their marriage, one that surely would not easily heal, if it were to heal at all.

Lying on the couch, for sleeping with her in the same room was out of the question, Jethro admitted, *My marriage is now an unsalvageable wreck.*

CHAPTER 13

JETHRO CONFRONTS BENNY

The next morning Jethro arose early and quickly left the house like a man on a mission. Sadie followed him out the door, berating him with renewed conviction on how the marriage between them was over. Jethro did not argue back nor respond to her at all. He got in his auto and drove off in search of Benny—that bastard.

"And for what?" one might ask. "To destroy Benny or at least beat him up?" In some circles in the border town of Laredo, that's the least that would be expected. For the sake of honor and the family name, a cuckolded man would be encouraged and even applauded for smiting his wife's paramour. Jethro, however, was a man cut from a cloth different from the normal garb—and he knew it. As he drove toward his destination, he reprimanded himself: *I'm such a coward. I've always been a coward. I should kill them both, but I won't lay a finger on either of them, and they know it. That's why they're enjoying themselves in spite of me; because they know I am no obstacle to deal with. They'll do whatever they want, and they and the entire town can have a laugh on me.* In spite of his verbal self-flagellation, Jethro formulated a plan.

Rather than a violent confrontation, Jethro had decided that he needed to *apologize* to Benny for the email reply he had sent him. In so doing, he was not putting into practice any

Christian ethic; he was not turning the proverbial cheek or loving his enemies. Rather, Jethro was making a deliberate, tactical move designed to enhance his strategic position in the ongoing war with his wife. The fight the night before had been terrible, and he had lost his temper to an awful degree. He could not afford many of those kinds of displays. Sadie would certainly go on about it with her friends and family, and whoever else might listen, and convincingly depict Jethro as the bad guy. Already the rupture between him and Sadie was quite serious, with the chance for any reconciliation growing increasingly remote if not altogether precluded. Moreover, and regardless of any reconciliation, Jethro would not allow himself to be painted in the wrong, and the goings-on of the night before certainly posed that risk.

No, Jethro would not allow it. *I might lack the courage to do what is expected, but I have the courage to do what is necessary*, he insisted. He would maneuver into position, swallow whatever pride he had to, and do whatever it took to gain an advantage and get to the bottom of it so he could walk away with a clear conscience, knowing that he had not quit when the going got tough. And, he assured himself, he would walk away only when it was clear to him, and to all who might notice, that he had been the aggrieved party—at least under the immediate circumstances. He needed to catch them in a way that would allow him to later demonstrate it in a court of law as the rules of evidence would have it— if it came to that. In the end game, he was determined not to let them get away with it. He would try to cool things down; gather intelligence; be certain of what was going on; and, once certain, he would find a way to wreak his vengeance. So on he drove toward his grim purpose.

Jethro knew that Sadie would certainly be talking to Benny—was probably talking to him at that same moment. And, Jethro considered, she was going to be as angry as a cheetah taunted in a cage when she learned about the email that

Jethro had intercepted. If he were to apologize to Benny, loathsome as doing so would certainly be, at least she might consider that he had tried to smooth things out. He would be allowing that he may have been wrong, and he would be admitting that he had behaved inappropriately. Maybe Sadie might give him some kind of credit, when what he wanted was more time. At the very least, the move would be unexpected and a response useful to Jethro's plan might result. *Let's see what happens*, gambled Jethro.

As he drove, Jethro thought, *The email spoke of spinning class. Maybe the scumbag's at the gym.* There were several gyms in town, but Jethro figured he'd probably catch the rat where the cheese is, so on he went to Sadie's gym and there he found Benny, in the cardio room, peddling away on a stationary bicycle, staring blankly at the wall before him. Looking rather smug, Benny seemed to be singing a song to himself; his eyes closed, and his lips were moving to an inaudible number.

Jethro stared through the glass door at Benny.

"Just look at that fucker," he muttered.

Presently, Benny glanced over in Jethro's direction. Benny's empty gaze met Jethro's scowl. Jethro beckoned him over. Benny raised an eyebrow, stopped peddling, dismounted the bike, and ambled over to meet Jethro.

Lanky and tall, Benny wore wire-rimmed granny glasses, a ponytail that reached his lower back, and carried his self with the laid-back casualness of a '67 summer festival flower child. Jethro detected, however, an almost imperceptible hesitation in Benny's demeanor that Jethro thought was meant only for him — the cuckolded husband. Indeed, Benny appeared to have preferred to keep matters between him and Sadie on sneaky terms, and it seemed to Jethro that as Benny walked toward him, he did so rather sheepishly. *Perhaps this hippie is wary of confrontation*, thought Jethro. *Or maybe he's ashamed of himself, or maybe he thinks he's a poster child for a Haight-Ashbury love-in.* Jethro's mood turned hateful. *I could kill the son-of-bitch!*

Benny passed through the glass door, wiping his brow with a dirty towel that had once been white. Jethro, with a sideways flick of the head, motioned Benny over to the farthest corner away from the door. They turned and faced each other.

"I assure you that I am a gentleman," Jethro began.

"I know you are."

"I'm here to apologize for the email I sent you; you must understand how upsetting this all is."

"What email?"

Jethro backed up with a pause and looked at Benny questioningly. "You didn't get my email?"

"No, when did you send it?" Benny stared blankly at Jethro. "What email?"

"You emailed my wife last night about some photos and about getting together with her, and I sent you a response telling you to fuck off. I need to know what the hell is going on between you and my wife."

Benny shrugged his shoulders as though he had no clue.

"Well, it's like, I'm like giving her support, you know? She has a lot of good energy, you know? And like I pick up on a lot of that energy and she picks up on a lot of my energy, and like, you know, there's a lot of good energy between us, and I sort of give her positive support, that's all. But look, in case you're worried, you know, we've done nothing like to violate your marriage or anything."

Jethro stood there nodding as though Benny's talk of energy made any sense at all, and he dismissed this last of Benny's assurances as something he expected Benny to say and nothing more.

"I can appreciate all that," Jethro responded, "but you need to understand that this energy business between you and my wife is causing my marriage, our marriage, a lot of problems. It is upsetting my home life, you get it? So I'm telling you straight up to fuck off, okay? Do you understand me?"

Benny had grown silent as Jethro spoke, but did more than merely stand there looking at Jethro through his granny glasses: To Jethro's sickened dismay, Benny performed "The Gesture."

CHAPTER 14
BENNY GESTURES

There it was, that same gesture Sadie had performed the Saturday before: a shallow shrugging of the shoulders, pursed lips as though to say, "Oh well," and a slight shaking of the head, a faint trembling, as though he suffered from a mild nervous disorder. *If that doesn't beat all*, cursed Jethro. Only for a fraction of a second, however, did Jethro have time to ponder Benny's gesture and its implications before Benny tried to make things better.

"I believe that marriage is sacred," Benny offered.

Jethro looked at him incredulously.

"Oh, so you think marriage is sacred, do you? Well then tell me why you're sneaking around with my wife; and where in the hell did you go with her Friday night until almost four in the morning? What the fuck did you do with her?"

"That's for Sadie to tell you," was Benny's smug reply.

"Oh, I see, you have principles; well okay then, tell me this: you speak of all this good energy. Do you think that this energy you have between you and my wife might become something more than friendship?" Jethro was being sarcastic, but in answering, Benny was not.

The groovy photographer looked about, as though considering the possibilities, and then turned to Jethro and said most casually:

"Yeah, it could."

Jethro had to consciously restrain himself from kicking Benny's teeth in. Instead of instant gratification, however, he focused on the larger picture of where this all might go; the proverbial end-play. Still, he could not deny the gravel in his gut.

"Listen, you fuck-wit, I'm warning you," thrusting his index finger in Benny's face, Jethro warned. "You'd better stay the fuck away or I'll take this out into the street; I'm fucking warning you, I'll take those cameras of yours and shove 'em up your ass!"

Benny again said nothing, but just stood there instead, making that strange gesture of his.

Jethro felt nauseous with anger and his head had begun to swim, when a noisy woman in an adjoining room suddenly caught his attention. The woman was speaking excitedly into her cell phone, and loudly enough for Jethro to clearly hear what she was saying. And he recognized her voice: It was Shirley, the originator of Sadie's former lip routine, and the biggest gossipmonger in the business.

"He's still here, yes, right now, yes, yes ... talking to him ... right now ... yes!" The excitement in that gossiper's tone of voice was palpable, which was to be expected, after all, for she had a ringside seat to the melodrama, and fresh fodder for her soirees as well.

Within minutes, Sadie waltzed through the gym entrance, appearing calm and collected. *She must have flown here*, surmised an astonished Jethro, then realized that she had probably been on her way to the gym anyway—right on schedule with Benny.

Most pleasant in demeanor, and fresh with makeup, Sadie strode in as though nothing were amiss, as if she were about to have a leisurely chat with her girlfriends. She betrayed no surprise at seeing Jethro there at the gym at such an odd hour and dressed in a suit as she casually eyed the two men squared off in the corner.

"What's going on?" she asked with absurd calmness.

By way of reply, Jethro explained about the email and his apology, and that he was a gentleman, to which Benny added mumbled affirmations. Jethro's explanations, however, quickly trailed off into awkward silence as he took in what developed before him: as he was speaking, Sadie had taken Benny's side. They stood there now, Benny and Sadie, side by side as though on the same team, both of them staring mutely at Jethro, Sadie with growing impatience and Benny with renewed boldness, and telling Jethro by their silence that he was unwelcomed company and should take his leave.

Jethro could have kept talking, and started to, but he spoke in a vacuum. The stares they both gave him clearly said, "You may go now." And, to add insult to injury, both were now gesturing as well — not talking, nothing but that shallow shoulder shrug, with pursed lips and eyebrows raised, and that slight trembling of their heads as though their heads were perched on a pair of Slinkys.

Not sure whether he was having a bad dream or whether this was real, the feeling of nausea that overcame Jethro was tangible enough this time.

Sadie, finally snapping out of her Benny mimicry, gave Jethro a look, not glaringly, but shaking her head slowly as though to say, "You really screwed up this time."

Jethro had lost this round, and he knew it. Feeling quite small, he turned and left while Sadie stayed with Benny.

As Jethro got into his car, he glanced back toward the gym entrance several times. He thought Sadie might hurry after him, but Sadie seemed to have other things to do. Jethro drove away, crestfallen, bewildered, and confused. He made slowly toward downtown Laredo and checked into a fifteen-story hotel along the riverbank, insisting on a room facing south, overlooking the Rio Grande and the Republic of Mexico beyond.

CHAPTER 15

JETHRO TAKES HOTEL REFUGE

At mid-morning, Jethro called his workplace and reported in sick. He wanted to withdraw, and withdraw he did, taking shelter in the hotel room for most of the day like a hermit crab in a seashell. He considered that perhaps he was wallowing in self-pity, but he didn't care. Looking around the room, Jethro spied a mini bar that stood next to the TV. He opened it and surveyed the selections at hand. Without much deliberation he made his choices. Along with a bag of peanuts to keep him busy rather than suppress any hunger, he downed a little bottle of tequila, and then one of rum.

Jethro had rented a small room in the hotel on the riverbank. Cylindrically shaped, and rising fifteen stories above the city, the hotel was Laredo's tallest structure. Jethro's room was on the ninth floor. The southward side of the room consisted of a giant, wall-sized window overlooking the Rio Grande below. Ahead and beyond lay the spread of Laredo's sister city, Nuevo Laredo, Tamaulipas, Mexico.

Jethro lay about his hotel room for the better part of the day. When not flopped down on the bed, he'd stand at the huge window and peer out on the buzz of people on the pavement, maybe sipping another mini bottle—this time scotch, next time vodka or whatever. Below him, on the streets and bridges, the international movement of people and cargo between the two

Laredos kept up as usual. A throng of pedestrian traffic, mostly shoppers and day workers, was now crossing Laredo's oldest bridge, the Lincoln-Juarez, on its way back to Nuevo Laredo after a day of working and shopping in Laredo. Feeling pent-up, Jethro decided to join them for a stroll. The walk would do him some good, if only to help clear his head which had grown foggy from the events of the day and the mini-bottles. He had by then munched disinterestedly through several bags of peanuts and some pretzels, mainly to keep busy because he wasn't exactly hungry. But it would soon be dinnertime, and he needed something solid in his stomach.

It was now late afternoon, approaching the close of normal business hours, and Laredo, Texas showed it. Laredo's narrow streets were clogged with cars as people tried to get out of the downtown area. The stores were clearing out as shopping was over, and the store attendants were closing their cash registers. By seven o'clock, downtown Laredo would be dead: its stores closed; its streets empty. Nuevo Laredo, on the other hand was full of life at the start of every evening, and would continue in its liveliness until well past nightfall.

Walking across the bridge into Nuevo Laredo was, for Jethro, the most charming diversion that Laredo, Texas had to offer. The bridge itself was not too long for a walk, and the view it offered was alluring. After paying the pedestrian toll, Jethro wove his way through the package-laden crowd that shuffled along the bridge's pedestrian sidewalk, headed south into Mexico. The view of the Rio Grande flowing underneath the bridge had its natural dazzle. Its murky waters gliding slowly eastward glittered as the sun began its descent. Underscoring its semi-wild character, the banks on either side were thick with vegetation and Carrizo making the river appear to be out in the raw country instead of in the middle of two bustling cities, and two different countries. In spite of its name, however, the Rio Grande was not so *grande*. Not very wide, and certainly not deep, it looked more like a big stream. Still, Jethro, like everyone else who led their lives in the Laredo river cities, had the image of the river indelibly stamped in his mind as the essence of the local vicinity.

At the southern end of the bridge, now in the Republic of Mexico, one first encountered Mexican customs guards who, invariably, would be found scattered about their station, lounging around in chairs, and engaging in casual chat. When a car triggered the red inspection signal, requiring a secondary review, the Mexican customs guards would respond by nonchalantly directing the car to park in a slot flanked by aluminum tables for the placement of luggage. There they would peer about and into the car with uninterested looks on their faces before waving the driver off on his way. The guards paid little if any attention to the pedestrian passers-by, who flooded into the street like a school of fish pouring into a retention pond.

Early evening found people finishing their day jobs. Instead of scurrying directly home, however, as one did on the American side of the river, people here took their time and went out for a leisurely *paseo*. It was as though a new part of the day started at twilight. The parks would fill with characters of all sorts. There were hustlers, and hawkers, and hookers, and thieves. There were beggars, and shoe-shining boys, and sidewalk musicians filling the air with music. Open-air bars were filled with tourists, laughing and drinking Margaritas and beer. It was only them, and not the locals, who dared to wear those outrageously brimmed *sombreros* as they sang their drunken songs. And it was only the tourists who would buy the cheap trinkets that the hawkers were selling.

Every street corner had its street food vendors of various sorts, but Jethro wasn't interested in street food. For dinner, Jethro went to *La Principal*, a restaurant on Nuevo Laredo's main drag that specialized in the northern Mexican delicacy of *cabrito asado*, or roasted kid. Admittedly a raunchy place, *La*

Principal could not be beat for character. The front of the restaurant featured department-store-type show windows proudly displaying freshly slaughtered *cabritos* splayed on spits, slowly roasting over smoldering coals: an odd spectacle, indeed.

The main street, lined on either side with stores displaying their wares, showed what one would expect to see on any commercial strip, in this or in any city in any Western country: store windows displaying dresses, wedding gowns, shoes, leather goods, Mexican trinkets and curiosities, records, musical instruments, jewelry, home décor, art, liquor bottles...and then, in the midst of such normalcy, would appear the carcasses of baby goats, spread-eagled on spits over a fire. To the uninitiated, a commercial non-sequitur such as the window of *La Principal* might be considered vulgar. But to the unfussy locals of Nuevo Laredo, it was normal, and it worked.

Although roasted kid was among Jethro's favorite dishes, he barely remembered whether he enjoyed it or not that evening. The emotional toll of what he had been through was beginning to register by way of slapping him back and forth between waves of anger and deep plunges into sorrow— a slow descent into what could become a bona-fide depression if left unchecked. He felt emotionally brittle and was given to lapses of silence and vacant stares. To help himself nosedive into a pit of misery, Jethro kept his waiter busy fetching tequila shot after tequila shot from the bar.

After dinner Jethro stumbled through the streets, smoking a Cuban cigar he bought at a nearby tobacco shop. The cigar made Jethro's head spin even more than the raw liquor, and he became nauseous the more he smoked it. Yet he kept on smoking it, determined to enjoy it. He never smoked cigars. *God, my life sucks*, he thought, as he staggered about the streets of Nuevo Laredo. The cigar was beginning to make his tongue ache.

Slowly he reeled back toward his hotel. The evening had long since become night; the merry crowd had cleared the streets, and Jethro had had enough. He was tired. His head felt heavy, and his feet like lead. He tossed the half-smoked cigar into the river as he labored across the bridge back to the American side. Once in his room, he flopped onto the bed like an overripe piece of fruit falling from its tree to the ground. The last sensation he remembered before passing out was provided by his tongue: it felt swollen, like a cigar flavored dill pickle.

CHAPTER 16

DECEMBER 23

On the morning of December 23, a Wednesday, Jethro readied himself to go to work. A cold front had blown in, and the weather was freezing. A hard, steady wind was having a blast. *This is as cold as it ever gets in Laredo*, observed Jethro as he put on his heavy topcoat and black fedora, garments he seldom used, given Laredo's normally mild winters. He had dumped them into the trunk of his car when he had hastily packed that awful Sunday before.

As he buttoned his coat, Jethro's gaze settled on another of the items he had also taken with him, a gift he had given himself for his previous birthday: a Smith & Wesson Air-Lite .22 revolver. When concealed-carry permits had become available to law-abiding citizens of Texas, Jethro had obtained one and then bought the gun. Made mostly of aluminum, the pistol weighed a scant ten ounces, and represented S&W's response to the market's growing demand for easy-to-carry, self-defense weapons. Designed for pocket carry, the small pistol had an internal hammer so it could be easily retrieved from a pocket without getting snagged on loose clothing. It could even be fired from within a pocket, thus maximizing its availability for self-defense.

Jethro considered the revolver lying on the dresser, then picked it up. It was loaded with .22 Stingers – the hottest .22

bullet on the market. He thought about the debate among handgun experts regarding the effectiveness of the "anemic" .22. It was said to be wholly ineffective for self-defense purposes. Referred to as a "mouse gun" with no stopping power, the lowly .22 was hailed as a gun to have when one could not have a gun. Although better than pepper spray, no serious armchair *pistolero* resorted to a .22 caliber weapon for self-defense carry. Jethro thought how he'd hate to be shot with one as he stuffed the revolver into his coat pocket.

At the office Jethro felt restless and caged. Work for the day would be out of the question, given his state of mind. He was lucky, however, in that it was the eve of Christmas Eve and work was not really an issue anyway. Throughout the bank building where Jethro's law firm was housed, office parties were being prepared and would soon be in full swing. Jethro's firm had its Christmas party arranged for that afternoon. Bank officers would certainly stop by at least for a courteous hello, and all the lawyers, including Jethro, were expected to do likewise at the various bank departments. Jethro groaned and popped three aspirin, fending off the tequila headache from the night before. The last thing he wanted to do was exchange social pleasantries.

Outside his window, Jethro had a full view of Laredo's main international bridge. With the holiday crunch in full swing, the bridge was at a standstill. Cars and trucks were lined up in all its lanes, both coming and going, like single-file parking lots. On either side of the vehicular traffic, the bridge's sidewalks were crowded with hoards of people bearing boxes and packages and groceries, laboring their way in and out of the U.S. and Mexico.

The streets of downtown Laredo were a buzz of activity. The stores were enjoying their busiest day of the year. On storefront sidewalks, stacked every few feet towered small mountains of cardboard, paper, Styrofoam, plastic wrap, and the discarded wrappings of the many purchases by Mexican nationals who, once rid of cumbersome packaging, wrapped whatever they'd bought in a manner more convenient for carrying into Mexico, and hopefully for escaping the lazy eyes of the Mexican customs inspectors. *So much traffic,* thought Jethro, *and almost all of it Mexican.* Indeed, the international bridges belonged to Mexico on any 23rd day of December in the Port of Laredo, for no native Laredoan would venture into such a mob scene on such a day. Driving a car to and from Laredo and Nuevo Laredo was impossible: it would take hours just to cross the bridge. The locals knew to stay away from driving into Nuevo Laredo the entire week before Christmas unless one had a fondness for traffic jams, a huge bladder, or no choice.

Jethro turned his attention to the goings-on at the firm. Outside his office door, the festive air had become more pronounced, and he could hear laughter and music floating freely about, even though it was only ten in the morning. The workday would come to an early end, and all were expected to gather in the firm's spacious conference room to enjoy a luncheon that the secretaries were now spreading on the conference table. There would be Christmas celebrations throughout the building, and at night the bank's grand Christmas party, featuring dancing to live music and a full-service bar, would commence.

Jethro's mind was elsewhere, however, for today was the day Benny had suggested lunch with Sadie in that wretched email he had intercepted on Sunday night. Given the fiasco at the gym on Monday, Jethro had stayed away and there had been no room for any follow-up on the subject. Jethro could not be sure what Sadie was bent on doing. He had to find out, and for that he would have to go see her — but he needed a reason. He looked around his office and found among the piles some home insurance forms that needed signing. Lord knew the papers had languished there for some time, and could have continued gathering dust until well after the New

Year. But Jethro was grateful for them now, as they satisfied his need for an excuse—any excuse, however flimsy—to go see Sadie. Jethro didn't have time to waste on considering the ridiculousness of his having to invent an excuse to go see his own wife.

He called her. She seemed calm. He told her he would be coming over for her to sign some papers. She said okay, so off Jethro went, thinking as he drove how transparent his document-signing ruse was, and how Sadie didn't seem to catch on. Since when did Jethro ever care about insurance papers enough to leave work to have her sign them? If anything, he'd have sent a courier if he needed something in a rush.

Arriving at the house breathless with nerves, Jethro rushed inside and found Sadie in her dressing room, standing before the mirror, applying makeup. Jethro noticed how carefully she was fixing herself up, as though she were going to a formal dinner. He offered her the papers, which she briskly signed without so much as looking at them. *There's that bad habit of hers again*, reflected Jethro. Although he did not expect her to read any fine print, she had been living with a lawyer for almost seven years and should have known to at least determine what kind of papers she was signing. But this she never did. Jethro had never liked this negligent tendency of hers, thinking that some day it could get them into trouble. As she scrawled her signature in haste, however, he pretended he did not notice, for a certain thought struck him: Her hastiness and lack of diligence could indeed cause trouble someday—for *somebody*. He stuffed the papers back in the manila folder and said thanks. She, on the other hand, was already back at the mirror, leaning over the counter as she applied her mascara.

"Where are you going?" he asked casually.

"I'm going Christmas shopping and I'll be gone all afternoon," was her matter-of-fact reply.

"Well, I'll be at the office. Why don't you call me later? Maybe we can meet for lunch or something," he suggested.

"I'll see, Jethro. It's going to be a busy day; I have a lot to do."

And that was that.

Jethro left. *So far so good*, he thought. *She's going shopping.* Still, he spent the rest of the morning in a state of agitation. Sadie's telling him that she was going shopping did not preclude her getting together with … well, that lousy bastard. He couldn't, however, confront her like a jealous hothead about it; he knew he was walking a tightrope. If he was going to get to the bottom of this problem on his terms, for better or for worse, he would have to keep his cool. He also considered how Sadie had kept her cool. She didn't scold Jethro for the recent troubles, or even mention them at all. It appeared that she was also interested in avoiding disturbing disputes. *Or maybe she's also acting on a plan*, Jethro's thoughts whispered in his ear.

At 12:30 Sadie called Jethro to tell him that she was at a home decoration shop, buying her mother a carving set. Jethro felt a comforting relief and quickly offered to meet her at the store to help her in the selection of it, but she quickly said no, and stayed with "no" in spite of Jethro's protestations.

"Let's do this together," he repeated.

"No," she insisted, and informed him that she wanted to continue with her shopping on her own. From the home decoration shop, she would be going to fight the mobs at Toys-R-Us to buy gifts for the nieces and nephews. They hung up, and Jethro was left to while away the hours, putting on a happy front at the office Christmas parties.

In spite of his efforts to appear relaxed and engaged, however, he could not laugh at all the jokes, and with his mind elsewhere, his responses were absent. Jethro was sure he had offended more than a few revelers with his apparent lack of interest in anything said to him. But regardless of what anyone might have thought of him, all he could think of was the tormenting question of Sadie's whereabouts and company, and how miserable life had become.

CHAPTER 17

JETHRO ON THE HUNT FOR SADIE

At about four o'clock, compelled by his anxiety, Jethro called Sadie's cell phone. She answered the phone with a cheerful "Hi," as though she were having a great time at a wine bar instead of a wearisome afternoon struggling with the crunch of Christmas crowds in the shops and stores.

"What are you doing?" Jethro asked, now decidedly bothered.

"I'm crossing back from Nuevo Laredo. I'll call you later." With that, she abruptly hung up.

Jethro was baffled, and a sinking feeling grew in his stomach: Nuevo Laredo on December 23 made no sense. He called right back. Again Sadie answered with a "Hi" that was as cheerful as it was bizarre. Her voice sounded excited, and, it seemed to Jethro, mocking in its tone.

"You went to Nuevo Laredo?" He asked with a tone of voice signaling disbelief.

"Yeah!" She answered most bubbly.

"What for?"

"To buy a bottle of tequila!"

"To buy a bottle of tequila in Nuevo Laredo, on the day before Christmas Eve? Why would you do that?"

"Well, why else? To drink it!" Her tone of voice was one of merriment.

Jethro was stupefied by how out of place this all was. But Sadie didn't stop.

"I'll call you later." She stated flatly as though she had something better to do at the moment.

"Are you with anyone?" Insisted an impatient Jethro.

"Nope!" was her uninformative reply, and with that, Sadie cut Jethro off by hanging up.

For a few moments, Jethro stood there with a vacant stare, the phone still pressed to his ear. He felt as though he had just received a diagnosis of malignancy. There was a certain something about her voice. It sounded exactly like it had that Friday night, or Saturday morning, at close to four AM when she had finally called home: somehow hurried, or evasive; certainly curt, yet full of nervous energy. On top of that, as Jethro knew, Sadie never went across the river into Nuevo Laredo alone, she was afraid to—and much less to buy a bottle of tequila. To do that, she would simply go to the neighborhood liquor store and buy an expensive bottle. Jethro looked out his window at the bridge packed full of traffic.

"She's fucking around," Jethro grumbled, and he was sure of it.

Jethro called Sadie's cell phone — no answer. He called again — no answer. Ten calls later — still no answer. *It's Friday night all over again*, he agonized. He snatched a phone book from a desk drawer and looked up Benny. There quite plainly was his address: 143 Lovers Lane. *Lovers Lane; whose sick joke is that?* he wondered, shaking his head. *God's or the Devil's?* He rummaged through a pile of papers stacked on his desk and retrieved Sadie's November cell phone bill. Among the list of calls there were several to and from Benny's number. *Well that doesn't mean anything*, thought Jethro. *Or does it? What will her phone bill for December reveal?* Jethro grabbed his hat and coat and fled the office, leaving the partying gang wide-eyed.

"Hey Jethro, where are you going?" called one of the partners.

"Are you coming back?" asked another.

"I think he's having problems with his wife," remarked a third in a loud whisper.

Jethro didn't pause to acknowledge their concern. His secretary, shaking her head slowly side to side with a sympathetic frown, watched him go with a sad little wave.

Jethro drove through traffic like a man late for work. His car was on empty and the fuel light was on. *I'd better not find her car at his house, that's all I have to say*, he swore to himself.

Lovers Lane ran parallel to the street that the old hospital was on, Jethro knew, but he wasn't sure whether the street's low numbers were toward the east or west end of the street. Jethro opted for the east end and headed down a main boulevard that also ran parallel to Lover's Lane. Driving far enough to the east side of the city, Jethro turned on an intersecting street, only to learn that the low numbers were to the west, in the opposite direction. He had overshot his destination by a considerable distance. His throat tightened with anxiety. There was no time to lose, and no time to gas up. The mere thought of standing there while the gas pump took its time filling the gas tank up taxed his patience enough given his anxious condition. He turned the car around and now drove west on Lover's Lane, apprehensive about what he might find, yet fearful that his car would run out of gas and prevent him from finding out.

Block after block he drove — 1300 block, 1200 block, 1100, 1000, 900, 800 — not long to go, and the gas-empty-indicator light now seemed to glow a brighter yellow. Jethro's heart pounded as he drew closer to his goal. He felt short of breath, and his mouth was parched. The street rose to a hill now, just beyond which had to be the house in question. His car had made it, getting him there on fumes. As he topped the hill and looked down the street below, however, a faint feeling overcame him, and his vision blurred as though he were peering through a fish bowl full of water— everything seemed to be melting. He focused his vision, and behold There was Sadie's Suburban parked in front of Benny's shack.

Jethro had been hoping that there might be a crowd of cars there, and that a party might be going on, or maybe no one home at all. But no, only Sadie's car was there, along with one other: an old SUV, faded red in color, presumably belonging to Benny. And, there was no party going on, none but their own, for they were definitely alone.

Jethro was crushed, and as angry as a rattlesnake.

CHAPTER 18

SADIE IN FLAGRANTE DELICTO

Jethro screeched to a halt in front of Benny's house and alighted from his car before the dust had settled, leaving the car door wide open behind him. He marched boldly up the sidewalk to the front door and rang the doorbell — three times. There was no answer. Jethro thought he had heard it ring, but now he wasn't sure. He tried it again; the doorbell appeared to be broken. Jethro could hear not a sound from within. He pulled open the rickety screen door, which screeched loudly like a stuck pig. Peering through a triangular peep window on the door, he surveyed a small, dingy living room cluttered with trash and debris.

Jethro looked about as much as the little peephole would allow. Inside, a large window facing the street was covered by drab yellow curtains through which a putrid light glowed, faintly illuminating the living room. Against the far wall stood a brown, cloth-covered couch that was lumpy and deformed, its armrests frazzled and frayed as though having been clawed at continuously by a cat. There was an armchair to match the couch, only it was piled high with wrinkled clothes that seemed destined for, or had just returned from, a trip to the laundromat. Before the couch, a small coffee table was stacked with old newspapers, magazines of various kinds, and a multitude of photographs. Numerous photos were strewn about the floor, only they had some order to them, as though they had been the subject of recent scrutiny. Jethro briefly focused on the photos. All of them depicted what appeared to be Indians engaged in ritual activities. Jethro's brain automatically questioned what tribe they were from, but just as quickly dismissed the query, for Jethro, at the moment, did not care about any Indians.

He knocked on the door and simultaneously tried the doorknob — it turned. Edging the door forward, he crept his way in imagining a scene with them panicking under the sheets. Instead, he encountered them walking questioningly toward him. Benny and Sadie appeared to have been seated at a small breakfast table, next to a filthy kitchenette — a cozy spot among the squalor. On the table were two shot glasses, with a tall, blue tequila bottle standing in between. How long the two lovebirds had been sitting there Jethro could not know, but he saw that the table was rather close to the front door, tiny dwelling place that it was. *Surely they heard me approaching*, he calculated.

Benny looked at Jethro with an indignant glare that said, "How dare you intrude into my home!"

What gall, thought Jethro, as he realized that he had, indeed, barged into Benny's residence. But then what was Benny doing there with his wife, anyway? Who was intruding upon whom?

Jethro strode to the middle of the small living room and stood there, feet spread apart, his hands in his coat pockets, his hat on his head, his right hand resting on the .22 revolver.

"What are you doing here?" Sadie opened the exchange.

With a calm reserve, Jethro mumbled awkward sentences about his just passing by the neighborhood.

"You don't mind if I join you, do you?" He proposed.

Benny, with an incredulous "harrumph," swept his arm toward the table. "Sure, why not? You're already here, aren't you?"

Sadie apparently at somewhat of a loss, stammered nervously, "We were trying out this new tequila, and I was just leaving."

Yeah, but my car got here first, thought Jethro.

To which Benny sputtered before she could finish, "I was showing her my photos."

With Sadie interrupting, "We went across the river and had lunch …"

Jethro wondered whether they had been seated at that little table for a while before he intruded upon them, or whether that's where they had posed after hastily throwing their clothes back on. He noticed that Benny's hair was not tied in a pony tail— it fell loose, over his shoulders and down the length of his back. The .22 throbbed in the palm of Jethro's hand. His head was swimming. He turned to Sadie and demanded, "What's going on, because I need to know."

Benny began responding, "Well, you know, it's like, we have this really good energy—"

"Yeah, I know, Benedict," Jethro cut him off. "You already told me about this energy stuff and how it could go further and become a relationship."

Benny rolled his eyes, but one lens of his granny glasses was blocked by glare, so only one rolling eyeball showed through making him look like Popeye with a monocle.

"I don't remember exactly what I said, man," the groovy photographer went on, "but yeah, that's true. You know, there's a lot of good energy between us, and it could develop into something very *spacial,* you know? And the name is Beneford, not Benedict."

" *Spacial?*" Jethro grilled, his tone filled with sarcasm. "Do you mean as in the outer limits, or is that east-Texas for "special"?

Benny rolled his popeye again.

What balls he has, thought Jethro. He had glanced at Sadie just as Benny so qualified the future prospect of his relationship with her. It happened fast, but Jethro could have sworn Sadie had suppressed a smile of heartfelt joy upon hearing Benny's admission. It was only an instant, however, and just as quickly her face turned to stone. Jethro now stared coldly and evenly at Benny as he went on, no longer speaking of any support role for Sadie, but of a one-on-one relationship instead. The chunk of metal felt warm in his hand, and the blood in his veins ran hot.

Sadie stood next to Benny, gazing blankly at Jethro. She had now assumed a pose of relaxed confidence, leaning against the door frame between the dinette and living room with her arms crossed casually in front of her. She said nothing as Benny spoke, and by her silence, tacitly agreed with Benny's characterization of their relationship, or so Jethro thought. He looked at Sadie and asked,

"Is that how it is?"

To which she bolted off the door frame and barked, "You know the situation. I want a separation and a divorce; I don't want to be your partner anymore." Her arms were now braced to her side, her fists clenched in a defiant pose.

Her use of the word "partner" instead of "wife" caught Jethro in the gut. After thus delivering a verbal blow, Sadie again reclined against the door frame, crossed her arms in front of her chest, and stared cooly at Jethro, smug and overconfident. Her solemn proclamation might have been delivered in private. *Did she say that for my benefit or his?* Jethro wondered. He eyed Benny, who stood there sheepishly, his now familiar gesture being all the expression he could muster.

Jethro froze as he took in the significance of the scene before him, a scene that was as mocking of him as it was absurd: Three figures in a hovel, one standing in the center of the room, dark and menacing in topcoat and hat; and two other figures, one in an artificially relaxed posture and familiar to Jethro now only in form, and the other, flat-footed in nerve-bound tremble. Suddenly, like the wiping away of a mist, the threat of it all, the urgency that had sent Jethro racing through the streets like a madman in a car on empty, chasing something he desperately needed to see, melted away into the ridiculous, and Jethro almost felt like laughing. Standing before him now were two strangers, and he, Jethro, became an outsider. In this moment of lucidity, a feeling of resignation overcame him. He felt he could simply walk away from it all. That feeling of freedom was fleeting, however, for just as quickly the anger that had him breathing shallowly not long before rushed back hotter still, and he grit his teeth and clenched his jaw.

Benny, now feeling called upon to say something, broke the suspenseful silence. Adopting a paternal tone of voice, he said,

"I understand how you feel and that this is difficult for you—"

But Jethro would have none of it and stopped Benny mid-sentence.

"What, exactly, do you understand? Why don't you do me a favor and tell me?"

Benny mumbled something incoherent and quickly fell silent, resorting as a means of expression to that gesture of his — complete with shoulder shrug, raised eyebrows, twitching head, and lips pursed as though to say, "Oh well!"

Shoving herself off the door frame, Sadie jumped anew into the fray.

"I can't believe you followed me here," she lashed out. "You have embarrassed and humiliated me!" She then leaned against the door frame again.

Jethro could not help but notice how forcefully she slung her words at him, meanwhile maintaining her relaxed demeanor against the door frame; a pose that now appeared as contrived as that seventies fashion statement when men wore their shirt collars over the coat.

"I didn't follow you, I sought you out," answered Jethro.

"Well, I wish you'd leave," was her curt reply.

"Just like that, you want me to just leave, huh? Just turn around and walk away..." but he fell silent as he saw what developed before him: A mute Benny, standing there, continued with his gesturing, though a bit more pronounced, with his head really shaking now, as though attached to his shoulders by a coiled spring. Sadie, just as quiet, and as though there was nothing else to say, abandoned the door frame and was now standing next to Benny and doing the same, gesturing just as he was.

Jethro drew back and watched in bewilderment. They resembled matching bobble-head dolls, or performers of a modern, interpretive dance of low-level energy.

Jethro could feel his temperature rise; he had had just about enough of both of them. He gritted his teeth tightly and clenched his fists.

KA-BOOOM! The gun in Jethro's pocket went off with a deafening explosion. Caught up in the red heat of anger, he had lost awareness of the gun he was gripping and had squeezed it without realizing what he was doing. So startling was the effect of the blast that for a moment Jethro did not know what had happened. Benny, however, stiffened in his shoes as though electrocuted, and, throwing his hands upwards into the air, let out a high, piercing wail as though he had been shot. Sadie, in shock with fright, threw her arms up as well and joined Benny in a high-pitched scream.

Jethro, by reflex, looked down at his right foot and saw a neat little hole in the wooden floor board, right next to the sole of his right shoe. Had the gun been angled just half an inch over, he would have shot off his little toe. But there was wasn't much time to think of that because Benny had skedaddled by then, blasting past Jethro like flatulence in the winter wind and bolting out the door and into the street with Sadie chasing after him.

AMERICAN BITCH

"Benny…Benny…wait for me!" she called as she ran down the street.

Benny wasn't slowing down for anything or anyone, however, and was already well down the block, still screaming, frantically shaking his upraised hands at either side of his head as he fled, his long hair flowing in the frigid breeze behind him.

Jethro took off as well. Into his waiting car he jumped, bringing the engine to life with a roar, and tearing out with tires spinning and spraying gravel behind him. He was in trouble, he knew it, and he drove in the direction of his mother's house, which was not too far away. He had not noticed the thin wisp of smoke emitting from his right coat pocket. The blast from the gun—hot sparks, burning gunpowder and all—had lit a small fire, and smoke now wafted inside the car. Jethro rolled the window down and shoved the gun under the seat below him. He paid no heed whatsoever to the bright yellow gas light, which had been a source of so much focus and concern only a short time before.

Certain that the police would soon be after him, he screeched into his mother's driveway, and then into her garage. Jumping out of the car, he tore the smoldering coat off his shoulders and tried to beat the fire out by slapping it with his free hand, but to no avail. The coat seemed to smoke even more, and small sparks and red cinders floated slowly to the garage floor. Jethro went to a nearby hose and dowsed the coat. "Damn it, this thing is ruined." He stuffed the coat into a garbage can outside the garage.

Jethro went into his mother's house, only to learn from the housekeeper that she was not there. *Just as well*, thought Jethro, *she doesn't need to know about my troubles; the last thing I need is to have to deal with a worry bug.* He went into the kitchen, retrieved a phone book from a drawer, and called a cab. He had to get out of town fast, and Nuevo Laredo had frequent flights to Mexico City. *I doubt they're blocking any international borders for a small-town lawyer gone rogue*, he figured. He would take a cab to the bridge, walk across it, then get a Mexican cab to the airport. But he needed a lot more cash than he had on him. Up the hallway he went and into a closet where his mother's safe was. He knew the combination. He would have to hit her stash. *I'll explain later*, he mused. After grabbing a sizeable bundle of bills, Jethro parked his car in the spare parking space in his mother's garage and closed the garage door behind it. He then turned to the housekeeper.

"Juanita, now listen carefully. I want you to tell my mother that I will call her later. Tell her not to worry, but I had an emergency. I am going away for a few days. Tell her to leave my car there, and to leave the garage door closed, okay? It's very important that she do that. Do you understand?"

"Si, Señor Jethro, I will tell her."

"Remember," Jethro emphasized, "keep the garage door closed."

Jethro spent the next ten minutes anxiously waiting for the taxi to arrive. He listened carefully for the sound of police sirens, but did not hear any. *For sure they'll be swearing out a complaint against me*, he thought. *Damn it, why did the fucking gun have to go off?*" Speaking of which, he thought he shouldn't leave the gun in the car. He went back to the garage and retrieved the weapon, which he then hid in a closet in the hallway closet. Moments later, he heard the cab pull up the driveway.

Night had fallen, and Jethro stared out the taxi window at the houses sliding smoothly by. The homes, brightly decorated for a merry Christmas, passed in a blur of red, green, and white lights as Jethro stared at them with disinterest. There an ensemble of plastic reindeer and sled with Santa in it graced the front lawn of one home; a glowing snowman was featured on another in front of a house decorated with fake icicles and faux frosted front windows. On the grass of another lawn, neatly arranged, sat a nativity scene complete with a baby Jesus in a manger surrounded by glowing, plastic farm animals illuminated by inner light bulbs as were Mary and Joseph, the three wise men or three kings—Jethro wasn't sure and he didn't care. How quickly things had changed. Only hours before he had been in his office watching the bridge traffic, reluctant to participate in the Christmas parties he would have to attend, little suspecting that only hours later he would be riding in a cab, bound for Mexico City, evading arrest.

Soon the taxi arrived in downtown Laredo, and dropped him off near the bridge. Jethro paid the cabbie, and braced himself against the bitter wind as he began his journey into Mexico by walking across the bridge as he had only a couple of days before. Only this time, the bridge was empty, and the Mexican side appeared dark and lifeless. The weather was freezing. Jethro shivered as he walked the lonely bridge, his hands stuffed in his pockets with arms stiff at his sides in an effort to keep warm. His teeth began clicking together like castañetes. He thought of his overcoat in the trashcan back at his mother's garage and his hat lost somewhere, maybe in the car.

Arriving at the Mexican side, Jethro walked past a lone guard who appeared quite cozy inside a booth. Sitting upright with his eyes closed, he gave the impression of being asleep. Jethro barely glanced at him as he made straight for a taxi parked up the street.

"*Al aeropuerto.*" He stated flatly as he climbed in. Lacking his passport, Jethro hoped his driver's license would do for a visa.

"Aw, this sucks," Jethro growled between his teeth.

CHAPTER 19
MERRY CHRISTMAS MEXICO CITY

Mexico City around Christmastime is a quiet place compared to the frenzied beehive it is at any other time of the year. The rhythms of Mexico City, as they normally flow, range from the mild and romantic to the hot and frenetic, and everything in between. Christmastime, by contrast, is always steady and slow. A holiday season steeped in tradition, Christmastime is, in *La Ciudad Capitalina*, a time for family and friends, spent in intimate surroundings. But Jethro had not thought of this. Given his hasty plan of escape, he thought only of being caught up in the city's buzz; of being carried away by its teeming flow of energy; and, of being denied, by colorful distractions, of any time to mope. He had no intention of having a "good time," there being nothing for him to celebrate; rather, Jethro just wanted to get lost and forget about everything; to be swept out to sea by the city's energy like a corked bottle in a stream.

He arrived late in the evening and checked into a hotel near *La Zona Rosa*, a neighborhood near the center of the city famed for its parade of people, its many shops, sidewalk cafes, and open-patio restaurants. Jethro had been to the Zona Rosa before, although it had been years, and fondly recalled its vibrant nightlife. On any given weekday night and twice on weekends, throngs of people crammed the Zona for a leisurely *paseo* while sidewalk musicians filled the air with music. There were always plenty of street performers — jugglers, mimes, play acts, sketch artists, and hustlers handing out nightclub passes or invitations to the underworld of naked pleasures, where dollars would be most welcomed. Groups of teenagers could be seen lounging about, some dressed in punk garb complete with black lipstick, black fishnet hose, and spiked hair dyed blue, bright green, or orange. Many of them were modern primitives replete with tribal tattoos, all black or gray, and copious body piercings. There would be plenty of lovers, too. Jethro would be able to gaze at them and think about what they had and he didn't. Yes, *La Zona Rosa*, mimicked in miniature by the streets of Nuevo Laredo, would be a perfect place to get lost in. It was a fine setting for a promenade. *Maybe I'll have another cigar*, Jethro mused.

On this retreat to Mexico City, however, only two nights before Christmas, he found no such colorful crowds. After first belting down a couple of shots of tequila in his hotel room in order to get the juices flowing, eagerly he strode into the evening, much anticipating the soothing distraction of the mob. His pace slowed markedly, however, as the Zona Rosa emerged into disappointing view.

Not its normal, lively self, the Zona Rosa was dark and shadowed; its streets cold and empty. The air was thick with a dampness that made everything slimy and wet. Jethro walked half a block up one of the streets and paused to take in the absence of what he had longed to see, and to let his spirits fall freely. All the shops were closed; their many lights that would normally brighten the atmosphere were all turned off. Burglar-proof gates, made of wrought iron and secured by heavy chains and padlocks, blocked any access to most storefront alcoves. Other storefronts had stiff curtains of corrugated iron rolled down from the top of their entrances and padlocked shut to a bolt embedded in the cement sidewalk. The overall effect was one of eeriness: the dark, empty streets, flanked as they were by iron bars or walls, felt as sinister as a third-world prison courtyard during a lockdown.

Crestfallen, Jethro strolled aimlessly about the gloomy streets of the Zona Rosa. Most of the cafes were also closed, with those few left open void of any patrons—as it should have been: it was the eve of Christmas Eve. Unlike Jethro, most folks were home where they belonged. After wandering around aimlessly for a while, he finally settled into one of the few cafés that remained open—a small Italian bistro called *Il Buono Gustare*. Outside its entrance stood a small table dressed in a red and white checkered table cloth on which were displayed various cuts of meat from which to choose. Also on display were several bottles of Chianti to go along with whatever meal one chose. Jethro wandered in. A smallish waiter with a sommelier's cup hanging around his neck welcomed Jethro with a friendly smile, and motioned him over to a brightly lit table in the center of the small dining room. Jethro paused as he looked at the suggested seating, and, after surveying the rest of the tables, selected one tucked away in a corner, next to a dark window where he could gaze out into the blackness. There, he slumped into a chair, ordered a simple meal and, dining alone, ate the bread of sorrows.

CHAPTER 20

JETHRO AT THE HOTEL BAR

The nightlife seemed better at the hotel's cocktail lounge, which featured live *mariachi* music. Jethro peered in. Rather on the small side, the lounge had more than its share of dim lights, thick smoke, and a ceiling so low it made the room seem to frown. At the far end, opposite the entrance, a musical performance was in full sway with a dozen *charros* arranged in a broad semicircle on a tiny stage, in the middle of which stood the main singer. The *charros* wore traditional costumes, complete with broad-brimmed, embroidered sombreros, white silk shirts, embroidered jackets, tight waistcoats decorated with silver ornaments, tight-fitting cashmere trousers with silver buttons down the outer seam, and scarves around their necks. Boots, spurs, and six-shooters strapped to their hips in fancy, tooled-leather holsters completed the ensemble. At one end of the semicircle the musicians played big-bellied bass guitars; then a succession of guitars in decreasing sizes; then violins, followed by the trumpeters and the slide trombonists.

    Jethro lingered at the entrance, undecided about joining in, until his gaze settled on the lead singer. Dark-eyed, complexion Latin, and with a perfect, slightly upturned nose, she stood there with her fancy-tooled leather cowgirl boots spread slightly apart, holding a broad brimmed *sombrero* in one hand and the microphone in the other. Thus poised at the center of the semicircle formed by the band behind her, she warbled like a nightingale in a voice as clear as lightning.

Jethro no longer loitered as he stood there at the entrance of the lounge staring at her, and momentarily forgetting that he had to move. He looked over at the feature bill: *Araceli y Los Tradicionales*. And she was scheduled for the rest of the week.

Jethro now knew where he would be spending his evening hours—all of them. No crowd anywhere could compete with such a beauty singing ballads like that. And what ballads: about broken hearts, betrayal, and love gone awry. The lounge would be perfect to get lost in. He could sit there in the darkness, cry in his cups, listen to Araceli, and wear the shoes she sang about which would surely fit him well. And so it happened that Jethro spent his evenings seated at one of the lobby-bar tables, not too far from the stage. Always until closing time, he indulged himself with too much tequila and was carried away into numbing stupor, as he had wanted, by Araceli's sensitive *vibrato*.

Jethro could not carry on for long like that before his growing desire to meet Araceli demanded expression. Her entire stage manner worked like a salve on the ache in his chest, and made his recently acquired painful thoughts go increasingly away. She sang her songs, and Jethro, imagining that she was serenading him, hungered back at her, although he knew she could not see him beyond the glare of the stage lights. He thought to have lunch with her, but he would have to meet her first and somehow strike up a rapport.

The evening after he handed down his romantic self-conviction, he arrived a bit early, and as he strode into the squashed lounge, he almost collided with Araceli as she was making her way to some tables near the stage. As she passed him, Araceli snapped her head toward Jethro in what appeared to be an effort to give him a good look-over. However much the dark lounge prevented a good look at anything, Jethro was certain she had turned her head toward him in a double-take. His handsome face and manly form had impressed her; he was sure of it.

Thus encouraged, he sat at his usual table debating how to approach her when a man who was wandering around the lounge peddling Araceli's latest CD among the patrons came up to where Jethro was seated. With an outstretched hand holding a record with Araceli's face on it, he offered it for sale by quoting a price. Jethro was quick to reach in his pocket to retrieve the required sum and put it in the man's hand with the enthusiasm of a hearty handshake for this unexpected ticket to Araceli. The CD would provide the perfect excuse to talk to her, and he picked up a decent album in the bargain. Eventually, Araceli took a break from the music, and Jethro saw her step into an open closet near the entrance that housed stereo equipment. With CD in hand he walked over to the equipment closet, and there she was, reaching into her purse for who knows what. She looked up at Jethro as he stood in the closet doorway. She was much smaller in person than how she appeared on stage, but she was even more beautiful than the stage lights would allow.

"Hello, Araceli" Jethro began. "I love the way you sing."

"Thank you very much," she said with a ravishing smile. "That's very nice of you. Thank you very much."

"Look," stammered Jethro, holding up her CD. "I just bought your latest CD; will you sign it for me?"

"Of course. Here, give it to me. Are you from here?"

"No, I am from the border; I'm just here for a few days."

Araceli opened the CD and removed the cover jacket from inside the plastic case. "What's your name?" she asked.

"I'm Jethro. And you're Araceli, I already know; the poster outside told me." Araceli smiled while Jethro continued. "You're not from here either; how long will you be here?"

"I'm from Puebla. I'll be here a few more days. I was scheduled for the entire week, but I may have to leave sooner. Why?

"Well, because you know there's a lot to do in Mexico City; I could go wander around the crowds, but I'd rather listen to you."

Araceli beamed. "I'll be here tomorrow," she assured him. She then wrote, "For my friend Jethro, with affection, Araceli," on the CD cover and, slipping it back in its plastic, handed it back to Jethro.

Just then, the lights on the stage brightened up signaling that it was time for Arraceli's next set. She glanced over at the stage, and then back at him. By tilting her head slightly sideways towards the stage, she told Jethro she had to go. Jethro nodded back in understanding. His gaze fell on her single dark braid of hair that was draped over her shoulder, close to her neck. She smiled and turned towards the stage, but looked back at him as she walked toward it.

Jethro remained, listened, and drank, but it soon became evident to him that waiting to speak to her after the show would not do, especially as the tequila was now impairing his mental and physical faculties. If anything were to surely turn her off, Jethro reasoned, it would be an inebriated stranger named Jethro standing stupidly before her, awash in liquor, and stammering some drunken nonsense about wanting to have a quiet dinner with her. So he left the lounge and stumbled to his room. As he lay his clouded head to bed, through the fog he seized on a plan to visit the lounge early the following night and wait for Araceli's arrival before the show. There he would engage her in clever talk, then ask her out.

And certainly she would agree.

CHAPTER 21

HOT COFFEE

Jethro awoke late, and except for a dull ache pressing on his brain, his head was numb from the bludgeoning the tequila had given him the night before. It was mid-morning when he finally crawled out of bed. The mere thought of the unavoidable walk to the cappuccino bar he had seen across the park in front of the hotel made him feel weary. He wanted immediate relief— a strong dose of caffeine and three aspirin—but not a laborious walk beforehand. There was, however, no getting around it. The coffee served in hotel lobbies in Mexico Jethro knew to be weak, generally, and he doubted that the coffee served downstairs would be any different. He needed heavy duty stuff, and he wasn't taking any chances. To the cappuccino bar it would have to be.

He put on the same suit he had been wearing since he arrived in Mexico City and set out for a day about the town, wherever his whim might take him. He thought of his plan to meet Araceli that evening, but he was no longer sure of it, not now that the liquid courage tequila had lent him was gone. But he had an entire afternoon ahead of him, and plenty of time to think it over even if it had been only beer talk.

The elevator doors slid open, and Jethro walked into a buzz of activity. People were checking in and out of the hotel; bellhops pushed their way through the patrons, steering luggage racks full of cargo. People sat in the lounge areas, smoking and having a drink, and fashionable ladies in expensive resort-wear were promenading the lobby floor. On one side of the cavernous lobby an open-air piano bar offered a rather jazzed-up version of "Betcha By Golly Wow" at the hands of a blind pianist wearing mod sunglasses à la Elton John. Off to another side, the day restaurant echoed with laughter, conversation, and the clinking of knives and forks on china as waiters hustled about with heaping trays balanced precariously on the palm of one hand.

Jethro dodged his way through the mob, aiming for the street and the coffee bar opposite the hotel. His labored but determined stride was propelling him there with certainty when his steady pace slowed to a halt as his gaze landed on the billboard outside the hotel lounge entrance: Araceli was no longer the featured entertainment. In fact, she was not on the billboard at all. Instead, advertised on the bill was some male trio that crooned Mexican love ballads. Jethro paused for a moment, taking it in. "Just my luck," he sighed, and then pressed on to the coffee shop.

A small park separated the hotel from Jethro's destination. He walked across the park slowly, taking in the weather. His headache had not gone away, but the fantasy that was Araceli sure had. He looked up at the sky between the tree tops. It was a cloudy day, on the cool side, perfect for romance. Jethro sighed. And then, there was the coffee shop.

Jethro walked up to the order counter gazing up at the large menu on the wall behind the counter even though he already knew what he wanted. The attendant, a cheerful young lady, smiled at him nicely.

"May I take your order?"

Jethro asked for what he needed: a medium black with two shots of espresso. He looked around the counter in hopes of finding aspirin for sale, but found none. As the attendant went to fetch the coffee, Jethro leaned against the counter to casually survey the small café. The walls were decorated with posters advertising *"Faros,"* some really cheap Mexican cigarettes that enjoyed a cult following. Shelves against the walls housed an elaborate collection of antique espresso makers made of yellow brass and reddish copper. A few people occupied the handful of tables in the coffee shop, and Jethro's disinterested look made quick work of them—until his eyes bolted to attention as his gaze became fixed on one of the tables in a far corner. There was Araceli, sitting alone, a cup of cappuccino on the small table in front of her, an open magazine lying to one side. She wore a skirt made of suede that fell to below her knees, approaching her high topped boots. A short leather jacket accentuated her trim waist.

Jethro could not believe his eyes, and he looked impatiently over his shoulder for the attendant and his coffee, *Hurry up, damnit*, he felt like telling her. It was now or never, and he needed his coffee now, although not so much in order to drink it. The coffee arrived soon enough, and Araceli seemed engrossed in whatever she was reading. Jethro approached her table like a house cat stalking a sparrow, his eyes locked on her form, waiting to intercept her when she looked up. He neared the table, and she raised her head. Her eyes met his, but for a moment, Jethro detected non-recognition.

"Well, hello there." He spoke up. "Do you remember me? I'm Jethro."

Araceli paused briefly. "Of course, from last night. I signed your CD, Jethro. You have a strange name. Did you think I have a poor memory?"

"No, it's just that I thought that with so many people asking you for your autograph, you wouldn't remember everyone, least of all me."

Araceli gave him a hard look, but Jethro was quick on the repair. "You know I really love the way you sing. But what happened? I saw that you're not on the bill anymore. I thought you were still on for tonight?"

"There was a mix-up in scheduling, so I had to end early. My manager can't seem to get it right. I was supposed to sing there tonight, but that's what happens—too often." She gave a shrug of deliberate patience. "So now I'll just relax for the day. I'll be leaving tomorrow."

"Do you mind if I join you—for coffee, I mean?"

Araceli smiled at him and pointed her chin towards an empty chair at her table. Jethro took a seat.

"So how long have you been singing?"

"Oh, since I was a little girl. I've always loved to sing."

"Where are you from?"

"I'm from Puebla. You don't remember? I told you last night. It seems it's you who has a bad memory."

"Oh yes, that's right. It's not that I have a poor memory, though; I just wanted to show you how clumsy I can be at starting up conversations," Jethro parried. "I've never been to Puebla; I hear it's beautiful."

"It is very beautiful," Araceli answered with a genuine smile. "You should go there for a visit, you'd like it. You're certainly not from around here."

"No, as I told you, I'm from the border." Jethro answered.

"The border. I've never been there."

"It's very beautiful." Jethro teased. "You should go for a visit, you'll like it."

Araceli continued smiling at Jethro. "I've always thought the border to be a harsh place to live." Then her eyes looked over his suit. "Do you always wear the same suit every day, or did you not pack enough clothes?"

Jethro looked down at the condition of his suit which was rather on the crumpled side. He then studied Araceli, and now smiled at her. She gazed at Jethro through long-lashed, honey-brown eyes graced with small flecks of soft yellow and green.

Her hair, which had appeared black under the stage lights, was actually chestnut in color, and it flowed in loose waves to well below her shoulders, framing her angular face, which was more fair-skinned than olive. She had prominent cheekbones that caused near vertical lines for dimples on either cheek, and lips the upper outlines of which formed a perfect Cupid's bow. Her left eyebrow arched itself higher than the other, lending her an expression of half surprise, and half knowing realization.

"So, you noticed my wardrobe," he exclaimed enthusiastically. "I'm encouraged. I'm from Laredo, to be exact. I'm just here for a few days, and you're right, I didn't pack enough clothes. Don't worry, though, only the suit's the same. I equipped myself with everything else new from Sanborns." Jethro lied. He had not as of yet bought any change of clothes neither at Sanborns nor elsewhere.

"You didn't pack enough clothes. Hmmm….by the looks of it, you didn't pack at all. What is it, are you on the run? What were you getting away from in such a hurry?"

"Well, let's just say I had to go, okay? And you're getting a little ahead of yourself," answered Jethro with a cautious smile; he was enjoying this, but sobered up to how perceptive she was.

"Hmmm…did you do something really bad?"

Whether to speak frankly and risk repelling this brown-eyed beauty by sharing tawdry personal details, or try to woo her with clever, but superficial talk: that was the question. Jethro decided some middle ground would be safest.

"No, but what is happening to me right now is bad. It's hard to put it into words, and there are legalities involved."

"*Legalities?*" Araceli gave Jethro a look of perplexion. "What does that mean? Are you a criminal?"

"No, don't be silly. I'm just a lawyer." Jethro paused. He had already decided he could not tell her about the gun going off and a criminal complaint probably filed against him by his wife and her boyfriend. Then he dove in.

"Look, to be frank about it, my personal life is falling apart. In fact, it looks like it's headed for a crash, and I had to jump out of there for a few days, that's all."

"You had to jump out to avoid a crash, and you landed here in Mexico City, at the lobby bar for a few nights listening to my show?" Araceli slowly shook her head and smiled asymmetrically, half in disbelief and half having fun.

Jethro noticed that she had noticed his being there every night, and he thought she noticed that he noticed.

"That's pretty much it," he answered with a wide grin. "Aren't you the lucky one?"

Araceli returned a smile, amused by the back-handed compliment.

"So, have you always run away from problems?"

"I'm not running away." Jethro retorted emphatically. "Sometimes you have to pick your fights, you know? I needed to get away for the time being, but the problem isn't going to take care of itself with me here in Mexico City. I have to go back and deal with it. Sometimes, though, you have to use discretion and be careful about the right timing." Jethro paused with a stare into the black of his coffee. He was somewhat uncomfortable with how fast the conversation had travelled into personal details he would rather not have discussed at all. He looked back up at her. Her gaze had not left him.

"Araceli, have you ever been in a situation where something just happens to you, like an accident, even though you don't want it to happen, and even though you try to make it *not* happen, it happens anyway because people in your life insist on it being that way, and just do whatever they want to do?"

Araceli held her gaze on Jethro. Her face was pleasant; there was warmth in her honey-brown eyes. She seemed to understand.

"Maybe." She finally offered.

"Well, if you have, then you might know that sometimes things can get pretty difficult, matters can get ugly, and a confrontation at such a moment won't solve anything, but will only make the problem worse. If you understand that, then you'll understand why I had to go—for now. It's not running away; it's surviving to fight another day."

Araceli paused, slowly stirring the spoon in her cappuccino and then looked steadily into Jethro's eyes.

"I understand, more than you know," she said. "I've had troubles too, but unlike you, I couldn't just go. But that's another story, and speaking about having to go, I have to go soon."

"That sounds rather like a dismissal." Jethro playfully sulked. "And here I was thinking we might see the city together. Why do you have to go?"

"I'm not dismissing you. I'd love to continue our talk. But you know how work is. I still have a few loose ends to tie up at the hotel. I have to meet my manager in about half an hour. Then later, I'm supposed to go out to dinner with this group of promoters from the hotel. It's the typical ritual in my business. All I want to do is sing, but to do that, I have to put up with the industry."

Jethro liked her, this entertainer confronted with the inevitable reality of someone else controlling the stage she acted on.

"There are some artists," she continued, "who are such a big hit that they dictate where and when they will perform. Unfortunately for me, I haven't become one of those—at least not yet." She smiled mischievously at Jethro. "So I still have to pay homage to the promoters."

"You don't sound like you enjoy that part of your profession."

"I deal with it. I am an artist, but entertainment is a business, so it's just one of those things. It can be rough sometimes.

There are some compromises I am willing to make, and others I will never make. Some artists, regardless of talent, are willing to do anything for a shot at being a star. I was never one of those. So here I am; I think I sing well, but I'm not a big star. So tonight I'll have dinner with my manager and some promoters and listen to them exchange tales descriptive of their prowess. Besides, it's not like I have much else to do this evening." She looked at him with a pleasant smile.

Jethro raised his eyebrows, as though suggesting an alternate plan.

"Well, why don't you call your manager and tell him that you'll just have to see him later because you have something else to do this afternoon?"

"What do you mean, 'something else to do'?" Araceli gave Jethro an amused smile. "Do you mean something else to do…with you?"

"Exactly," invited Jethro with glee. "Let's go somewhere, Araceli. Let's go to the Zocalo and enjoy the atmosphere."

Araceli's eyes widened.

"Look, Jethro, that sounds nice, but I really—"

"No, you really don't anything," interrupted Jethro with a playful smile. "C'mon, let's get away; the hell with your managers and the industry. We can go to the Zocalo. The last time I was there, there were some dancers in Aztec costume dancing ritual dances, and there has been a lot of archeological digging going on there. They've uncovered much of Tenochtitlan's Templo Mayor; let's go see it. We can have lunch in a café near there that has a bullet hole in the ceiling— some guy during the revolution took his gun out and shot up in the air."

Araceli grinned. "The restaurant is called *La Ópera*, and the bullet hole was put there by Pancho Villa who galloped in on a horse," she said.

"Oh, then you know the place. C'mon, we'll have fun."

Araceli shook her head with a smile, as though she didn't know what she was getting herself into, but was going to do it anyway. Grabbing her purse and magazine, she inclined her head toward Jethro and breathed aloud, "Okay, let's go."

CHAPTER 22
LA ÓPERA

The *Zocalo* that they found waiting for them was as Jethro had anticipated, and a far cry from *La Zona Rosa* at night. Throngs of people milled about the square. Street vendors lined the sidewalks, while in the open stretches Mesoamerican dancers, beating their drums and tom-toms and rattling their rattles, wheeled around in patterned dances, their elaborate, feathered headdresses turning in cadence as they moved. Jethro and Araceli strolled slowly about the plaza, pausing to take in whatever interested them as they went along. They stopped for a good while at the now-exposed ruins of Tenochtitlan. Archeologists had recently uncovered the main temples: twin pyramids on which rituals involving human sacrifices were conducted by the ancient Aztecs. Jethro had often read about them and had seen artist's depictions of the pyramids. He thought they would be much taller than they appeared, exposed there, in ruins, in the heart of modern Mexico City.

"I thought they'd be much bigger," he remarked.

"Maybe they got squashed after being buried for centuries," suggested Araceli.

"Actually, the Aztecs built their pyramids overtime one on top of another like those Russian dolls that contain smaller and smaller dolls within each until you get to the tiniest one." Jethro went on. "After the Spaniards conquered the Aztecs, they destroyed the Aztec centers of worship thinking them to be satanic. What we're seeing here are the remains of pyramids older than those the Spaniards encountered. The ones we're looking at remained at ground level after the Spaniards destroyed the ones on top of those above ground. They must have buried these with the broken debris of those they destroyed leaving them for discovery in our modern times."

Jethro pointed to a small platform at the top of one of the pyramids. "Look, that's where they sacrificed human victims. They would spread the human offering over that small platform, with one priest holding the feet together while another held the hands. A third priest would then saw the heart out. Then they'd let the body tumble down the stone steps."

"Do you believe all that?" asked Araceli.

"Believe what? That they conducted human sacrifices? I think so. I've also read that they were cannibals."

"You know, I've read that the Spaniards exaggerated much of that because they had to justify their destruction of them," offered Araceli.

"Well, I wouldn't doubt it. The Spaniards had their own agenda, that's for sure. The Aztecs probably were cannibals, and the Spaniards were probably liars. I'm not sure what's exactly true. But have you seen pictures of Aztec gods? They look like monsters."

"They sure do. They have many of the original sculptures at the museum of anthropology not far from the hotel. Prehispanic Mexico has always fascinated me," said Araceli.

"Me too," agreed Jethro. "You know even if the Spanish exaggerated the extent of the Aztecs' ritual sacrifice, there's no question they did it."

"Yes," added Araceli, "they certainly did; can you imagine? Well into the sixteenth century."

"It is hard to believe, isn't it? Jethro and Araceli paused and stared at the ruins in silence. "One thing's for sure," he continued. "The Aztecs were delusional."

"What do you mean?" asked Araceli, glancing up at Jethro and then back at the ruined pyramids.

"I understand that they sacrificed humans to appease their gods so that the sun would keep rising and the rain would keep watering their crops. Well, all the human sacrificing they did had no effect whatsoever on the continued rising of the sun, or the seasonal rainfall. Did it? If it had, then the sun would have stopped rising after the Spaniards conquered them, and we'd still be sacrificing people today, having since recognized that their gods were for real."

"Okay—"

"And so we know that their gods were imaginary, and the Aztecs were delusional in believing in them to the extent that they did."

"Well, yes, Jethro," added Araceli, "but you could say the same thing about the Egyptians who built those great pyramids for the sake of what they thought their gods required, or the ancient Greeks or Romans who built all those temples for theirs—"

"That's right," continued Jethro, "they were all delusional."

"But Jethro," insisted Araceli, "even today, there must be hundreds of different gods that people all over the world believe in, and people engage in all sorts of different rituals, depending on the god they believe in…"

"Sure." Jethro conceded. "There must be at least a couple of hundred different gods that people believe in today. And until the real god speaks up so we can all gravitate to him or her, or it—I would say that all people who believe in whatever god are delusional to the same extent."

Araceli eyed at Jethro, who was gazing at the ancient Aztec pyramids

Jethro turned his face to hers, grinning with fun.

"It's just a thought, Araceli."

"No. It's not just a thought." She replied. "There's nothing ordinary about it." Their eyes met.

"There's nothing ordinary about you either." Jethro said without bothering to mask his admiration of her.

She smiled, and with that, they again turned to gaze at the ruins in silence for a while.

"Let's go eat at *La Ópera*; you want to?" offered Jethro after a time.

"Sure." Araceli smiled, and Jethro guided her into a tri-wheeled bicycle taxi.

La Ópera bar was among the most opulent *cantinas* in the city. Complete with gilded baroque ceilings and lengthy patches of beveled mirror, the restaurant featured cavernous, dark wood booths that were perfect for romantic interludes. Jethro and Araceli were lucky that afternoon, for although the place was teeming with people and tables were hard to find, they soon found themselves in a huge booth, and it was not too long before a large platter of clams lay before them, along with small glasses of classic tequila. The waiter suggested the specialty of the day, red snapper *Veracruzano*, with a sauce made of olives and tomatoes. Jethro and Araceli opted to share a plate, as the clams had provided almost enough for lunch.

"Well, that's a bullet hole up there, for sure," Jethro remarked as he peered up at the ceiling.

Araceli joined him in gazing upwards and studied the ceiling which was as decorated as a Faberge egg, however faded and musty with time. She glanced back at Jethro, who was holding a fork on which was balanced a bit of snapper, and shrugged as if to say, "I suppose so."

Jethro surveyed the crowded restaurant. Where there were no booths there were many linen-covered tables with people noisily enjoying lunch.

"I don't know, Araceli, I can't see how Pancho Villa could have galloped in here on a horse; I don't think he would have fit."

"Well, that's the story. Who knows?"

"If it wasn't Pancho Villa on a horse, then it was a drunken Villista, at any rate. I've read that those guys were really wild."

"Yes, it had to be a Villista," she agreed. "The Zapatistas were very respectful. They would never have shot their guns off in a place like this."

"Oh yes, they were very respectful; you can say that again. They killed just as many people as the Villistas, didn't they?" Jethro asked in a tone laced with sarcasm.

"Probably. But you know, the Zapatistas were *campesinos*. They were fighting for the land they had worked for generations, and they were against the wealthy landowners who basically enslaved them. When they killed, they did so for the sake of the revolution, which they believed in—but what they really believed in was the land they fought for. The Villistas, on the other hand, were bandits; they didn't work for anything, and they killed just to kill. For them, the revolution was one big killing spree."

Jethro mused back up at the ceiling.

"I see. The Zapatistas had principles." He teased. "I guess that makes them a better class of murderers than those raunchy Villistas."

Araceli gave Jethro a mocking sneer then smiled.

"You're a bit of a revolutionary, aren't you?" asked Jethro.

"*A revolutionary?*" She asked, pausing as she brought a forkful of sautéed spinach to her lips. "How so?"

"Well, here you are from Puebla, a traditional Mexican town, and you've sort of gotten away from the traditional role, right?"

"Do you mean the role of the woman who stays home, as they did in 1899?" asked Araceli taking a sip of white wine.

"Yeah, sort of. I don't mean it in a bad way, but isn't it less common for a woman to do what you do in Mexico than it is in America?" Jethro motioned the waiter for the bill. It was getting late, and he knew Araceli would have to talk to her manager at some point.

"I guess so. You know, I started as one would expect, in Puebla; I married young, and the role of homemaker was the norm, and that was what was expected of me. But my career led me away from that, as it turned out. I guess I'm not the traditional Mexican girl at all."

"What do you mean?"

"Well, I don't stay home; I travel a lot, for example. And show business being what it is, it can be a hard way of life, especially for a proper lady from Puebla." Araceli smiled coyly. "That doesn't mean that I've lost all principles, but I'm not exactly the sweet, innocent girl from Puebla one might expect."

"Oh, I see. So tell me, where have you been? Around the world or around the block?" Jethro teased.

"Oh, I've been all over Mexico, South and Central America," explained Araceli while smiling off the slight. "And, I've been to Spain; they seem to like charro music."

Jethro wondered what Araceli was trying to tell him. The road had not hardened her, at least not as far as Jethro could tell.

"And I've lived life, Jethro, if that's what you mean by going around the block."

"Well," he ventured, "maybe someday you'll find a reason to settle down once and for all." He raised his eyebrows twice at her as though to say that he would be the reason. Araceli smiled warmly.

"Shall we go?" Jethro rose from the booth and helped Araceli with her chair.

Mid-afternoon drew nigh. The Zocalo was not far away, and they strolled there to find a taxi back to the hotel. They were rewarded with a rare view on that fine day. Normally obscured by the city's dense smog, the snow-capped peak of Popocateptl, the smoking mountain, was clear to see. Jethro stood gazing at it with Araceli while standing among the ruins of Tenochtitlan and thought how the ancient Aztecs had shared the same view, albeit with a different reverence. And just then, a break in the clouds allowed the sun to shine on through, to glisten and glimmer in yellows and reds on the snowy face of the volcano. They turned to each other with smiles. It was a special moment, and before Jethro realized what he was doing, he bent forward to kiss her, and she met him halfway.

They arrived back at the hotel after a lazy taxi ride that made its way through the dense traffic without too much standstill. The lunch weighed on Jethro who now felt very sleepy. They walked into the lobby and paused at the piano bar. The blind piano player was playing mood music. They paused and looked at each other.

"What are you going to do?" asked Jethro.

"I really should meet with my manager. I had a lot of fun escaping with you, but I have to talk about what's next. For sure they'll want to go out to dinner. I hate those dinners."

"I'll tell you what. You go meet with them, and then let's you and I go out to dinner."

"You want me to tell my manager to go on his own, as though I didn't care, and then you and I go some place together, alone?"

"Well, I sure as hell don't want your promoters to come along with us. Do you?"

Aracelli gave Jethro a coy look and then snickered.

"Look, why not?" insisted Jethro. "We had a nice afternoon alone..." He shrugged slightly commenting on the comfortable, casual ease that marked their afternoon together. "We can meet in the hotel lobby and take a walk to the Zona Rosa. There's a little Italian restaurant there where I have been having dinner every night. It's not bad. We can have a glass of wine, or two, or three; a light dinner. It looks like it's going to be a nice evening." Jethro dared her with a grin.

Araceli seemed to give Jethro's invitation some thought.

"That's very nice of you, but I really have this obligation with the promoters, and they expect me to be there..."

"And aren't you always there? You never miss, do you? You always do what they expect, don't you?

"Well yes...of course..." Araceli answered with some hesitation that underscored her reluctance to frankly concede anymore resentment towards her handlers. Yet the corners of her lips widened, slightly, giving a hint of a smile as she acknowledged how well Jethro had read her.

"And still they have scheduling problems for you to put up with," he pressed. "They're unpredictable, aren't they, these unscheduled days off when you'd rather be on stage? I'll bet your absence this afternoon took them by surprise. I'm sure they didn't expect it. " Araceli took in his words. "Look," he continued while the iron was hot, "go meet with your manager. I'll go to my room and watch T.V. My room is number 747, like that big jet they used to have. I'll be there until around nine before I go to the Zona Rosa alone if you chicken out on me. Just think about it, okay? And if you would like to go out for a casual dinner or a glass of wine, or just go for an evening's walk, call me; I'll be there."

"Well, we'll see." Araceli made to leave, smiling longingly at Jethro as she did so. Jethro took her hand, but she went to him and embraced him, kissing him warmly on the cheek.

"I'll be waiting for you." Jethro watched her go and thought he would never see her again.

Before going up to his room, he went to the front desk to ask for directions to the nearest Sanborn's.

CHAPTER 23

ARACELI

What Jethro thought to be an alarm clock waking him from his deep slumber was actually the ringing of the telephone. Momentarily disoriented, he raised his head, looking about for the source of the noise, when he snapped to and lunged for the phone.

It was her.

"Were you asleep?"

"Actually, I dozed off a bit; I didn't think you'd call."

"I wasn't going to."

"And you changed your mind because..?"

"I didn't want to follow the same script. I don't know, I thought about what you said. And I had a really nice time this afternoon with you."

"Well, so did I, and you've come to the right place," announced Jethro as he sat up on the bed, fully awake now, planting both feet on the floor. "Shall we meet downstairs, say, in twenty minutes?"

"I'll be waiting."

At Sanborns, a fashionable department store adjacent to the hotel, Jethro had bought a fresh shirt and a few other things. Later, back in his hotel room he had summoned customer service to have his suit pressed. Now he called the concierge to have it brought up. It was ready, thank goodness, and so was he.

Jethro took a quick shower and climbed again into his only suit, which now looked fresh, as were his new shirt and other apparel. Smoothing his hair back, he headed for the lobby… and Araceli.

He found her at its far side, beyond the hotel's convenience store. She was leaning with her back against the wall, her hands together in front of her, clasping a small purse. She wore a simple, form fitting black dress that fell to just below the knees. Wrapped around her shoulders she wore an ivory colored shawl, or Mexican *rebozo*, complete with fringes along its edges. Several strings of irregularly shaped beads of Mayan imperial jade from pre-conquest Mesoamerica adorned her neck to add a dazzle of color to her appearance as did a silver clasp over her left wrist which also included a few bracelets of similar vein. The night was misty and cool, and her hair flowed loosely down the sides of her face just grazing her upper back. As Jethro approached her, she straightened herself off the wall and smiled.

"Shall we?" Jethro offered her his arm. She nodded and wove her right arm through his left. Together they walked out of the hotel and into the evening.

The waiter with the sommelier's cup around his neck smiled at Jethro as though to congratulate him as he uncorked the bottle of Spanish Rioja. He had come to know Jethro as a new, but increasingly familiar customer—the one who always wore the same dark grey suit, tipped well, and always dined alone with a somber look on his face. But not so tonight. Although Jethro wasn't laughing it up as he might, he certainly wasn't alone; and he wasn't somber.

Araceli sat across the small table from Jethro, gazing back at him. They didn't talk much at first, not so much out of shyness, but because of how suddenly their meeting, and now this moment, had arisen. With the day over, the relaxed mood had sobered a bit, and a frank assessment of the stranger before each of them was in order.

"So, you never finished telling me: you're on the run." Araceli started, going straight to the point.

"Not exactly, but I guess you could say that. I—"

"No, no, don't tell me from what; I want to guess. Let me think...you shot someone."

"I already told you, I'm not a criminal. I didn't shoot anybody. Just because *you* wear a cowboy gun on stage doesn't mean everyone packs a pistol." Jethro was aware that he had just met this striking woman he liked and already he was telling a white lie; but he wasn't about to tell her the truth—at least not yet, and maybe never.

"Did your promoter give you a hard time?"

"Not really. They market you where they think they can make money. They put my album out, and they keep scheduling me at different places. But they bump me when they need to in order to work in different performers. Now they've booked me for a few nights in Ixtapa-Zihuatanego. I'll go home for a long vacation after that."

"Ixtapa? Isn't that in the jungle?"

"No, it's on the Pacific coast, not far up the coast from Acapulco. Zihuatanego is really old-fashioned, and quite charming. Ixtapa is across the bay from Zihuatanego, and it's more modern and trendy. It can be fun. There's a really nice hotel there, where I'll be playing." Araceli raised her eyebrows at Jethro as she said this, as though to suggest a plan. She was clearly having fun, as was Jethro. "I must admit, Jethro, for its being your only suit, it is a nice one."

The waiter served their dinner—a beautiful veal *con porcini* to accompany the Rioja.

"You're still hung up on my only suit, just because I've worn it for days? Well, I'll have you know that I've had it pressed and laundered at the hotel. It is a nice suit: see?" Jethro showed her the label on the inside of the jacket. "It was custom made for me in China."

"You bought that suit in China?"

"No, no. Don't jump to conclusions," Jethro admonished. "I bought it from a travelling tailor. He comes around every few months, takes my measurements, shows me fabrics, and mails me the suit when it's made. Are you married?"

"Well, Jethro, given how quickly you run off to places, you might have gone all the way to China just to buy a suit." She smiled as she placed a piece of veal and a couple of mushrooms onto her fork. "I used to be married. I told you I married young. "

"Yes, I remember; I just wasn't sure if you still were. What happened?"

"It didn't work out. My ex-husband didn't want me singing. At first he gave me his support, but he seemed to grow resentful when my career began to show some promise. I don't know. We grew apart. I would have never left him. But he just didn't want me to be me."

"He was jealous of your career?"

"You know, I don't think it was that, exactly. It was more as though he wanted to rip my heart out for my *wanting* to pursue my career. I think he really believed that the only thing I should ever have wanted was to be there for him, and to stay at home most of the time. He could not understand my doing anything for *me*, and he took my pursuing a singing career as a betrayal of some kind; as though I had left his side. "

Jethro took a drink of wine as she said this, asking himself whether that sort of thing was at work between him and Sadie. Just as that thought occurred to him, Araceli interrupted it.

"I know! You were caught with another man's wife, and you had to skip town in order to avoid being killed by her jealous-crazed husband."

Jethro hid his surprise. She almost had it right, only it was the other way around. With that, however, the seriousness of his situation was brought home to him, and he no longer wished to play games. He frowned as his eyes darkened.

"That's it, isn't it? You broke up someone's home?"

The dark cloud over Jethro was not lost on Araceli. He laughed slightly at the irony.

"No, Araceli, I didn't break up anyone's home, and I'm not running away from a jealous husband. But that was a very good guess."

"It's partly true, then?"

"In a way." Jethro held her gaze as he answered. Her eyes didn't stray. "Araceli, I'm married, and it appears my wife is getting involved with another man. I left town because I didn't want to become a criminal."

Araceli put her knife and fork down.

"It appears that she is? You're not sure?"

Jethro wiped his mouth with his table napkin then laid it carefully by the side of the plate. He signaled the waiter.

"Would you like a cognac?"

"Later, maybe?"

"Sure. You don't mind if I have one now, do you?"

She shook her head, and to the waiter he said, "Un *Cordon Bleu*." He then turned to Araceli.

"Oh, so you really know your cognacs, huh?" she asked with a slight smirk.

"Not really. In fact, I hardly ever drink the stuff. Cordon Bleu is the only one I know by any name. I actually prefer tequila."

"So why are you having a cognac instead?"

"I don't know," he answered. "I figured what the hell."

Jethro paused, his gaze fixed on the pattern-less table cloth.

"Jethro, you don't owe me any explanations," said Araceli.

Jethro knew she was only being polite. She wanted a complete explanation.

"It's a rather long story," he said. "Do you want to hear it?"

"If you want to tell it."

The cognac arrived. Jethro swirled it around in its goblet, inhaled its fumes, and then knocked it back by the mouthful. He then told Araceli everything, including the dreaded tequila incident at Benny's hovel being careful to leave out the part about the pistol shot, of course. Araceli listened quietly, stopping Jethro only when necessary for clarification. She really seemed to care, and to want to understand. Jethro expected nothing more from Araceli but a compassionate ear, but then she lowered the boom.

"Jethro, you know you have to divorce her, don't you?"

Jethro paused at Araceli's audacity, yet he knew it was true.

"I don't know, Araceli, I just don't know. Maybe I'm being stupid. Maybe they're just friends, and I'm being a *macho*. Maybe I'm reading my own insecurities into it. Maybe I want to rip her heart out simply because she wants to go, regardless of where she goes, or with whom, or to what extent. That's what happened to you, isn't it?"

Araceli lowered her head and then pinched the upper bridge of her nose as though she were massaging irritation from wearing eyeglasses. She shook her head to shake off the astonishment, and then looked up.

"Jethro, Jethro, Jethro… May I have that cognac now?" She gave him a soft, knowing smile.

Jethro gave a short breath of a laugh.

"Sure, I'll join you. Would you like some flan? It's pretty good here."

"I'll share one with you." She said warmly.

Jethro signaled the vigilant waiter nearby. "*Two* Cordon Bleus this time, please, and a coconut flan with two forks," and then to Araceli, "Cappuccino?" She signaled no. Then a nod to the waiter that that would be all. The waiter gave Jethro a congratulatory grin so filled with enthusiasm that he might as well have given him a high five or two thumbs up on a good score.

For the sake of Araceli, Jethro gave no response to the waiter's gesture however positive its intention may have been.

"You're in a real mess, Jethro."

"You're telling me. I'm not sure what to do. Part of me knows that what has happened so far is fatal to my marriage. It's like a broken plate now. Even if you put it back together with great care, the cracks are still there, and it will never be the same. On the other hand, part of me thinks I'm being a macho ass, and maybe I'm the problem. What if they're only just friends? What's wrong with that? I seriously doubt they've slept together."

Araceli eyed him with maternal benevolence.

"That's not what matters," she flatly stated. "What is important is that in her heart, she abandoned you; she left you. Your wife stayed with that man instead of being with you; she took his side instead of yours. In her heart she is no longer your wife, Jethro. She has already left you — and that is what matters, nothing else. If you were to stay with her in spite of what's happened, you'll hate yourself forever, you'll hate her, and you'll never again be the man you are. You have to divorce her, Jethro; you have no choice."

Jethro sat there in silence gazing blankly into Araceli's eyes. She had struck him hard with the truth he already knew, but had denied with self-indulgent blather.

The cognac and flan arrived. The waiter placed the flan between the couple with a courtesy and care reserved for the most welcomed of patrons. Jethro nodded at the waiter in acknowledgement and then at Araceli invitingly. He then stabbed his fork into the creamy dessert with a dry disinterest. There was no smile in his eyes.

Outside, the weather had turned damp, and though it was chilly, they strolled slowly through the empty Zona Rosa arm in arm.

"It's really too bad you're leaving tomorrow. We should spend more time together," he said.

"Yes, it is a pity. You know where I'm going," she said looking up at him.

"Yes, I know," he answered pulling her closer to him, his arm around her slender waist. "But how much time would we have even if I went? I can't avoid my situation for too long—I don't think we would have enough time to get to know each other enough anyway."

"Enough for what?"

"Well, you know, when there's too little time, only the simplest of relationships can survive. Nice, friendly, platonic relationships. Which is fine; there's nothing wrong with that type of relationship."

"Oh, so are you aiming at something beyond a platonic relationship with me? You sure get right to the point, don't you?"

"Why wouldn't I? I don't need a lot of time to know that I want to be close to you. The problem is that without enough time, even a promising start can hardly undergo all the natural reactions that would happen between us, and which would be necessary for a meaningful relationship to form."

She paused at this, gazing at him and then at the sidewalk before them. The sound of their footsteps grew louder as the silence between them lingered.

"You could call me, and we could keep in touch," she said finally.

"Yes, of course, I would love to, and I will." Jethro assured her. "But even if there's a little fire between us, don't you think it will go out sooner rather than later?"

Araceli shrugged and smiled.

"Not if we don't let it."

"But I don't know where I'm going with my situation."

"Yes you do."

Jethro stopped and turned to her.

"Yes…I do." He took a deep breath and nodded. "Yes I do."

They resumed their slow stroll. They had by then left the Zona Rosa and before them now stretched the expansive *Paseo Reforma*. Given the lamps that lined it, the atmosphere of the spacious boulevard was brighter than what the closed Zona Rosa had offered. The glow of the park lamps was softened, however, by the mist that hung in the air. The streets that sandwiched the *Paseo* shone a pitch black instead of their usual pencil-lead grey. A modest traffic sailed by, their headlights reflecting in a pale, shimmering yellow on the wet pavement.

"But nothing seems to last in this day and age," Jethro spoke up. "I want something that will last. Don't you?"

"Yes of course, Jethro, I also want something that will last; I never wanted to be a divorced woman. It just happened. What I wanted didn't matter in the end."

"Did it get ugly?"

"We fought; it wasn't pretty. Eventually the fights became pointless. I saw that it was no use." Araceli sighed in resignation.

"Yeah, well I'm about to become a divorced man. But the fight's not over."

"There's no point in fighting, not if there is no hope," Araceli answered. "Do you really think there is a chance that you might reconcile with your wife?"

"No, I don't. But the fight is not over because I still have to go through the divorce, and they are not going to get the best of me, Araceli. Right now, my wife and her boyfriend think they've got me where they want me. I've been thrown out of the house and they're laughing at me, while I have to just take it because—well, I'm not going to just take it."

"What are you going to do?"

"I'm not quite sure yet. I need some time. I'll figure something out," Jethro answered dryly. "It's not her I'm fighting for; I'm fighting for myself—for my own dignity."

Araceli gave Jethro an admiring nod, and they walked in silence for a while.

Then she asked, "How will you recognize something that lasts if you think you found it; how will you know that it's it?"

Jethro considered the question and took time to answer. "I don't know that you can ever know for sure; a lasting relationship doesn't have a certain look to it, I don't think. No matter how sure you may feel, you're still making a bet out of life. Only time will tell. You know, it used to be that divorces were rare."

"Now everybody seems to get divorced," agreed Araceli.

"That's how it is. It used to be that society made marriages last a lifetime by not allowing an easy way out. Divorces were considered shameful, and it had to be somebody's fault for a divorce to be granted. It's very different today. All it takes these days to get a divorce is for somebody to be unhappy, it doesn't have to be anybody's fault; and, society couldn't care less."

"Do you think you are responsible for making your spouse happy?"

"No, I don't," answered Jethro. "Though I surely tried hard enough in my marriage. I think I tried too hard. In fact, I think that was my biggest mistake."

"Trying to make her happy was your biggest mistake?"

"No, what I mean is that I overindulged her," Jethro explained. "Her Daddy treated her like a princess, and that's what she thought she was, and I'm guilty of treating her like a princess, too. I mean I did everything for her. She couldn't do anything and wouldn't do anything except run around with her friends and go shopping. I thought I could make her happy by letting her do whatever she wanted and not making her participate in what had to be done. I wound up taking care of a child in an adult body. But by her being Daddy's princess, and with me perpetuating the syndrome, there was no way she would ever grow up. She was playing princess, and I was playing prince charming like an idiot.

"But is it wrong to try and make your spouse happy?" Araceli insisted.

"Not necessarily," continued Jethro. "But it becomes wrong when the happiness of only one individual is relevant, and the other individual has the job of making that person's happiness happen. That's what I now realize *happened* to me. In my marriage, only the happiness of my wife mattered, and I blindly did everything I could to make her happy. How ridiculous!"

"Yes, Jethro, but we all try to make each other happy," she responded. "There's nothing wrong with that."

"That's right, and the operative word is "we." What is important is reciprocity. If both are committed to each other and to each other's happiness, and both participate in making the house a home, a tranquil home, and in sharing a peaceful life together—that's what it's about." Jethro paused in silence for a moment. "But to answer your question, Araceli, I think that a person is responsible for his or her own happiness."

Araceli shuddered in the chill, and Jethro held her tightly. She leaned into him. They stopped. She met his eyes. Her lips parted slightly, the glint of her white teeth showed through. Jethro gently kissed her lips, holding her chin in his hand as he did so.

Arriving at the hotel, Jethro paused as they passed the lobby bar. But then he kept his gait. The look from Araceli was clear. They'd had enough with bars. At the elevators, both had to go up, with Jethro on the seventh floor with her on the ninth.

As the elevator made its noises, traveling down the shaft to give them a lift, Jethro and Araceli gazed at each other.

"You are irresistible, Araceli."

"Well then, don't resist me."

They entered the elevator, and Jethro pressed 7 and 9. Just before the doors slid to a close, however, Jethro heard the call of an old man trying to catch the elevator. "Wait, wait, wait for us…".

Jethro pressed the button that held the doors open. An apparent octogenarian with a cane was walking as fast as he could, which was labored at best, to reach the elevator. Slightly behind him shuffled an old woman—undoubtedly his wife.

Jethro glanced at Araceli.

"Here comes something that apparently lasted."

The old man and his wife reached the elevator. Haltingly, the aged gentleman reached for the edge of the elevator door to hold it open while his wife caught up but Jethro got there first and held the elevator doors securely open for the elderly couple. Hooking his cane on his arm, the old man reached for his wife and gently guided her steps as she boarded the lift.

"Watch your step there, my dear, you don't move like you used to," he said winking at Jethro teasingly. "Don't worry; the door won't close we've got a strong young man helping us here. Thank you, son." He nodded at Jethro.

The old woman, in labored half-steps, positioned herself at the rear of the elevator, in between Jethro and Araceli. The old man then joined her by her side.

"*Buenas noches,*" they said in unison to Jethro and Araceli.

"*Buenas Noches,*" they answered.

Jethro and Araceli looked at each other over and above the senior citizens now between them. Araceli smiled. The old couple stood arm in arm in dignified silence. The elevator had not yet moved. Jethro asked them what floor they wanted and pressed 5 for them.

As quickly as the elevator began its climb, it stopped at level 2. The doors slid open and a young couple clattered halfway in, the female of the pair stopping mid-entrance, blocking the elevator door from closing. They were dressed in formal evening attire—he in a tuxedo with a carnation pinned to his lapel, and she in a lavender evening gown, her hair done up in a beehive bound by a matching lavender ribbon. A corsage of the same shade was attached to her wrist. The elevator was immediately engulfed with a strong smell of cologne, overpowering perfume, and the distinctive aroma of cigarette smoke the young couple had apparently absorbed while with a crowd of elegant partiers in one of the ballrooms on the second floor, sipping champagne and smoking cigarettes and cigars. The couple was in the throes of an emotionally charged argument.

"No I was not flirting with her," insisted the young man from inside the elevator. He had backed into it, oblivious to his almost bumping into the elderly gentleman who raised his cane to ward off the collision.

"Yes you were," the girl with the beehive insisted. "I saw you looking at her and the way she looked at you." She leaned against the elevator door, in need of support given her rather advanced state of inebriation. Her lipstick was a bit smudged and the eyeliner under her left eye had begun to run.

"You're delusional," he insisted." Your own insecurities are causing you to see things. She's not even my type. Besides, you sure were having a good time with Rodolfo. You never danced like that with me!"

"He's just a *friend*, you insecure *machista*!" she yelled. "And you don't even know how to dance. It's not my fault you don't know how to have any *fun*!"

Araceli questioned Jethro with her eyes. The elevator was going nowhere, and it didn't seem like the estranged couple's dispute would reach any resolution soon.

"Uh...listen you two," Jethro spoke up. "Maybe you could take this elsewhere?"

The quibbling couple stopped and stared at the inhabitants of the elevator as though they had not realized before that moment that anyone else had been there at all. While the young man looked at them with a wild disregard, the young lady dashed off down the hallway. The tuxedo rushed off in pursuit.

"Where the hell are you going?" He called out loud as he took off after her.

The elevator doors slid to a close.

As the elevator crept its way up again, the old lady turned to her husband and asked in a hushed tone, "Are you sleepy, old man?"

"I'm a little tired. We can watch some TV; your favorite program will soon be on." The old man gave his wife a twinkly smile as he said this. And then the elevator arrived at the fifth floor.

Jethro stepped forward and held the elevator door with his outstretched hand.

"Thank you, young man," said the senior citizen as he grabbed his wife's elbow to guide her out of the elevator.

The old woman turned back to Jethro and Araceli as she left the elevator, "Have a good night."

As he moved past Jethro, the old man paused long enough to look Jethro in the eye. Smiling, he flicked his head slightly toward Araceli, looked over at her, and then back at Jethro. Araceli straightened up in anticipation of what the old man might do or say.

"Don't let go of her, young man; she's just right for you." He said while tapping the crook of his cane on Jethro's chest. "Have a good night, both of you," he smiled warmly at both Araceli and Jethro before shuffling slowly away.

Jethro and Araceli smiled at each other. The elevator doors closed and up it went.

"Do you think that old couple rediscovered what they meant to each other when both were young?" wondered Araceli aloud.

"I don't know; maybe their love never dwindled," said Jethro. "For some people, it's not the having but the getting that matters. That old couple seems to appreciate what they have."

"They never let go of each other," she said. "That much is for sure."

The elevator stopped at the seventh floor. The doors opened. Jethro held them open, and studied Araceli.

"Maybe we shouldn't let go of each other."

Araceli looked long and hard at Jethro. She then walked out of the elevator with him.

CHAPTER 24

IXTAPA-ZIHUATANEJO OR BUST

Jethro awoke the next morning with a start. Opening his eyes, he raised his head, and blinked around the empty room. Something was different but for an instant he did not know what. Then the thought of Araceli struck him as did the impression of her having left very early in the morning. Jethro sank into his pillow and closed his eyes. He well recalled her goodbye kiss, and blissful memories of the previous night came flooding back. Now, hours later, she was gone. Jethro rolled over onto his side and lay there breathing into the pillow next to him where she had slept. The smell of her perfume still lingered. Jethro rolled onto his back and closed his eyes. "I can't believe this," he groaned. But then he thought of her lovely face, the sweep of her hair, the way she carried herself, and how she looked at him. He missed her.

He crawled out of bed and made his way to the bathroom. There on the dresser lay a note from Araceli. She had left her contact information, and then, "Jethro, I will be in Ixtapa. You know where. Find me if you can. You will be in my thoughts. Yours, Araceli."

Jethro studied himself in the mirror. His smile grew broader as the conviction to go to Ixtapa appealed to him more and more. He would find Araceli. He would start a new life. *Yes*, he kept thinking, *Ixtapa-Zihuatanego; Araceli*. He decided to go there at once and quickly gathered his things.

The airport was a madhouse packed with families trying to get out of town. Unbeknownst to Jethro, it was the custom of the well-to-do in Mexico City to vacation during the Christmas and New Year's holidays. Flights were oversold. The airline counters were besieged with mobs of affluent Mexicans demanding their tickets out, as though they were fleeing a calamity and getting out meant survival.

Jethro pushed and jostled his way through the crowd, headed for Mexicana Airlines. The ticket counter was packed to the gills. A long line of would-be travelers stood ahead of him. People were arguing and children were complaining. Husbands were impatient with wives. At the counter, an irate traveler whose luggage had been sent through to his destination, but who himself had been bumped off his flight, almost came to blows with the ticket salesperson. Adding to his fury was the fact that some members of his family had managed to get on the plane, while others, like him, had not. The infuriated traveler was yelling at the top of his lungs, demanding that he be allowed to take his place on a jet plane that was already pressure-sealed and taxiing its way down the tarmac. The irate traveler's contorted face was as red as a tomato, spit was flying, and his veins were bulging out his neck and forehead. Jethro watched with anticipation of witnessing a physical altercation in which a member of the Mexican elite, educated and refined, was about to take matters to the primitive level of the street.

Suddenly, whistles could be heard blowing from a distance and coming nearer, quickly. Security had been summoned, and there, weaving through the crowd, came the security guards in a determined rush. They were dressed in blue uniforms with black Sam Brownes, wielding billy clubs in hand. The irate gentleman turned his bulging glare on them. He did not get far with his sputtering demands, however, before they grabbed him and forcefully hustled him away.

Jethro surveyed the throbbing crowd, pressing against each other, heaving to and fro, and shouting at the ticket personnel. There would be no traveling by airplane today. Slowly he shrank away. Ixtapa-Zihuatanego had been a nice, frenzied dream. And that was all it would be. He would have to let go of any desire for Araceli, at least for the time being. He took a taxi back to the same hotel, rented the same room he'd occupied before, tossed himself onto the same bed, and stared up at the same ceiling.

CHAPTER 25

JETHRO SPOOKED AT MUSEUM

Jethro stood by his hotel window. Below him stretched the *Paseo Reforma* — the huge boulevard that bisects the Aztec capital. And there before him, in full view from the window, stood an iconic Mexican monument: a golden angel, the "Winged Victory." The golden sculpture depicted the Greek Goddess of Victory, Nike by name, having just flown in, her wings spread wide as she alighted with one foot atop a single Corinthian column while holding aloft a laurel wreath in an outstretched hand signaling victory, her golden robes draped by the wind against her glittering form. Only Mercury could marshal speed with similar grace and beauty.

On the seventh floor of the hotel, Jethro was almost eye level with the angel. The base of the monument housed, on display behind crystal sepulchers, the bones of heroes of Mexican Independence. Jethro had wandered in there once to look at the heroes' remains; but they didn't interest him much now. Cars circled the monument, and people were walking on the sidewalks and in the park opposite the hotel. Jethro thought of Araceli. How he wished she were with him now. Not having anything else to do, he decided to visit the Museum of Anthropology she had mentioned. It was about a mile or two from the hotel—a nice walk up the *Paseo Reforma*.

The midday sun warmed Jethro's face as he strolled along, but he arrived at the museum hot from a hike that took longer than he thought it would. The entrance of the museum appeared cavernous and dark, and a mass of cooled air met him as he bought an entrance ticket and pushed through the turnstile. Ahead lay a maze of inky chambers, each faintly illuminated by soft, pastel colored lights aimed at the various displays. He wandered around, gazing at the many fine examples of Pre-Columbian art until he arrived at the immense Sun Stone, that magnificent Aztec calendar. It was bigger than he had imagined, for he had only seen it in photos. Inspecting it from a close distance, he noticed that it still had original paint here and there — not enough to allow one to behold its original color scheme, but enough to tell that it had originally been brightly painted with many colors. The calendar was once a relief sculpture, with part of the wall it had adorned still evident about its edges. The conquering Spaniards had tried to destroy it in their effort to stamp out the ancient Aztec culture, which they believed to be Satan-infested. The Spaniards had succeeded in knocking it down, but they failed in its destruction. Unearthed centuries later, the Sun Stone was now the pride of Mexico; its iconic symbol.

 Elsewhere in the museum, Jethro encountered an array of stone sculptures some of which the Aztecs had used as receptacles for the hearts of sacrificial victims. One of the sculptures consisted of a massive, squat cylinder, resembling the drum of a gigantic unfinished column. The top of the cylindrical sculpture served as a platform, a spacious bowl hewn at its center. It was into this stone bowl that the Aztec priests tossed the still-beating hearts of sacrificial victims. Emanating from the bowl were small channels, like rain gutters or storm drains, where the blood in little rivulets flowed away to be collected, perhaps, in portable receptacles dutifully held by would-be altar boys. Something about how thoughtful the Aztecs had been in engineering their sacrificial furniture caught Jethro in the gut. Relief sculptures of great skill and artistry decorated the sides of the platform, lending a sinister delicacy to its appearance. Jethro backed away from the object and the inherent contradiction it embodied: exquisite artistic beauty celebrating the macabre.

Jethro retreated away from the death sculpture. Backing into an adjacent vestibule, he collided with a glass case where, on display, lay a collection of magnificent sacrificial daggers. Originals, these were knives the Aztec priests had practiced their bloody rituals with, using them to saw the hearts out of the chests of countless victims offered as sacrifices for their gods. Objects of the highest craftsmanship, their black obsidian blades displayed fantastic knap work of machinelike precision. Again the strange dichotomy of high art blended with sinister purpose disturbed Jethro in spirit. *How appropriate that the daggers should be adjacent to that weird table over there*, thought Jethro as he reflected on his own heart and how much trouble it had caused him. How many fatal decisions had his heart led him into? How much heartache had the results brought? Aztec gods, apparently, needed hearts more than humans. *They can sure have mine, if they want it. Then I wouldn't feel a thing.* Something began to turn in Jethro's stomach, and his head began to swim.

Jethro backed away from the daggers on display, crashing into yet another object of art. But this one hurt, it was made of stone. Spinning around, he came face to face with the statue of *Coatlicue*, the mother of the Aztec god *Huitzilopochtli*, in whose honor the obsidian daggers and stone receptacle for pulsing hearts were put to blood-dripping use. A veritable monster from hell, Coatlicue loomed over Jethro scowling down at him with gnashing teeth and glaring fangs, and draped in human skulls and rattlesnakes.

Jethro's spirits began to plummet. He was surrounded by objects from hell, which only served to underscore what his life had become. *I shouldn't be here*, he thought to himself, his reeling mind now swimming with depressing thoughts. *What am I doing here in Mexico City? What did I do last night? What the fuck is my life coming to?* With deepening shame he realized that he had perpetrated the same insult to his marriage that he believed Sadie was doing. *I'm no better and no worse; I'm just as bad,* ran the stubborn self-accusations. Wasn't he still a married man? The grotesque images began to swirl around in his head, adding to the distortion in his mind and amplifying the moral hangover he had begun to suffer.

Jethro felt a strong urge to get the hell out of there, fast. He rushed for the exits, and a feeling of nausea overcame him as he fled the museum.

CHAPTER 26

JETHRO BEATEN BY ALLEY CAT

Treading wearily down the avenue on his way back to the hotel, Jethro felt sweat dribble down his back, and his feet grew as heavy as a pair of cinder blocks. He wanted now to get out of the sun, and to hide in the darkness of his hotel room with the air conditioner on high. But he had quite a distance to go. So, on he lumbered, with stooped shoulders and head downcast.

Presently, Jethro noticed over to his right, atop a grassy knoll that sloped down to the edge of the sidewalk, a cat, jet black in color, sauntering in his general direction. Walking not quite parallel with Jethro, the cat, with silky gracefulness, traveled at a shallow angle set to intersect Jethro's path further along the sidewalk.

Not particularly superstitious, and at any rate not believing that a black cat crossing one's path was of any significance, Jethro nevertheless, but without any special heed or effort, casually sped up his pace so he would cross ahead of the cat. As he quickened his pace, however, the cat did as well. Jethro went a bit faster, and the cat did too. His interest now sparked, and no longer slouching but walking upright with added determination, Jethro sped up some more, to which effort the cat responded by breaking into a light trot.

Jethro was now wide awake, his lazy stroll having become a competition between him and this purposeful black feline.

How quickly Jethro's sluggardly pace had turned steady, then sure; determined, then brisk; but the cat had matched him, to Jethro's growing dismay. The cat could have darted off at a speed Jethro could never compete with; or it could have simply turned off in another direction, ignoring Jethro altogether. But that was not happening. Instead, the cat kept its pace measured with that of Jethro so their paths would inevitably cross, with the cat just in front of his.

What had begun as mild amusement had turned into utter astonishment as Jethro realized that the cat was as determined as he to win what had become a race. Jethro began to run, but so did the cat. Jethro now sprang into a dash, full blast, as though having just been handed the baton in an 800-meter relay. But the cat was faster and slipped across Jethro's path just inches away from his feet, close enough to be kicked.

"That's it!" howled Jethro.

The cat sped on and out of sight, and Jethro, now panting, sank to his knees in defeat. It wasn't so much having lost the race with the cat, nor was it that a black cat had crossed his path in spite of his efforts to prevent it; rather, it was everything: his mess of a life; his being in Mexico City instead of where he should be; his not being able to go home even if he went home. It was the string of hangovers he had but shouldn't have because none were the aftermath of a good celebration, but the residue of pity parties that lingered painfully to remind him that he couldn't get away from anything; it was the moral hangover he also suffered as the thought of what he had done the night before left him feeling raw; it was his aching heart he could not stop from aching, nor could he have it ripped out and dropped into that bowl of stone back at the museum. On top of it all, he couldn't even beat that damned cat. This was the final straw. He had had enough of Mexico City; enough self-imposed exile. As he continued his walk back to the hotel, now with steady determination, he contemplated the fix he was in.

Divorce laws were tough in Texas, and they favored the woman. He'd already moved out of the house, and the courts would probably award it to Sadie. And, as he was the breadwinner, he'd probably get stuck with the mortgage especially in view of the fact that Sadie was not, and never had been gainfully employed. *I could kick myself for letting her off so damn easy all this time; treating her like a fucking princess,* Jethro cursed. *I only set myself up.*

Her having a boyfriend wasn't much help. A judge might see her involvement with another man as nothing more than a symptom of how their marriage had become incompatible, if not love-less. It was only natural for grownups to move on and form new relationships, legalities aside. Jethro imagined himself pleading in open court that she had had a paramour, and thus had insulted the marriage and was clearly at fault. If he pled loudly enough, however, soon the judge and jury might be looking sideways at him, wondering what it was they didn't know about him that made her run off. Maybe they'd wonder whether or not he was truly the macho man he seemed to be; maybe they'd wonder whether he had difficulty in satisfying his woman—any woman; maybe they'd think he liked boys—or goats. Jethro didn't like the picture.

He then thought of the boyfriend moving in with Sadie while he, Jethro, paid the bills. And then there was the question of alimony—allowed in Texas. Jethro would probably have to give her a paycheck on top of it all. He could lose everything, get fleeced in the bargain, and wind up working for her—and him. As Jethro strode on, with these thoughts cruising through his head, he clenched his jaw and fists. "They're not going to get away with this," he muttered. "I'm going to make them pay for it." Suddenly he couldn't wait to get back to Laredo. He wanted a fight; he wanted to kick them both in the hienie.

Back at the hotel, Jethro collapsed onto the bed and lay there, exhausted, staring up at the ceiling. It was time to go home to whatever awaited him. He rolled over to one side and reached for the phone. He needed to call an old friend first to find out if anyone was looking for him in Laredo—anyone official, that is.

A certain Manfredo answered the phone.

"Listen, I need you to do something for me right away," Jethro told him. "I want you to call the Webb County jail; check with complaints. Find out if there's anything filed against me and if there's a warrant pending for my arrest. It's a long story, so just do it, would you? I'll call you back in fifteen minutes."

It was understandable that Manfredo, Jethro's private eye of choice, should be surprised at Jethro's request. Manfredo knew Jethro only as a respectable lawyer who often represented criminal defendants wanted by the law with arrest warrants pending against them. To have Jethro on the other side of things was most unexpected. Being the professional private detective that he was, however, Manfredo simply answered, "You got it, Boss."

Jethro took a few minutes to stare out the window at the angel and the street scene below. He walked over to the wet bar, poured himself a tequila, and downed it in one gulp. He walked over to the sink and splashed water on his face. He then called Manfredo again.

"Nothing, man," said the private detective. "You're clear."

"No complaint, no warrant? Are you absolutely sure?"

"I promise you, if there was anything there against you, they'd have told me. There's nothing. Damn, Jethro, what the hell did you do?"

"Oh, I just had a little incident with my wife and this guy she's seeing, and my gun went off, that's all."

"Your *gun* went off?" Manfredo blurted. "*You shot it?*"

"It was an *accident*. I had it in my pocket and I only shot the floor. I'll tell you about it later. I'm gonna need your services"

145

"Sure, boss, you got it."

Jethro then called the airline and booked the next flight out. He had no problem in getting a ticket: no one thought of Laredo as a vacation destination.

Neither did Jethro.

CHAPTER 27

LAREDO AGAIN

Jethro landed in Laredo with the new resolve he had lathered himself into while on the plane. He was now one of made-up mind, determined to go to his proper home. He was not going to be pushed around and thrown out anymore; he would simply not allow it—especially since he might have to pay for it all anyway. He would demand to stay there as was his right. After all, he had done nothing to deserve being kicked out like a dog. He had left, willingly, only to avoid violence. "Well, there will be no violence, and there will be no leaving," Jethro swore. He would read Sadie the riot act, state the law of the household, and tell her the way things were going to be from now on!

Jethro arrived home, however, to an empty house.

She had left no note behind, nor anything else to tell him where she might be. Of course, he hadn't told her where he had gone, either, the week and a day he'd been in Mexico City. Nor had he called.

Jethro suspected Sadie had gone to California to visit her family. Now, at least, he could stay home without having a fight. But he felt strangely out of place—like a visitor—a guest, or an intruder, somehow, like a stranger in someone else's dwelling. He certainly did not feel at home. Without his wife; without that closeness they had shared, whether by custom or by habit, this place he had once called home was just a house.

Jethro walked through it, surveying the rooms. Little changes here and there told him that she was fast replacing her old life with Jethro for a new one without him: a new potted plant; sofa and chairs rearranged; and what had been his nightstand was now a piece of furniture on which were displayed several new picture frames, none with him in them. Gone were his bedside books. He did not want to sleep in his former bedroom—in her bed. Instead, he slept in a spare room that might as well have been a hotel accommodation. Jethro had to admit to himself that he no longer belonged there: he had no home.

The following day, Tuesday, Jethro went to the office; he needed to work. He felt nervous and anxious, and found it hard to sit still. He could not help but wonder about Sadie. He didn't want to call his in-laws. She might be at her mother's or her brother's, or maybe her stepmother's house, but he did not want to unnecessarily involve anyone. How much did any of them already know? Surely they would ask what Sadie was doing in California during the Christmas and New Year's holiday without her husband. Undoubtedly, Sadie had told them how "abusive" Jethro was, and how she finally had to flee in search of refuge. They would certainly believe the break-up of their home to have been entirely his fault. They would by now be poisoned against him — Sadie would have made sure of that, injecting them all with heavy doses of her venom. No, he wouldn't call; not yet. He would have to wait.

Jethro could not wait long, however; he needed to break the ice. In all likelihood, she would be staying with either her mother or her brother. The mother Jethro knew to be a witch who would not hesitate to unload a gratuitous pile of invective on Jethro, based wholly on whatever Sadie had told her. He certainly did not want to talk to her. Sadie's brother, on the other hand, was nicer, and perhaps more discerning. He might consider hearing the other side of the story before assigning guilt. Jethro decided to call there first.

The brother's wife, Abigail, answered the phone. She sounded as though she were expecting Jethro to call. Normally as warm and friendly as any southern Californian could be, her tone of voice was now icy cold. *Sadie sure got to her*, considered Jethro, *and if she got to her, so much for the rest of them.* Undaunted, he forged ahead.

"Let me speak with Sadie, please."

"I'm sorry, Jethro, but she doesn't want to speak with you, and I can't say that I blame her." Abigail sounded not at all comfortable being stuck between Jethro and Sadie, but comfortable enough to deliver a jab of her own.

"Look, Abby, I don't want to cause any problems or disruptions, even over the telephone," Jethro persisted, "but please tell Sadie that it's me, and I need to talk to her. We're going to have to deal with this sooner or later, and it might as well be now. Would you tell her… please?"

Silence ensued as Abigail conveyed the message to Sadie, who most assuredly was standing next to her the entire time.

"I'm sorry, Jethro, but she won't talk to you," said Abigail.

Strange, thought Jethro, *why doesn't she just hang up on me?*

"Abby, come on, this is childish. She is going to have to talk to me eventually. I'm not going to get ugly with her; tell her please …" Silence again. A few moments passed. This time Sadie took the call.

Immediately, she launched into a verbal diatribe, berating Jethro for disappearing on Christmas Eve without so much as a telephone call.

"What were my mother and family going to think when they called to wish us a Merry Christmas only to find out that you abandoned me?" *Abandoned? Is this what Sadie had turned it all into?* But Sadie wasn't finished. "You are being extremely irresponsible. You need to tell me where you are in case there is an emergency!"

Sadie was yelling this through the phone, into Jethro's ear and into the ears of all others present who, standing there next to her (Jethro was sure), probably enjoyed witnessing Sadie put it to Jethro, as would any righteous woman of a household who takes no nonsense from a wayward husband like Jethro.

After that initial outburst, the conversation shifted in tone to one mixed with anxiety on Jethro's part and impatience on Sadie's. She spoke as one triumphant, as though she had defeated a grossly disrespectful bully of a husband, and was now all dignity. And while in that vein, she could not contain her disdain toward Jethro, the vanquished. She was curt and rude, snapping Jethro off mid-sentence as though utterly tired of him and his many excuses. She had become a tyrant sitting in judgment over one of her subjects, this lowly Jethro, who was increasingly sinking into insignificance as a person and deserving of only the worst treatment.

"I'm coming in on Saturday," snapped she, "but I don't think I want to see you."

In the face of such odds, Jethro had nothing to lose by his persistence.

"Why don't I stop by the house, Sadie? We have a lot to talk about." He needed to find out where she was with her plans. Had she reported him to the police for the shooting incident? Had she hired a lawyer? Were divorce papers being prepared? How much time did he have? He could not accept her words. While she spoke in front of her personal audience, Jethro believed, she was like a politician before the media: the words were tailored to the expectations of the listeners and what the speaker wanted them to believe, irrespective of the truth.

On she bellowed. "You need to give me an exact time if you're going to pass by. I'm not going to be waiting around for you."

Jethro wavered. "Do you want an appointment so you'll know exactly when I won't be around?"

"You're not going to control me, and what I do is none of your business," she screamed. "And just for your information, in case that's what you're thinking, I like Benny a lot, and I'm going to see him — and just so you know, he's probably gay, so don't blame me for your insecurities."

Jethro pondered this last comment of hers. For whose benefit was she saying this—for his or those in the room she was in, there standing next to her, hanging on every word that came out of her mouth? *Well, of course,* thought Jethro, *she probably told them that I'm freaking out in jealous madness over a mere friendship she has with a gay man, to which they probably said to her, "Well, that's what you get for marrying a Mexican; you know how macho they can be."*

"You will give me an exact time when you intend to pay me a visit so we can talk, or else don't call and don't come around," she thundered. "I'm not doing this under your rules. You're trying to control me."

Not much had changed since his trip to Mexico; Sadie appeared to have stayed frozen in time and issue, and was ready to pick up where they had left off.

"And you really embarrassed me at the gym," she continued with her scolding. "What you did to that poor man, in front of everybody is unforgivable."

"I didn't do anything to him," Jethro protested. "What are you talking about?"

"You attacked him. Everyone saw you, and you made people think that I was involved."

"I did not attack him," was Jethro's meek reply as he lapsed into dismay.

"Yes you did," she thundered. "There were people there who saw you, and it put me in a bad light. You damaged my reputation." She was now yelling from deep lungs.

Why is my wife doing this? Why is she so ready to distort facts against me? And now she has witnesses? He thought of Shirley, the gossipmonger. *I guess she went talking about this with her gang of vipers, so they'll be arrayed against me now.*

Jethro barely had enough time to consider the implications of what he was dealing with, for Sadie was on a roll now, and launched into discussing the scene in Benny's abode. She was adamant she had done nothing wrong, meanwhile adding that she was free to do whatever she wanted.

"I'll see whoever I want, and yes, I'm going to see Benny, and have lunch with him, or whatever, and you'll just have to get over it."

Jethro could not leave it at that, so he questioned, "What about Benny characterizing your relationship with him as something that could go further than just friendship?"

"I asked Benny about that, and he denies ever having said that to you."

Jethro was beside himself with frustration. "Sadie, you were there standing right next to him when he said it, don't you remember?"

"That never happened, Jethro, it's simply not true. There were three of us there, and two of us don't remember it that way. And another thing, that firecracker stunt you pulled was really low class. You scared us into thinking you had gone postal. All you did was convince both of us that you need help, Jethro; you need therapy. And you are not welcome in Benny's home ever again. Just so you'll know."

Firecracker? Jethro wondered in disbelief, but he did not argue the point. *Is that what they thought it was?* Regardless, Sadie kept speaking in the plural, and he realized they were teamed up against him.

Sadie and Benny were now a "we."

CHAPTER 28

A NEW YEAR'S RESOLUTION

The next day, December 31, Jethro hit upon a plan that he thought might work to get closer to Sadie. What he needed was time to formulate and implement a strategy, and to do that, he needed to disarm her. He would first admit fault for being such an insensitive macho ass. Certainly she would accept this as true with no argument. At any rate, he was confident of better success than he had had with his failed Benny-apology plan. Then he would appeal to her emotional and psychological needs, as best he could surmise them to be at this point, and tell her how, because of his self-centered ways, he did not know how, or what, she had been thinking or feeling over the last few years, and for everything that happened to have happened, he would recognize that much has been going on that he must have been completely unaware of, all due to his insensitivity, and to the horse's ass that he must be. *That ought to buy me some time*, he assured himself.

With his new plot in mind, Jethro called California ready to put it into action. It was about nine PM, over there. Tom, Jethro's brother-in-law, answered.

"Sorry, Jethro, She won't come to the phone right now."

"Tom, will you please ask her? It's New Year's Eve."

"I'll tell her, but don't get your hopes up; you've really screwed things up."

Sadie said hello in a flat tone of voice, Tom having spoken in haste. Jethro jumped on the moment as though he were starving for attention.

"Sadie, I've had a lot of time to think about everything, and I realize that by allowing you some space, things might get better between us. I want to be your friend, Sadie. If I've caused trouble, or if I've appeared troublesome, it's because of the difficulty I have with the idea of losing you and moving out of the house. I don't want to move out, but I realize that my staying at all costs will only aggravate the problem."

Sadie expressed a measure of glee at Jethro's having come to this frame of mind.

"I'm so glad you feel this way! I really appreciate your understanding me and your willingness to give me my space." So excited was she to be free, and so eager was she to have Jethro be so compliant, that she never stopped long enough to consider whether Jethro might be pretending. And his was a star performance.

"Well, of course, Sadie, that's what being friends is all about. I'm willing to give you *all* the space you need, and as often as you want." *She'll be sorry yet*, he murmured.

With enthusiasm, she promptly responded by suggesting that every weekend she should be free, and then suggested that Jethro might come for visits during the weekdays, for dinner, and that Jethro could even do the cooking. Jethro rolled his eyes around at the ceiling as she said this.

"As long as you are cooperative in this way, Jethro, we can take our time and work it out before going to the lawyers."

Jethro agreed. It appeared he was winning the delay he sought.

CHAPTER 29

JAN.2—A SATURDAY

Jethro waited anxiously at the airport. Sadie was scheduled to land in a quarter of an hour. He peered out over the landing strip through the wall-sized windows in the waiting area. *How did I get here?* He wondered. *How did it all come to this?* Everything had happened so fast, so many events that could shatter any confidence or marriage had occurred with a suddenness that bewildered Jethro. Jethro was not sure how to react, what to say, or even do. Anger was one prominent emotion, but so were sadness and dismay. How could she haul off and do what she did, for goodness sake? On the one hand, Jethro wanted to take her out with one good sock to the jaw. On the other hand, he also wanted to plead with her to wake up and stop the madness. Slowly brewing deep within him, however, was the thought of a new life; the thought of Araceli; and, a desire to be rid of Sadie— but not before getting even with her for all she had done. It was not so much that she wanted out—such things happen. Jethro could accept that. Rather, it was for treating him like a piece of shit—which was totally unnecessary, as Jethro saw it.

Jethro paced the waiting area of the airport, constantly watching through the floor-to-ceiling windows for the plane. And soon there it was, flying in towards the runway from the north. And then it landed and taxied to the gate, and in no time,

Sadie emerged from the aircraft with a somber face, the wind tossing her hair, and her head canted forward and low as she worked her way down the narrow stairway. "Fucking bitch," muttered Jethro through clenched teeth.

He stood silently before his wife, who stifled a smile as she said hello. Quickly, however, her face became quite serious. Maintaining cordiality and a sympathetic tone, she spoke evenly as she said, "Everything will be okay, Jethro," and she then embraced him in a hug.

Jethro went along with it, not quite sure how to respond. It was clear that regardless of any appeal, and in whatever form, Sadie was determined to go her own way.

"I need my solitude today," she told him. "I'm tired. Emotionally I am drained from all I have had to put up with from you, and so I want to be alone; I need my space."

Jethro burned in his shoes. For a moment the role of husband appealed to him as did his plane-ride resolution. He would put the proverbial foot down, demand an explanation, deny any apology that surely must follow from her, and then, with thunderous voice, usher her home to exact a deserved punishment of harsh words, stern looks for an extended while, forced labor for an even longer while, and the denial of any sex until he determined otherwise. Of course, this idea presupposed that Sadie cared and would respond to such treatment with true repentance. Good luck.

Meanwhile, there at the airport, unrepentant she remained. There would be no atonement today. Her attitude clearly said, "Don't push it, Jethro, you're lucky I'm being nice to you at all."

Jethro, like a pathetic gentleman who clings to his high-toned manners as a badge of honor, helped her with her bags and then watched her drive off after he dutifully loaded her luggage into a her Suburban. Struggling to maintain a semblance of calm, he drove off in the opposite direction for a weekend alone. He would have plenty of time to think it all through and to deal with the formidable distraction that thoughts of Sadie's whereabouts would present. Let alone the rage.

Faced again with the question of where to go, Jethro opted for a change of accommodations. He would take refuge in a small cottage in the woods that he leased from a local ranch owner. The ranch was some miles beyond the city limits, so he settled back into a drive that would take about forty minutes, allowing for reflection as the city thinned out and the countryside grew before him.

There on the edge of town, along the way, Jethro spied a small booth selling firecrackers left over from New Year's Eve. Impulsively he pulled over. *Firecrackers*, he thought. *How ridiculous; how was I even supposed to light them from inside my coat pocket, with a smokeless match? Absurd!*

Jethro walked up to the makeshift counter and perused the colorful array of fireworks.

"Hey, I know you, you're Jethro the lawyer, right?" said the old man behind the counter, grinning a toothless smile at him. "You helped my nephew stay out of jail. Hipolito Menchaca? You remember him? The *federales* caught him running drugs."

"Yeah, sure, I remember him," answered Jethro after a pause. "They caught him not just running drugs, but running *a lot* of drugs; he was hauling over a ton of marijuana, if I remember correctly."

"*Si, señor*," the old man chuckled. "And you got him off scot free."

"Yes, well your nephew's very lucky, because he might have gone to jail for a hell of a long time," said Jethro emphatically.

"Maybe he still will; he hasn't learned his lesson," replied the old man with his smile unabated.

"Well, if he's still in the business, maybe he'll create a little more business for me if he gets caught again. But he may not be so lucky next time—you oughta tell him. How much are these?" Jethro picked up a packet of black cats.

"Those are five dollars, but you don't want those."

"I don't? Why not?"

The old man leaned forward and whispered, "Because I have something *way* better."

Jethro detected a strong smell of liquor on the old man's breath. It appeared that with the waning fireworks business on the second day of January, the old man had kept himself warm by nipping at the bottle. The old timer reached below the counter and produced a handful of small explosives that looked like serious ordinance. They were about an inch long and about as wide, with fuses out one end. They looked like TNT in miniature.

"Try one of these."

"What are they?" asked Jethro, dubious.

"They're cherry bombs," said the old man. "Oil riggers use them for some kind of tests." Then, leaning forward so as to speak in hushed tones, allowing Jethro to again smell the strong odor of alcohol on his breath, the old man confessed, "They're illegal." He drew back with a naughty smile, which he quickly covered up with an upraised index finger pressed to his pursed lips. "Shhhhhhh ... " And then he stood there, proudly grinning his toothless smile.

"Why are they illegal?" asked Jethro.

"Because these are serious," responded the old man. "These are not playthings; they can blow your hand off."

"How much are they?"

"Ten dollars each," responded the old man self-righteously.

Jethro looked at him, amused. *Cagey old crab*, he thought.

"Let me have three of them."

The old man laughed as he put the three cherry bombs in a small paper bag. Jethro handed him three crisp ten-dollar bills, stuffed the paper bag into his pants pocket, and drove away.

Finally at the ranch, an empty, one-room ranch house offered him a simple army cot to sleep on. Austere and rustic, the ranch house was far away from the city, out in the country where the stars, unhampered by city glare, could still be viewed in all their splendor. Although lacking in modern amenities such as a heater, the country cottage offered the succor that only unadulterated nature could provide: there was silence in the air, with only the wind whispering through the bare trees. A great horned owl, whose call Jethro had learned to recognize as a boy, made its home nearby the little ranch house. Out there in the country, Jethro was completely alone, which, as it happened, was exactly what he needed: a place to get away from it all. *It's better to live alone in a bark hut than with a brawling woman in a fashionable home*, thought Jethro as he reclined on the cot, and stared out the window into the dark of night.

Better or not, a bark hut was now his lot.

CHAPTER 30
LAWYER TALK FOR DINNER

On Sunday, Jethro sat on a large rock by a lake, gazing out over the water. The weather was cold. A steady drizzle had stopped. The lake was as smooth as glass and as grey as the sky. A mass of ducks floated lazily at the back of the lake, away from Jethro. The trees were leafless, their soggy trunks, wet and cold, almost black in color. Except for the ever-green mesquite trees, wearing their olive drab, everything else was dressed in monotone. A meadow in the distance hosted a collection of white tail deer grazing quietly. A great horned owl, probably the same one that hooted for Jethro at night, was perched somewhere not far away, hooting now for 'who, who knows who.' *How peaceful*, Jethro reflected. He looked down at the palm of his hand on which lay one of the cherry bombs he had bought the day before. He recalled the old man's words about how the little device could blow one's hand off. Clutching the firecracker in his left hand, he lit the fuse with a plastic lighter he held in his right.

The fuse burned very fast, so fast that it shocked Jethro with alarm. In a knee-jerk reaction, he flung the cherry bomb as far away as he could before it exploded with a mighty blast, which was echoed by the sudden thrash of wings flapping water as the huge flock of ducks took to the air with much commotion. The deer grazing peacefully in the distance darted off for the cover of the woods, leaping with their white tails raised high.

"Damn!" Jethro exclaimed. "The old man wasn't kidding."

Back inside the ranch house, he tossed the other two cherry bombs, still in their bag, onto the small dresser that stood next to the cot. He then took a shot of tequila. He had unfinished business to tend to. Jethro needed to talk to Sadie. And talk to her he would.

It was about five PM when he finally called her. She answered.

"Sadie, do you mind if I come over for a while so we can have a calm discussion? I think we need to talk."

Sadie hesitated at first, but then consented.

"Only if you come over for a short while and then you leave, understand? I mean it, a short while."

"Why don't I come over for dinner?" he proposed. "We could have dinner together and talk. I know you're angry, but I'm interested in being your friend."

Somehow, this last remark served to soften her up. She stopped with her invective and said, "Look, Jethro, I also want to be friends, and you're welcome to come over tonight for dinner as long as you promise not to linger."

"That's fine; I have other things to do tonight anyway, so I'll only stay to eat." Jethro had lied, of course, for he had nothing to do that evening.

Jethro arrived at the house (until recently his own) at about half past seven. Sadie opened the door, appearing friendly enough. She gave him no kiss for a greeting, but she didn't meet him with a scowl either. Jethro followed her into the kitchen and set himself to helping with the cooking — not so much because he wanted to help with the cooking (although he usually would anyway), but in order to appear cooperative and to demonstrate that he was together with the program.

The evening went seemingly well. Jethro and Sadie sat at the dinner table and ate in silence. Jethro was glad for a moment of quiet in Sadie's presence while the strife took a break. However, he was not altogether well received. Although she was polite, Sadie behaved toward Jethro as though he were an unavoidable bother, like a repair person in one's home, a plumber perhaps, who, of necessity, must be allowed to inspect the inner sanctuary of the toilet.

"What did you want to talk about?" Sadie began.

Jethro took a deep breath as he absorbed the slight.

"Don't you think we have a lot to talk about?" His mood turned level and serious.

"Look, Jethro, I'm tired of all the pressure you keep putting on me to make decisions; I want to take one day at a time, and I do not want to go back to the negativity and the fighting, do you understand?"

"Of course I understand. I don't want troubles either, but we also have a lot of unfinished business, Sadie, and you're not just going to throw me out like I'm some kind of garbage. You're going to have to deal with this situation and resolve it with me one way or the other, so let's stop the bickering and the tantrums, and let's just deal with it, shall we?"

Sadie seemed to consider this. For a moment, Jethro thought he had her thinking twice, but then came her decided response.

"I want us to maintain separate residences, Jethro, and I think we should start legal proceedings soon."

"W-when do you want to do that?" Jethro stammered, momentarily caught off guard by the divorce business, and still suffering from divorce-phobia.

"Soon, Jethro, soon."

"Well, soon can be anytime. Do you know what lawyer you want to use?"

"Yes. I've considered several, and I have talked to a few, and I think I will use Porter Swinefellow."

Sadie paused long enough to let the intended effect take its toll on Jethro. A wry smile crept slowly across her face as she enjoyed the spectacle of a struggling Jethro trying to conceal any outward manifestation of the turmoil now surely raging within. And, indeed, Jethro was rendered speechless as he registered the shock. The prospect of divorce filled him with fear, and Porter Swinefellow was the most ruthless shyster in the business.

Swinefellow had been, in his prime about twenty years before, Webb County's District Attorney, elected by popular vote. Webb County was the sixth largest county in the State of Texas, and Laredo was the biggest city in Webb, accounting for about 90% of Webb's population, or about 250,000 souls. The borders of Webb County, however, stretched far beyond the city limits of Laredo and included a number of small hamlets within its territorial limits. During his tenure as D.A., Swinefellow had forged a considerable reputation in the border town of Laredo by exercising his prosecutorial discretion along factional lines. Thus his friends, mainly the power-brokers, the wealthy, and those to whom he was politically or financially indebted, enjoyed a marked degree of privilege under his watch. The progeny of those so privileged drove about town recklessly and in violation of speed limits while under the influence of various intoxicants, only to have any resultant charges somehow disappear.

During Swinefellow's term of office, he allowed assistant district attorneys to maintain private practices so long as doing so would not interfere with their duties as prosecutors—a contingency difficult to assess, given the lax work ethic that Porter cultivated at the offices of the Webb County District Attorney. To this liberal custom of enjoying a private practice on the side,

Lawyer Porter brought scandalous new meaning, with the cooperation of a certain judicial ally.

At the time of Swinefellow's rule, the district had enjoyed the services of one particularly odious judge whose dispensation of justice could well be described as daring if not cavalier. Frequently this esteemed jurist turned his courtroom into a forum for kitchen debates where, in the style of the ancient Spartans, the lawyer with the loudest shout carried the day and the rule of law was relegated to the dusty books on the shelves of the law library, where they remained forever undisturbed as though painted on the walls. Porter Swinefellow took to this legal environment like a serpent in a grassy field, and enjoyed a prosperous private practice representing the same criminal defendants his office as District Attorney prosecuted. With the judge turning a blind eye to such obvious conflicts of interest, Porter managed to orchestrate a most satisfying disposition for his clients, win or lose, meanwhile always treating the bench and bar to the greatest of bombast, designed to impress the largely unlettered public of Laredo.

And loud he was, his voice booming with unchecked authority, for the private bar cared little for legal correctness and more for jockeying for position with Porter and the judge. To an ignorant public, and judge, so much noise from Mr. Swinefellow surely indicated that he knew what he was talking about, and so he was warmly embraced by his large following, who considered his losses as miscarriages of justice and his victories hard won and well deserved. No one seemed to notice how terribly he fared on appeal: results that came long after the fact, and never publicized by the one newspaper that served as Laredo's only media organ.

It was to this gentleman that Sadie was turning for legal representation. By now, Porter Swinefellow was an old man—biologically that is, because chronologically he must not have been a day past sixty-one. But a life of excessive self-indulgence had worn on him, and he now looked not a day short of eighty-two. His tired, gibbous figure was a common feature of the courthouse hallways, moving in a shuffle, labored and slow, indicative of circulation problems. In the courtroom, though, he could still manage to summon sufficient energy to deliver his famous oratory, loud and long, however devoid of any technical finesse.

He had two assistants to do the fieldwork for him, and these were his spinster daughters. Well intended though they were, the Misses Swinefellow had never argued before a jury since their licensure years before. Professionally, they lived entirely by trading on the reputation of their father. Still, the Swinefellows were formidable opponents, as the memory of Porter's legal exploits yet lingered in the collective consciousness of the community. Together as a team, the Swinefellows could make plenty of trouble for the unwary—and for Jethro.

"Do you know Porter Swinefellow's daughters?" Sadie asked casually.

"Sure I know them; I see them at the courthouse all the time." Jethro kept a straight face, but he thought he would be sick. He felt unprepared to deal with either the process of divorce or the tactics of the Swinefellows.

"Then you know who you'll be dealing with, and believe me, they'll make sure I'm treated right and that I get everything I deserve."

"Oh, you're gonna get everything you deserve, Sadie, I'm sure of it."

Sadie frowned at him for an instant as he said this, but she was too fired up to think too much about any double entendre. Instead, on she gushed.

"I don't want to be your wife anymore. I don't want the pressure that that entails. I want to be free, Jethro. I am becoming a new woman, and I don't want to be held back!" The exclamation point she added to this last statement was audible.

Then, almost as an afterthought, she added, "But I always want to be close to you as a friend, to talk to and do things with." This she said as though she were saying 'farewell' and felt pity for Jethro. Her voice held a hint of nostalgia, as though she were fondly recalling their days of old.

"I thought you wanted a severance." remarked Jethro.

"I do, but only a severance of legal ties."

"Well, that would mean a severance, wouldn't it?"

Sadie stopped and looked at Jethro as if coming to a sudden realization.

"Jethro, we need to take one day at a time," was her considered response.

Jethro pondered Sadie's ambivalence. Apparently she wanted to remove the intimate aspect of their relationship, with all else remaining status quo: a liberal "open marriage" it would seem. And she really appeared to believe it could be easily arranged — a simple procedure, nothing more, involving the amputation of a small aspect of the marriage that no longer functioned as she desired. In short, she wanted a marital appendectomy. The rest of the marital corpus would go on living just fine, with all the conveniences that marriage offered, such as having Jethro as a handyman about the house to mend things as men are supposed to, and, more to the point, to labor and pay all the bills.

Jethro looked away in disgust. *She wants to relegate me to the barn like a gelding*, he thought, *to keep me there for when she needs some ordinary task performed; except. of course, stud services. She would turn to her new steed for that.*

"What is this new woman you are becoming?" He wondered aloud, and then asked, "What does that mean?"

"I want to be free," was her only reply. As Jethro pondered this, she continued, "And I don't want to have sex with you anymore. I can't stand you anymore. You pollute my life. When you are in the house, I feel cornered and trapped. I want you out! Either you go, or I'll get you out legally!"

In an effort to lighten the mood, Jethro changed the subject to matters insignificant about which they spoke little for the remainder of their supper.

What makes her think I even want to have sex with her? What a bitch.

CHAPTER 31

THE INTIMATE FOUL

After dinner, Jethro loitered about for a while, helping to clear the table and tidy up the kitchen. Soon, however, all chores were done, and he began to gesture as one does when leaving time approaches, walking about as though searching for his car keys and openly declaring as though to the furniture, "Well, I guess it's getting late." He was biding his time, hoping that something would come up to keep him from following through with any departure. He wanted a confrontation, though he didn't want a fight. He still wavered on a divorce and vacillated between conceding that his marriage had indeed failed and hoping that maybe things could be worked out—somehow. Lapsing into a state of denial, he wanted to put everything back on track, and then start working toward the relationship they'd had for so many years.

And matters seemed to be going in that direction. As Jethro said goodbye he paused at the door, and, to his surprise, Sadie moved forward with open arms to hug him. She seemed quite emotional, devoid of any anger. Jethro believed she was now in a receptive frame of mind, and he could thus speak to her seriously, sternly, and lend a sound effect on her future choices. Her simple gesture of wanting a hug convinced him that her heart was finally melting.

Deeply angered though he was, Jethro recognized that he needed to treat Sadie with a measure of severity sufficient to have her recognize and concede the magnitude of offenses she had perpetrated against their marriage. His treatment of her, however, he knew had to be tempered with mercy so as to allow for personal redemption if sins were admitted and if sufficient remorse were demonstrated. Outwardly, like the final judge with the books about to be opened, he maintained an austere demeanor as Sadie (to his continuing dismay, which he endeavored not to show) drew close for the hug.

Jethro was overcome with emotion as the longed-for moment arrived with Sadie surrendering herself into his arms. How he wanted to enfold her and hug her tightly. He wanted to tell her how he loved her, and regardless of all the insults that he and their household had had to recently endure, he wished to be there for her, with her— and for them— with both feet on the ground, steadfast, and ever the same in spite of all the adversity. He wanted to be her pillar of strength; a man for all seasons. Yet he faltered in his humanity. His pent-up emotions revolted. Jethro turned away from her entreaty and marched straight out of the house.

Almost instantly he recognized his demonstration for what it was: all melodrama; a mere acting-out of his wounded pride. Halfway to his car he turned and went back to the house. He wasn't going anywhere and he knew it. He walked back slowly, with faked delay this time, and opened the door at will. It was unlocked, he noticed, and he went right in.

The open-hearted, warmed-up Sadie he had just left was, however, no longer there. Instead, he encountered an angry Sadie who now behaved as a spurned lover.

"How dare you walk out on me like that?" she protested.

What did she expect? Jethro made it clear to her that his leaving at all was only on her account. The ensuing argument did not last for long. Sadie came to him again, and this time Jethro relented. He took her in his arms, and they kissed with passion.

At such a moment, no words were necessary. They went to the bedroom and engaged in a wordless communication as in days of old. But then something went wrong. As they were making the beast with two backs, Sadie began to sob uncontrollably. Jethro was not sure if it was Hollywood drama he was witnessing, or if she were truly disturbed. She behaved as though she had been forced to lie down against her will. He felt at once baffled and horrified. Why was she doing this? What was she trying to say? Thoroughly confused and distraught, he was instantly disabused of the notion that he was in control of anything.

Sadie stumbled into the bathroom and then stood there, miserable, crying and shaking as though she'd been raped. Jethro pleaded with her to tell him what was wrong. It was clear to him that something terrible must have happened. That male fear of being cuckolded erupted. Had she? And was her guilty conscience now getting the best of her, such that the truth would of necessity force itself out? The recently formed impression of Araceli panting under the weight of his body as he buried his face into her luxurious hair and bit into her hot neck as she moaned raced through his mind. *No*, he told himself, *that's got nothing to do with this*. And Jethro was not going to say anything about it. Sadie, on the other hand, was acting very strange.

"Sadie, I mean it; I want to know right now what the hell is going on." He demanded, fed up with the melodrama.

"Nothing, just leave me alone," she cried.

"No! It's not that easy, Sadie, I have a right to know. What happened Sadie?" Jethro spoke accusingly, the volume of his voice steadily rising.

"Nothing happened. Just leave me alone, Jethro. I want you to go, please." She walked back to the bed and put her clothes on.

Jethro's mind was racing as he dressed himself as well. If she was not romantically involved with Benny, then what was her plan?

"Okay, Sadie, I believe you. Really I do," he lied, "but I just don't understand. You're destroying everything we have; you want out, you want to get rid of me, but where are you going with your life, and how?"

"I'll find a way." She proclaimed as convincingly as a runaway teenager.

"Find a way? To what? And you have the means to do so? Do you have an inheritance you haven't told me about that will allow you to go on this new adventure?"

"No, no, there's no inheritance." She had recovered her composure by now, and lifting her chest, declared, "I am going to be a professional woman."

"A *professional* woman? Where? Doing what?"

"I don't know where. And I don't know how yet, but it's none of your business anyway, and it's time for you to go."

Jethro stared, flabbergasted. He couldn't imagine Sadie as anything but a professional shopper.

But she was right—it was time for him to go. She had reverted to nonchalance as she now went about her room, oblivious of Jethro. She walked over to the stereo and began browsing through her music collection as though choosing a CD to listen to. Jethro stood there watching her. She turned to him, as cold as a reptile, and repeated in a flat tone, "It's time for you to go."

"When will I see you again?" Jethro asked as though they were lovers married to other people.

"I don't know, maybe tomorrow; you can come over for dinner." She spoke in a tone of voice now laced with impatience, as though to say, "Why are you still here?"

And so he left, driving back to the country house he now called home.

Dinner tomorrow? He thought. *Why does she keep having me over?*

CHAPTER 32

SADIE CALLS THE COPS

The next morning, Jethro awoke from a blank sleep feeling disturbed and not sure why. He lay staring at the ceiling for a moment before the reason for his unease struck him with an ugly, sinking feeling. Sadie's reaction to their intimacy the night before was appalling and bizarre. *She behaved as though I forced myself on her, completely against her will*, reflected Jethro. *There is something very strange about it*, he thought as he visited the images his memory had stored of her weeping bitterly in the bathroom. *She cried for real*, he believed, *but something isn't right; it seemed rehersed somehow.* His doubts and uneasiness continued until he was driven into compulsion and decided to conduct a bit of reconnaissance. It was early yet, and a drive by Sadie's gym, the locus of his confrontation with Benny, might provide a bit of intelligence. *Maybe I'll see Sadie and that damned photographer friend doing something—anything—with each other. Maybe she'll be crying on his shoulder, given how violated she felt last night.* Dressing hastily in an old pair of warm-ups, he headed for his car after calling Idalia, his loyal secretary, to tell her he wouldn't be in for the day.

Jethro drove into the gym's parking lot, slowly creeping toward the entrance. He didn't want to be seen by anyone who might recognize him and tell Sadie he was there. He parked far enough away to be discreet, but close enough to see into the gym through its glass doorways, and into the mirrored room where the aerobics classes were held. As perfect timing would have it, he had arrived right after an aerobics class had ended—the session usually attended by Sadie. Enough time had passed for most of the patrons to have left—all but two.

The classroom was empty except for Sadie and Benny. They were in the middle of their own private yoga session. They stood on separate yoga mats, opposite each other, so that they could look at each other as they flowed through the poses. At the moment Jethro saw them, they stood frozen, face to face, in a warrior pose: arms extended out to their sides, legs apart, lunging on one leg with the other straight. Their eyes were fastened on each other, eyeball to eyeball. *Oh, how groovy*, sneered Jethro to himself. *They're looking into each other.* He didn't wait around to see what pose they would flow into next. He felt sickened by the sight. They seemed so alone together, and although Jethro wasn't sure, he thought he saw blissful smiles on each of their faces as they maintained a lock on each other's eyes, and Sadie's face had a certain glow about it as though she had at last found nirvana. He drove away in disgust towards his mother's house where he would spend the afternoon watching TV while flopped on the carpeted floor until it was time for the dinner date his wife had invited him to in spite of the intimate foul.

Six o'clock rolled around soon enough, and it was time for Jethro to keep his dinner appointment with Sadie. *Should I dress up for the occasion?* he wondered, but then decided to go in his sweats as he was in order to induce a relaxed mood for the evening. He wanted everything to be casual and easy; no stress, no pressure, only comfort if possible.

While en route, Jethro called Sadie to tell her he was on his way. Her mood seemed positive.

"I'll be here, waiting for you," she said pleasantly.

And everything seemed fine once at the house. Sadie answered the door warmly, there being no hint of combativeness to her demeanor. Right away, however, she put Jethro to good use.

"Why don't you go get some wine and a few groceries?"

A compliant Jethro agreed, although with some resentment.

Why is she being so nice? he wondered as he drove to the store, impatient by having his meeting with Sadie delayed by this last-minute errand, meanwhile ignoring his inner radar that told him he was being used, or something.

He returned to the house and prepared supper, which went well. Sadie behaved warmly towards Jethro, touching his hand several times as they dined. Their conversation was fluid and varied, and it seemed like they were friends again. They drank much wine. As they did, however, Jethro could not help himself and asked too many questions about Sadie's friendship with Benny. The image of their squared-off warrior pose jeered at him in his mind. Perhaps the wine emboldened him, or maybe Sadie's friendly disposition and easy behavior that evening disarmed him. But either way, by returning to the subject too many times, he aggravated the mood of the evening. Sadie grew irritated and retreated into the bedroom. There she sat on the floor and busied herself with a pile of magazines from which she was cutting fashion photos.

Jethro moseyed into the bedroom, trying to appear calm and collected. He trained his focus on several books that lay on the bed and casually thumbed through them. Sadie made no protestations about his presence, and the mood simmered down. Presently, Jethro went over to her. Her demeanor had indeed changed: gone were the anger and the bitterness. Now she was pleasant, her eyes appearing moist and warm. With the most casual ease, she leaned over to Jethro and kissed him. Jethro kissed back, eagerly, not so much for the physical sensation, but for the emotional need. He kissed her neck, and she melted into a rising passion. An amorous exchange developed, headed toward intimacy. Jethro, wanting desperately to return to normalcy, interpreted Sadie's behavior as a surrender—a concession that the strife might be headed toward an end.

Then the amorous exchange ceased abruptly as Sadie suddenly stood up and announced that she needed a smoke. She strode to the bedroom door and locked it. She then went straight into the bathroom, with Jethro following her like a loyal dog. Standing by the sink, Sadie lit a skinny marijuana cigarette — a "pinner." She drew deeply on the slender joint and paused in between hits, lifting a brow at Jethro as though to ask if he wanted any. Jethro, eager not to detract from the moment in any way but to maintain a lighthearted mood, took a puff but did not inhale.

The happy mood persisted after the smoke. Jethro likened the pinner to have been, perhaps, a peace pipe. At least that was his hope. But then the mood became too carefree for Jethro's liking, with Sadie now completely mellowed by the effects of cannabis. With eyes closed she began dancing in the bedroom with increasing abandon to the music that flowed energetically from the stereo. Jethro, never having been much of a dancer, stood there and watched as she wiggled and spun about. She looked like a hippie in the Summer of Love, lacking only flowers in her hair. Jethro grew increasingly discomforted as she became lost in her own world—a world where Jethro did not exist and did not matter.

It was now about 11 PM. Sadie, having tired of dancing solo, resumed her place seated on the floor and quietly continued with her clippings though with less interest. Jethro wandered over to the bed and again, for what seemed like the longest time since he had left the house in December, lay down in his usual place, by his former nightstand, and felt the familiar indent on the mattress that received his body like a pod.

He relaxed, gazed up at the ceiling, and sighed deeply. He realized just how much he missed his bed—that one spot in the whole world that was his.

Midnight approached, and Sadie turned to Jethro, who was now enjoying a sleepy reverie, and asked, "Are you going to leave?"

Jethro looked at her for a moment, not knowing whether to take the question as an invitation to stay.

"I'm really tired, Sadie, so if it's all the same to you, I think I'll stay the night and leave tomorrow."

Sadie, with her eyes narrowing and her jaw tightening, exclaimed in a shrill voice, "You're staying?"

"Yeah, Sadie," Jethro responded with a tone of resignation that said, "Give me a break."

"Relax, I'm just tired, really," he pled.

Sadie sprung to her feet for a full frontal confrontation. With fists tightly clenched at her sides, she began demanding, her voice increasing in volume,

"You get out now. I want you to leave. You have no right to stay here!"

Jethro was fed up. *If it's a good fight she wants, I'm gonna let her have it!*

"No, Sadie, *you've* got it wrong. I do have a right to be here. This is *my* home too; I left only out of courtesy and to be fair and to avoid needless fighting, but I have a right to be in my home just as much as you do, and tonight I think I'll stay; okay? I'll leave in the morning."

Jethro's feeble attempt to restore his authority was to Sadie the proverbial gauntlet thrown to the ground before her, and her anger erupted like volatile price action in the markets after a black swan event. She began screaming at the top of her lungs; her face turned a beet red, and awful veins bulged at her neck and forehead. She looked like a rabid animal.

"You leave now, *you bastaaaaard!*" She yelled in a guttural tone.

Jethro ignored her and began leafing casually through a book, aware that his heart was now beating fast and realizing that he was in a lot of trouble. He peered over at her from behind the book, and with a calmness he was proud of under the circumstances, decided to call her bluff.

"No, Sadie, you leave, I'm not going anywhere."

Sadie shut her mouth and stared at Jethro. It seemed she did not know what to do. To Jethro's surprise, she then climbed into bed.

Jethro was beside himself with astonishment. *You see*, he thought. *All I had to do was put my foot down. I'll get to the bottom of this yet.* But just as he finished that self-congratulatory assessment, Sadie jumped out of bed and strode over to the television, turned it on, and put the volume at full blast. She then turned to measure Jethro's reaction. Jethro, hiding behind the book, thought, *Well, I guess this means no quiet reading in bed.*

Sadie, not happy with Jethro's lack of response, now stood before the bed and spat, "You pig! Fuck you, you bastard, fucking pig, you're imposing yourself on me and invading my space. You fucking pig, I hate you!" She began sobbing with rage.

Why isn't she frothing at the mouth? Jethro wondered. He calmly put the book down and said in a fatherly tone of voice, "No, Sadie, you're a little tyrant, and you're a spoiled brat having a tantrum. If you'd just settle down, you'd realize that my being here is not such a big deal. Why don't you just ignore me and I'll ignore you; in no time we'll both be asleep, and I'll leave in the morning. I understand you want nothing to do with me, and besides, as this bullshit continues, I'm wanting less and less to do with you. But this is my bed and my place too, so why don't you just deal with it?"

Sadie stood at the edge of the bed, looking at Jethro with a blank expression, as though she were waiting for a pebble to hit the bottom of a well. Then she began to shudder and turn a darker red. Her anger blew like a hot spring, and as it boiled over, she began to spew obscenities at the top of her lungs.

"I hate you, you fucking asshole, you fucking pig, get out, get out, *gggeeet ooooouuuut* !" Her eyes were wide and bulging in their sockets. As she screamed vulgarities, her head shook nervously side to side, and spittle sprang from her gaping mouth as though— Jethro thought—a bottle rocket had been fired up her rectum.

She stormed over to her nightstand and retrieved a small address book from her purse. Frantically she rifled through the little pages, and then, picking up the phone, began dialing a number.

Jethro could take it no longer. *Who is she calling*? He asked himself as he sprang from the bed and reached for the phone to take it from her.

Sadie began striking Jethro with the phone receiver as though it were a hammer, then socked him in the neck with her other free hand— the address book having since become airborne. The blows rained down wildly on Jethro's back, and then came the kicks. Sadie had fallen back onto the bed and started kicking Jethro freely now, employing a paddlewheel technique. Jethro endeavored to gain control, braving the foot storm with upraised arms in defensive posture. In the ensuing melee, the lamp on the nightstand tumbled with a crash.

With that, Sadie stopped her thrashing of Jethro, leapt up, and announced, "I'm calling the police!" She grabbed the phone again and dialed emergency 911.

Jethro took his index finger and pressed the hang-up button on the telephone cradle, thus provoking Sadie into another violent outburst. He then, in a show of bravado, and so as again to call her bluff, grabbed the phone, dialed 911, and calmly handed it to Sadie. Jethro's move would prove to be ill-advised.

"Hello," Sadie blubbered into the phone, "I need the police, my husband won't leave … Yes he has weapons; he's threatening me with a knife! His name is Jethro (speaking up his name so that it would be loud and clear). You all know who he is, yes, the lawyer. Yes ma'am, yes, thank you, I'll be waiting..." She then calmly placed the receiver on the cradle and turned to Jethro with a triumphant sneer.

"I told you to go, but you wouldn't leave," she calmly stated as though what had just occurred were entirely Jethro's doing and he was about to get what he deserved.

"I can't believe you called the police," muttered an almost speechless and totally deflated Jethro. He stood with his arms hanging limp by his sides, his shoulders sagging.

"Well, you dialed the number."

"But you filed a police complaint against me, and a false one, Sadie. I can't believe it."

"You'd better just go, Jethro; just leave before the police come," she said with a measure of resignation in her voice.

"No, I'm not leaving. Let the police come and take me." Jethro could now hear the sound of sirens screaming in the distance, getting louder and coming closer with each passing second.

Hastily, Sadie put some shoes on, and within minutes (admirable response time), three police cars had rushed up to the front of the house with the roar of the screaming sirens, and revolving red and blue emergency lights of the squad cars now blazing through the windows and dancing surreally off the walls and furniture.

The police cars arrayed themselves on the street facing the house and fixed the glare of their spotlights onto the façade, lighting it up like an eerie stage. Sadie ran out of the home to meet the police, arms outstretched before her with hands wide open and calling out in a loud, clear voice, "I'm not being hurt, he's not hurting me...it's just that my husband won't leave. We're separated, and he won't leave. All I want is for him to go."

Jethro walked boldly onto the front yard as no waylaid husband had gone before. The cops immediately converged upon him, commanding him to stop and raise his hands. As Jethro did so, two police officers swiftly approached him from the side. One of them ordered Jethro to place his hands on the back of his head with fingers interlaced. As Jethro complied, another cop clasped Jethro's hands in order to secure them and grabbed a fistful of Jethro's hair as well, pulling it in the process and violently yanking Jethro's head sideways. At the same time, another overzealous cop pushed one of Jethro's upraised elbows so as to make him turn around and then slapped a heavy hand on one of Jethro's shoulders so as to hold him steady. The cop then kicked Jethro's legs apart in order to conduct a pat-down weapons search.

Jethro was wearing the same loose fitting gym sweats with no underwear he'd lounged around in all afternoon at his mother's. As the aggressive cop frisked him, he reached between Jethro's legs and accidently grabbed Jethro's balls, giving them a hard squeeze which made Jethro yelp. The affront was not intended, and it happened fast, but to Jethro it had come as a mean surprise. What with pulled hair, yanked head, and now manhandled balls, Jethro felt totally humiliated. He glared at the cop, and for a split moment they locked eyes. The cop, whose adrenaline-charged stare betrayed an underlying stupidity that allowed him to take up the cudgel with such zeal, gave Jethro a brutish look that said, "Don't move."

Jethro, remaining steady under pressure, said flatly, "Careful, they're loaded."

The wild look in the cop's eyes subsided. He eased his grip on Jethro and told him to relax. A higher-ranking police officer had now walked up to them.

"Okay, Jethro, what happened?" he asked.

Jethro looked about and noticed that several neighbors were now standing on their lawns peering over with necks outstretched.

"It's her, Officer. I promise, I live here, and we were fine, when all of a sudden she wants me out. She became violent when I refused to leave. I mean, I live here too. This is my home, and she just wants me out. I was not threatening her at all, much less with a knife. That is complete bullshit. I was just laying there with a fucking book. She's using you all to get me out. This is a fucking set up!"

The police explained that they had to effectuate a separation — one of them, either Jethro or Sadie would have to go. The ball-squeezer cop, his adrenaline high sufficiently subsided, addressed Jethro evenly and with appropriate firmness.

"I understand what you're telling us, but our orders are clear; we're supposed to take you in. We're supposed to take any aggressor in a domestic violence situation straight to jail."

There was a pause. Jethro looked at both policemen.

"Look Jethro, those are our orders," said the ranking cop, "but I'm going to cut you a break. I'm going to give you a choice; either you leave voluntarily or we will arrest you. It's the law; you know it better than we do. We have to separate you, and since your wife called in the complaint, it's you that has to go. We'll even escort you into your house so you can get your clothes or whatever you need, but you're gonna to have to go."

Jethro argued the point no further. He thanked the police for their consideration, and then got in his car and slowly drove away.

Okay Sadie, he swore inwardly, *the gloves are off.*

CHAPTER 33

JETHRO CONFRONTS THE INEVITABLE

"ENRAGED EX-HUSBAND SHOOTS EX-WIFE ON COURTHOUSE STEPS." As he drove home from his confrontation with the police, Jethro remembered that headline and the news story he had read years ago. There was even a dramatic film clip on the nightly news broadcast. Apparently, the final divorce had just been entered. The ex-wife was walking briskly out of the courthouse, an accompanying girlfriend at her side. They must have been a prominent couple, because a media person was following her with the camera rolling. Just then the nascent ex-husband, enraged, rushed up behind the ex-wife and shot her repeatedly in the back of the head with a .22 automatic. She dropped like a stone after the first shot, and then he stood over her pumping bullets into her head until the pistol was empty. The girlfriend had run off shrieking in panic, but the Zapruder like newsperson had caught it all on film. *That ex-husband was one pissed off dude*, thought Jethro, who now well understood how a woman, a member of the weaker sex no less, could drive a man beyond the brink.

Why the memory of that news clip entered Jethro's mind he did not know, but other thoughts followed. There was something off about how Sadie kept inviting him over for dinner. She was doing it on purpose, concluded Jethro, and the cop call was a strategy designed to put him in a cage. She was preparing the groundwork for a successful divorce, findings of fault, and an uneven distribution of the marital estate. *That's what's she's up to,* Jethro calculated. *She's setting me up, and I'll bet that fucker, Benny is in on it. We'll see who wins.* He arrived at his new ranch home with his desire for confrontation as intense as his knowing resolve to stay away.

He went into his room and poured himself a glass from the bottle of tequila he kept on a small barrel standing on end by the bed for a bedstand. Outside the night noises were in full concert, as if nothing had happened. The crickets went on with their usual tenor chirping, while the bullfrogs were croaking the bass from their muddy homes at the back of the lake somewhere. Other chirpings and creepings that Jethro did not recognize accompanied those sounds, and the horned owl hooted, as though to tell Jethro it had told him so.

Jethro gulped several tequila shots and lay down knowing he would not be getting any sleep. The sirens from the police vehicles, the emergency lights, and how badly everything had turned out played over and over in his mind. There was no way to repair the extent of the damage. Regardless of any feelings, or insistence on reconciliation, Jethro could not trust Sadie anymore—at all; she was dangerous to his character and professional reputation. *She wants to destroy me so that she can get everything.* He thought. *And just how does she expect me to pay alimony if she ruins me and my career?*

Lingering in doubt and denial about what was really going on was one thing, but having the cops brought in on false charges was quite another. She was trying to bury him. It was certainly over, their marriage, and it was now a question of getting out as best he could, getting even, and gathering what evidence he could to make sure he would win. Jethro walked over to the door and stood peering out into the darkness. A faint wind rustled through the trees, and the night sounds welcomed him.

"This is war," he vowed. "This is fucking war, and I'm going to kick that bitch's ass and that skinny hippy she's with, too."

Jethro spent the next several days expecting to hear from the Swinefellows, to the effect that his wife had instituted divorce proceedings and he was not to communicate with her unless it was through them. As the days passed, however, no such communication came. Perhaps she thought that the police intervention had taught him well enough to stay away, he speculated. He recalled, however, that she hadn't filed charges after his gun had gone off that other day. *Surely, they didn't think it was a firecracker*, he reflected. *I mean really, are they that stupid or are they using a firecracker story to guard their little secret? Had she said it was a gunshot they would have wanted to know why she hadn't called the cops.*

A week and a half passed. Jethro paced in his office, his life in suspense. Continually waiting for what might happen was almost unbearable. He decided to call Porter Swinefellow and ask him whether legal action was afoot.

"Hello Jethro," Swinefellow bellowed. "It's been a long time. What can I do for you?"

"I understand you have been in touch with my wife, or she's been in touch with you, so you know my situation. I need to know where matters stand. Has she hired you, and where are you with divorce proceedings?"

"Yes, your wife has contacted me, and we have talked about it. I can't tell you much else; you know the rules."

"Yeah, I know the rules, Porter, but you can tell me if you're about to sue me or not." Jethro stated flatly with a hint of impatience. "Are you?"

"Well, she's only talked to me about it, but you know I have to protect her interests. It would be really helpful, for both of you, if I knew your income; I mean, everyone knows you're the breadwinner, and she needs to be taken care of. These issues are going to have to be addressed, and we can take care of them up front if you cooperate. Why don't you just prepare an accounting for me—you know, your assets, revenues, and liabilities—so we can get this taken care of?"

Jethro could just see Porter licking his chops at the chance to size up the economics of the case and determine his potential fee.

"Porter, if she's hired you and you've taken the case on, then sue me and I'll see you in court." Jethro retorted with contempt. "Otherwise, I'm not giving you jack."

The call ended. Jethro clenched his fists as he stared out the window. But then he tension eased: Porter was clearly not in attack mode. Rather, he was still fishing for a payday. *She didn't call Swinefellow to have him file because she doesn't know what she's doing*, concluded Jethro. *She's got an affair to keep secret, and she'd have to tell Porter the Pig and she's probably afraid of how he'd take it. I have all the time I need.*

The thought of how David ran toward the army to meet the Philistine arrived unsummoned in Jethro's mind.

CHAPTER 34

JETHRO CANCELS MAKE-BELIEVE PLANS

After having spoken to Porter Swinefellow, Jethro called Sadie. On this occasion he needed, oh what should it be this time, oh yes, tax information, that might work. Sadie answered the telephone, but was engaged in a conversation with some teacher at the local college and had put the person she was talking to on hold.

"What do you want, Jethro?" She barked with rudeness.

Hmm, thought Jethro, *the college*.

"This is a business call, Sadie," Jethro announced. "So just calm down. I wouldn't call you if I didn't have to. I think I'm going to go to Mexico City for a couple of days, but I need some copies of our tax returns before I go." Jethro improvised this part about Mexico City on the spur of the moment. *Give her plenty of rope*, he thought.

"That's your business; I'm on the phone," she answered curtly.

"That's fine, I don't mean to intrude, but like I said, I need copies of our tax returns," said Jethro.

"Well, I may be going downtown in a while; I have some errands to run. I could drop off the tax information if you want," answered Sadie as though preoccupied.

"No, that's okay. Why don't I just go by the house and pick up the tax returns myself? It's not a problem."

"I don't want you coming around the house. How long are you going to stay in Mexico City?"

Jethro noted the sudden interest. "Oh, I don't know, just a few days. Look, all I need are the returns in the folder that's in the desk in the study. What are you going to do, call the cops on me and file false charges again?"

"Just stay away, Jethro, and there won't be any problems."

"Yeah right, Sadie."

"Jethro...I don't want to argue with you."

"Okay, well look. On second thought, if you are going to be around this area, just drop the tax returns off with the receptionist. Okay?"

"Yeah, fine. Have fun in Mexico City."

Early the next morning, Sadie called Jethro very early and most unexpectedly, greeting him cheerfully.

"What are you up to, Jethro? Are you getting ready to go to Mexico City?"

"Yes, in fact I was just packing. I think the trip will do me some good."

Jethro was lying, of course, and the ploy yielded an intriguing development—just the sort of tidbit that Jethro was fishing for.

"When you're in Mexico City, will you email me a number where you'll be, in case I need anything?" she asked casually.

"Sure," replied Jethro as nonchalantly as he could. That she would appeal to him for anything was hard enough to believe, but that she might need help while he was away was absurd. Jethro didn't have to guess for long before grasping that such a transparent request had to do with mapping his whereabouts so she could go unimpeded with hers. Exactly what she was up to he did not know, although he had a good idea; what he did know for sure was that she wanted to be certain that he would be far, far away.

Jethro waited until the following day before calling, only to learn from Lupita that Sadie was not there. Nor did the housekeeper know where Sadie had gone or when she would return. He recalled that the academic fair was scheduled to begin at the local college the next day—the academic fair that Sadie had helped organize and which was to include a photograph exhibit. The day of its opening would also feature a social gathering in the evening to celebrate the commencement of the fair. *An academic fair ... photographs ... evening cocktails ... Benny ... This is it; I'll turn the tables yet.* With that, Jethro would have cancelled his trip to Mexico City if he had really planned one.

"*Send me an email with the telephone number of your hotel...*" *How stupid does she think I am?*

CHAPTER 35

THE LOOMING CONTEST

Jethro called Sadie the following day. For a change, Sadie sounded nice in her greeting, but he detected her unwelcomed surprise to hear from him at all.

"I thought you went to Mexico City," she stated flatly.

"No, I decided not to go after all; I had too much to do around here."

"Are you intending to go to the academic fair?"

"*Ah ha*," thought Jethro. "Uh, I don't really feel like it. I have other things to do. Maybe I'll go later, I don't know," he answered in an innocent tone of voice, taunting her with the prospect of his presence at the photographic event that evening. *Won't her style be cramped if I show up*, he considered with a mischievous wringing of the hands.

Her anger rose quickly. "You can do whatever you want, but it is not fair for you to walk out on your responsibilities. I need to know where you are in case I need something. As it is the bills need to be paid, and you need to come pick them up."

"Sadie, I know my responsibilities. I'll get the bills later, okay?" Jethro ended the testy call.

Almost immediately, however, Sadie called Jethro back, demanding to know why Jethro was being so curt.

"Curt? I'm not being curt, Sadie. I'll go by in about an hour or so to pick up the bills. You can leave them with Lupita if you have to go somewhere, okay?"

Jethro mused with a half smile, *Now why would she be so angry?* It was noon. How would she be one hour later? He reflected on her erratic behavior. Would she, in an effort to enjoy her photo fair, call the cops on him again and this time have him jailed? He already well knew how capable she was of false accusations. He had to be very careful indeed.

One hour passed soon enough, and as Jethro pulled up to the front of the house, Sadie emerged from inside, walking boldly toward him with an outstretched hand, holding a large, overstuffed envelope. She thrust it forward like a speeding ticket from an arrogant traffic cop.

"I've decided we're officially separated, Jethro, indefinitely, and while we're separated, I am free to do what I want, and I'm no longer under any obligation to be loyal to our marriage. And don't try to get me to go to marriage counseling, in case you're thinking about it. I'm going to file for a divorce as soon as I feel ready for it, and you'll find out when you get the papers."

Jethro studied her. He questioned whether Porter would go along with her rather neat legal assessment. She was wearing her mouth-full-of-vinegar face, with lips pressed so tight they were white.

"Look, Sadie, I've really had about enough of your moods and your threats, so why don't you just file the fucking divorce and let's get on with it."

"I don't know what my intentions are right now; I only know maybes."

"Maybes? What are you talking about?" Jethro stared long and hard at her as she stood there before him in a defiant posture. It seemed to him that she had lost some weight; she looked thinner, and she looked older. Her left eye seemed to sink into her skull, somehow, which gave her a look of dementia.

"And I have plans tonight," she went on. "You know I helped organize that event, so you'd better just stay away; I don't want you there."

It was an event that Benny had also helped organize, Jethro suspected, and whose photos would be on exhibit; maybe from among those Jethro had seen spread out on the floor in Benny's house on that cold December afternoon just a few weeks before when his gun had gone off like a firecracker.

"Does the event last all night?" He asked, foolishly perhaps.

"No, Jethro, but afterwards, we're going out for dinner and drinks, Carla and I, and whoever else wants to come along."

"Carla or Benny?"

"If Benny wants to join us he will." Her tone of voice was angry and impatient. "Why are you asking, Jethro?"

Jethro, by contrast, had retreated to cautious ground, like a snake charmer before a cobra.

"You're right, you're right, I'm sorry I asked." He quickly interjected. He examined her again. That left eye of hers appeared strange; it looked like the dead eye of a fish on a bed of ice in the seafood section of the grocery store. Jethro shook his head and drove away.

As he was driving, the cell phone rang, snapping Jethro out of a morbid meditation. It was Sadie calling from her cell phone while driving somewhere, and she sounded extremely upset.

"Why does it have to be so antagonistic between us?" she demanded.

"I didn't think I was being antagonistic."

"Well, you are, Jethro, and you're being distant and cold, and too formal, and I don't appreciate your asking me questions. You interrogate me, and I resent it."

"I wasn't interrogating you. I was just curious, that's all." Jethro's replied. "Why are you so touchy? You're behaving very weird."

Sadie got all fired up.

"How am I acting, Jethro? Just what exactly do you mean? Have you been watching me or spying on me? Are you following me, is that what you have been up to? What behavior are you referring to?"

Her voice was shrill, and Jethro listened not so much to the content but to the tone. *She sure jumped at that one*, he thought. *I must have struck a nerve.* So he continued.

"I don't know what you do, Sadie, and I'm not following you or spying on you, that's ridiculous. I'm staying away from you."

Sadie arrived at the school where the evening's event would be held. With Jethro still on the phone, she told Jethro at least that much, adding that she was there to deliver some things for public access. Jethro could hear her car door open, and then he heard her greet someone who had apparently arrived at the same time and had walked up to Sadie's car. "Hi," he heard Sadie say. And what a cheerful, bubbly hello it was.

A second or two passed before Sadie cut in and curtly told him, "I have to go; I'll call you later." She then hung up.

Yeah, thought Jethro. *We'll see about that.*

CHAPTER 36

HELLO CARLA

Jethro spent the remaining hours of the afternoon driving about aimlessly, finally stopping at the local mall just to have a place to stroll around in and do some people watching. For dinner, he parked himself at his usual Chinese restaurant for his favorite comfort food: Chinese fried rice and beer. He took his time, and this time enjoyed the meal. It certainly was not his intention to go to the event and sit there among the crowd while having to put up with Sadie's antics. Instead, he had enlisted the services of Manfredo, his trusted private-eye, to follow Sadie around and maybe get some photos that might come in handy in the fast approaching future.

He went back to the mall after dinner and loitered until it closed at nine o'clock. With nowhere else to go, he headed for a nearby tavern to drink a few beers.

Seated at the bar, Jethro was into his second glass when a familiar voice spoke up behind him.

"Well, well, if it isn't the macho-man himself, and all by himself—Jethro. What's the matter, Mr. Popular, all alone here? Don't you have any friends, or have they left you, too?"

Jethro swiveled slowly around to be met by the singular beauty of Carla, the feminist on a mission to destroy her fellow man. And how she looked the part. Tall and slender, and with ample bosom, hips, and bottom, she had a narrow waist that lent her torso the S-curve of a Gibson Girl. *She must have modeled for the Venus de Milo*, said Jethro to himself, already feeling the hypnotic effects of the vision before him. Her facial features were almost symmetrical with wide, prominent cheekbones narrowing up toward her forehead and down to her jaw and chin. She was smiling as only she could, with a perfect row of white teeth and one dimple on her left cheek, her almost violet blue eyes sparkling behind long, long lashes. Her chiseled nose came to a tip that seemed hand formed into an almost perfect little circle. And all of this framed by a volume of the blackest hair which fell to her shoulders in a waterfall of the loosest curls. Always at ease and fashionable, Carla wore an elegant dress wrapped around her hourglass figure, stopping just above her knees to show off a pair of well developed calves shaped like upside down Cupid's hearts.

"Hello, Carla," he deadpanned. "What are you doing here?"

"I just came in to have a drink, like you, Jethro. Or did you think women don't do that?"

"I don't know what women do, Carla. I only asked you what you did. Why does everything have to be a challenge to your gender?"

Carla shrugged and, much to Jethro's awareness, performed the Carla giggle complete with a jutting of her lower jaw while affecting a hint of a smile, achieved by her moving only the corners of her mouth by pointing them in opposite directions, all of this finished off with a slight chuckle, or rather a small, double-syllable trill.

"I do whatever I want, and what I want is a drink. Do you want to buy me one?"

Jethro sighed. Buying her a drink was the least he wanted to do with her.

"I see your feminism is not above tapping on traditional roles for free drinks, eh, Carla?" Jethro motioned to the bartender.

"You're such an ass, Jethro; I don't need you to buy me a drink. I was actually offering you my company, which is something you *do* need, because you really don't know anything about anything." Carla said with her giggle.

The *Margarita* she'd ordered came right up, and Carla didn't ask for a tab.

" 'Anything about anything.' What does that mean?" Jethro asked casually as he took a sip of beer.

"You know, that stupid stunt of yours the other night, with the knife. You're lucky you have a wife like Sadie who had mercy on you, because if you didn't, you'd be in jail right now (Carla giggle). You should be grateful she let you off the hook. I sure as hell wouldn't have."

"Oh, so you believe her?"

"Jethro, you're such a macho asshole; I feel sorry for you."

She said this with the sweetest smile that only her lovely face could offer. Jethro smiled back in male appreciation. As rotten as she was, she was hot.

"Yeah, well I appreciate your sympathy." He said sarcastically. "That's very nice; thank you."

"You know, Jethro, you really don't know what's going on, do you?" (Carla giggle).

"What are you talking about, Carla? Why don't you just spell it out?"

"You know, all this fuss you've made about Sadie's friendship with Benny—I know all about it, Jethro, how you confronted them and pulled that ridiculous stunt with the firecracker. They're friends, Jethro, *friends*, okay? Benny's gay, just so you'll know, you macho ass (Carla giggle). You don't know anything; you don't even know your own wife." With that said, Carla knocked her *Margarita* back in one gulp, and slammed the empty glass onto the bar as would a sailor in a port of call.

"I'd like another." She announced.

Jethro had turned from the glass of beer in front of him and after noting the gusto in her performance, took her at her word and summoned the barkeep.

"What do you mean, I don't know my own wife; what are you saying?"

"I'm saying that you only see the world in black and white. Boys and girls. Well, I hate to be the one to break it to you, but the world is actually grey. There are boys and girls, boys and boys, and girls and girls."

"Thank you for pointing that out to me, Carla. I feel wiser already." Jethro took a long swig of beer.

Carla paused, slowly stirring her fresh *Margarita* with the tiny straw it came with. She studied Jethro as if to measure whether she could confide in him.

"Jethro, Benny is gay. That means boys and boys. And you don't know your wife—that means girls and girls."

"Are you saying that my wife is gay?"

"Good God, Jethro, you really are dense." Carla grabbed her handbag as though to go. "Jethro, I can't explain everything to you. Every macho pig has his learning curve, and you have yours, only yours is unusually steep (Carla giggle). You have a long way to go and you're just going to have to wait and see for yourself. That is, of course, if you don't lose it all before you run out of time. Sadie knows as well as I do where all this is headed and we're all behind her, and *you*, Jethro, are dead meat."

With that, she swilled down her *Margarita* and slid off the stool.

"Hey Carla, aren't you late for dinner?" Jethro asked on impulse, taking note of what she had said and how well it matched Sadie's purposeful behavior.

"Dinner?" Carla asked with a blank look. "What are you talking about?"

"There's an arts festival tonight over at the college. I thought for sure you'd be going. Those festivals always end in dinner parties..." Jethro didn't want to show his hand.

"I'm not interested in any art festivals, Jethro."

At that, Jethro took a swig of beer.

"Relax. Why don't you have another drink?"

Carla hesitated for an instant and then sat back down. Placing an elbow on the bar, she ran her fingers through her luscious patent-leather hair. She looked at Jethro and smiled with her eyes.

"I'd like another *Margarita*, please."

"So, my wife is gay, huh?" Jethro played along. "And just who is her lover—you?" Jethro nodded at the waiter who was leaning against the liquor display by the cash register.

"You're not supposed to know, and I'm not gonna be the one to tell you. Sadie is a friend of mine, and I respect her, so I don't want to talk about it anymore." Carla laughed.

"Oh, okay, well thanks a lot for telling me." Jethro went back to his beer. He thought of the Sadie he knew, and considered what Carla was telling him. *She's full of shit*, he thought, taking another swig.

The drinks flowed, with Jethro sipping his beer and Carla guzzling her Margaritas. Carla's talk on feminist subjects and her declaration of war on manhood waxed on. Jethro participated in the discussion as though part of a theater audience and counted fourteen Carla giggles she added to her soliloquy. But Jethro had business to tend to, and the time for the festival's end had passed and the time for any dinner party was underway.

"Carla, as much as I have found your discourse on the uselessness of men intriguing, I have to get going," he said.

"Okay," she agreed as she gathered her purse. "I'm leaving too."

Jethro called for the bill, and as he did, Carla excused herself for the ladies room. As she stepped down from the barstool, she lost her balance and Jethro caught her arm and steadied her. The Margaritas had had their effect.

"Are you okay?"

"Yeah," she assured him. "I'm just a little dizzy; that's all, but I can take it; let go of me!" She snapped while snatching her arm away from Jethro's hold. "I'll be right back." Carla seemed quite unsteady in her gait, and Jethro watched after her as she tacked her way toward the ladies' room.

Just as Jethro paid the bill, Carla reappeared over by the entrance to the bar. Jethro made his way toward her. Carla, on the other hand, didn't bother waiting for him. After seeing that Jethro saw her, she sashayed out of the bar well ahead of him. She didn't get too far, however, before Jethro stepped outside and into a cloud of perfume that wafted off of Carla who must have doused herself with the entire bottle of perfume while in the ladies' room—or so Jethro thought.

As Carla walked slightly ahead, Jethro held his breath at the spectacle before him. Perhaps the Margaritas had deadened her sense of self perception; or maybe the tequila in her cocktail had warmed her enough that she couldn't feel any differences in surface temperatures; or, maybe, whatever she did feel, if a slight coolness somewhere perhaps, she attributed it to the contrast in climate one would normally feel after having stepped out of a warm bar and into a cool evening. Whatever it was, she was unaware that the back of her dress had gotten caught up in her lingerie, exposing the right of her derriére—a cheek largely unprotected from complete exposure, and view, by the scant fabric of her cosabela soire thong. Jethro held his breath in amazement, and swallowed hard to clear his mouth which had suddenly turned into water. There she was, walking confidently across the parking lot, as though she owned it, with half her stern on display.

Jethro caught up to her.

"Carla, where are you going?" he asked.

"I'm not sure." As she answered, she raised her head slightly as though considering several choices. By not returning the question, however, Jethro understood that he did not figure in any of them.

"It's a little chilly out, don't you think?"

"No, Jethro, I'm fine." She glanced over at him. "The weather's nice."

"But, don't you feel a breeze?" He insisted.

"Well, yeah," she answered as though bothered by him. "There's a slight breeze, but so what?"

Working quickly, Jethro leaned backwards as he walked in order to make a frank assessment of her gluteal fold, which, based on the visuals Carla now provided, appeared to be perfectly shaped—like a red delicious apple.

"What are you doing?" Carla asked with a frown upon detecting Jethro's strange ambulatory attitude.

"Nothing." He answered, snapping back to a normal walking posture.

"You've always been such a weirdo, Jethro." Carla said in a dry tone of voice.

"Thank you, Carla." Jethro answered sarcastically. "I've always thought highly of you, too. And I want to thank you, really, for just being you. Where are you parked?"

Carla gave Jethro a look in an effort to measure whether or not he was serious.

"I'm right over there," she answered, signaling with her head.

Jethro walked her over to her car. She, in the meantime, fumbled inside the depths of her purse in search of her car keys. When her hand emerged clutching them Jethro reached over and gently took the keys from her. Unlocking her car door, he opened it for her, and taking her left hand in his right, guided her in. He then handed her the keys so that she could start it. She still had not reacted at all to her half exposed fundament.

"Do you feel anything strange?" Jethro asked her.

Carla made a face.

"Jethro, the only thing that is strange around here is *you*." With that, she slammed her car door shut, and drove off at a high rate of speed.

Jethro walked over to his truck, peering back at her as he did. *Carla's beauty, what a waste — like sugar on the floor,* he sighed. He then drove away as well, only more slowly.

It was now about 10:30. *The event should be well over and dinner on,* considered Jethro. After some deliberation he decided to drive by the festival, just to see what was left of it.

The art show was being held at a local college, in one of its big convention rooms that often hosted community events in order to promote the local culture. As at any college, expansive parking lots had been built adjacent to the various buildings. The lot next to the art show was about the size of a football field, and almost empty. There were a few cars there, next to the building. The rest of the lot was vast emptiness except at the far, opposite end away from the building where a few cars were parked — and there among them was Sadie's car. *Why would she park so far away from the buildings?* Jethro asked himself. Indeed, Sadie's car was so very far away from the buildings that one might not have seen it unless one looked about deliberately as Jethro had.

He grabbed his cell phone and called Manfredo.

"I'm here at the college looking at her car; where are you?"

"I'm trying to find your wife," said Manfredo.

"What do you mean, 'trying to find her?'"

"Well, I saw her leave the contest, or whatever it was, but I lost her in traffic."

"Lost her in traffic? What car was she in?" Jethro asked while staring at her parked Suburban.

"I saw her get into a reddish SUV-type vehicle, and then she took off. It was all very fast, so I'm looking for her."

"Well forget that, Manfredo. You've gotta come back to the college. Her car is parked here. At some point tonight, whoever she's with will bring her back to her car. I need you to be there, and take some photos. I don't care if it takes all night. I'll settle with you later."

"You got it, boss," Manfredo assured him. "Give me the description of the car again, and tell me exactly where it is. I'm on it."

"Good. Keep me posted."

Jethro considered the few cars left near the building and thought to have a look inside at the exhibit. He parked and walked in.

The exhibit was held in a large conference room on the second floor. Partitions were arranged in semicircles about the room with photographs on display. Along one wall was a lengthy table covered in white cloth and arranged with pastries, finger sandwiches, plates filled with grapes, melon balls, and cheese squares with toothpicks sticking out of them. A large punch bowl sat in the middle of the spread. A few people stood around the table nibbling on the refreshments. Staff workers were folding chairs, stacking them on rolling platforms, and generally cleaning up.

Jethro ate a few grapes, poured himself a cup of punch took a sip and then ambled over to view the exhibits. There Jethro recognized photos of the sort he had seen strewn on the floor of Benny's living room. There were photos of Indians dancing; others featuring Indians sitting in a circle; and some of Indians holding their hands up to the sky performing incantations. There was one photo of an Indian standing there looking at the camera with a large melon tucked under his arm—a far cry from his warrior predecessors. Jethro walked about them slowly but scanned the photos quickly. They were of no interest to him. But then, one photo made him stop and stare.

It was a photo with Sadie in it. The camera caught her looking at it with a half smile—that is, with only half her mouth smiling asymmetrically, and her eyes not smiling at all. Depicted in the background was the inside of a shallow cave or hollow, its back wall of stone decorated with what appeared to be ancient petroglyphs. Jethro stared at the photo in disbelief.

Where the hell was that taken? Jethro wondered. *And when?*

He set his cup of punch down and left the building.

CHAPTER 37

PRIVATE EYE REPORT FOR WORK

The morning after the arts festival, Jethro went to work early, eager for the investigative report. Stepping into his small office, he closed the door behind him, and called Manfredo who answered his cell phone in hushed tones.

"I'm on another job, Jethro, so I can't really talk right now."

"Well, damnit, tell me what happened," demanded Jethro.

"I saw your wife get dropped off at three AM by a woman in a red SUV that was maybe ten years old, or older. It was either a Bronco or Ford Explorer, I'm not sure."

"Who gives a damn about the vehicle, Manfredo; you said a *woman*? What did she look like?" Jethro remained unsettled. *A woman in a red sports utlility vehicle*, he repeated to himself. He thought of what Carla had said to him. His thoughts then focused on the red SUV. Something about it nagged at him, but he couldn't put his finger on it.

"Look, I've gotta go. I'll call you sometime later today," whispered Manfredo.

Jethro tried to focus on work as he waited for the phone to ring.

At about 10:30 that morning, Jethro's secretary called over to him, "Jethro, it's Manfredo, line one."

"Thanks Idalia." Jethro shut the door to his office, and then eagerly he grabbed the phone.

"Okay, Manfredo, tell me exactly what you saw."

"It was a red Explorer or Bronco, about ten years old, maybe more. It drove up quickly and parked alongside the white Suburban. The driver and passenger got out, but they were standing in between the vehicles, so I couldn't see them very well from where I was positioned. They said a quick goodbye, got into their own vehicles, and drove off. That's it. They were there for just a few seconds."

"What did the driver of the Bronco look like?"

"Average in height, maybe a bit taller, and she had long blonde hair, but it was straight blonde hair. I didn't really get to see how she was dressed, but it looks like she was wearing jeans. They were parked in a way that I couldn't see."

"A slender *woman*?" Jethro asked incredulously.

"Yeah, not fat or heavy at all."

"Manfredo, that wasn't a woman." Jethro stated flatly.

"Jethro," Manfredo insisted, "I was there; I saw them. I'm telling you it was a damned chick."

"Manfredo," Jethro almost barked. "That was Benny, her boyfriend. He's tall and skinny, and has a pony tail down to his ass."

Manfredo remained silent as he tried to resolve the conflict now in his mind. Just then the red SUV struck Jethro in the brain. He now remembered the red SUV parked in front of Benny's residence alongside Sadie's suburban.

"That red SUV is Benny's; I remember seeing it parked in front of his house."

"Well I'll be damned," exclaimed Manfredo. "I could have sworn he was a chick. He looks like a girl. But I'll tell you what: his hair was not in a pony tail. He had let his hair down."

"Well, one of Sadie's best friends assures me that he *is* a girl. Did you get any photos?"

"No, I would have, but university police made me move from my original location, so I had to park a good distance away. It was the best I could do." Manfredo confessed. "They took off in opposite directions. The Bronco went south, and the Suburban went north. I decided to follow the Bronco, but I lost it. The thing is that at three in the morning there was very little traffic, and I couldn't follow too closely because I was afraid that the driver would spot me."

"All right, Manfredo, thanks a lot. Good job." *Fuck*, muttered Jethro.

Later that morning, Sadie emailed Jethro. She wanted to meet. Jethro sat back in his chair, wondering why. His musings precluded any rush to respond. As he stalled, he reflected on how, only days earlier, he would have jumped at any invitation from Sadie to spend any amount of time with her — anything to have a chance to appeal to her; to maybe make her reconsider the course she had taken. By now, however, matters had changed. He was now of decided mind. It had only been a month and a half since the real troubles had begun, and he didn't feel confident that his feelings now, or then, were truly reflective of all that was happening to him. Feelings, after all, varied and changed as did the time of day. But his mind was well made up and his feelings would just have to catch up. In the meantime he vowed to catch the love-birds. He was determined to be the victor.

Although Jethro had worked with clients who had gone through what he was now undergoing, always he had maintained the clinical detachment of the professional. That objectivity, valued by his clients to the extent they paid his fee, was wholly absent now. After all, unlike in the case of his clients, what was happening was happening to him.

Jethro continued reflecting and busied himself with work until later that afternoon, when Sadie called. She was extremely angry with Jethro for his not having responded to her email of that morning and accused him of spousal rape because of the intimate foul a few weeks before.

"You refuse to talk to me, and I think that is abuse." Sadie's anger gathered momentum as she went on accusingly. "You need to understand that I need to talk to you, and you're unwillingness to talk to me is cruelty."

"Sadie, I haven't refused to talk to you. You only emailed a few hours ago. In fact it has been me urging that we talk about everything that is going on. What are you saying?"

"It's you who doesn't communicate; you're screwing this all up," she growled. "You're not going to turn your back on your responsibilities!"

Jethro was almost speechless with incredulity, and just basically sick of this.

"What do you mean, turn my back on my responsibilities? I have always been there; it's you who wants out. Look, I really don't know what you're talking about."

"Wrong, Jethro, you're the one who is ruining everything." On she went, shouting. Jethro shook his head from side to side. He was now convinced that his wife was either insane or childishly naïve in thinking her designs viable.

Just then Jethro was interrupted by his secretary.

"Jethro, Mr. Derecho is here to see you on. You have an appointment with him about the Australian meat case against Border Cold Storage; remember?"

"Oh, yes." Jethro responded mechanically. "Tell him I'll be right with him."

Automatically thoughts about a cargo of beef, several commercial containers of it, from Australia bound for Mexico via Los Angeles and then Laredo flooded Jethro's mind: there was something about a warehouse receipt, storage costs in dispute, and only a few short weeks left before the beef could no longer be shipped into Mexico due to expiration dates of cold-stored meat and something about the health and safety code. Several hundred thousand dollars worth of beef were at stake.

But Sadie went on with her grossly inconsistent diatribe, and Jethro could not readily break away.

When Sadie finally hung up, Jethro remained in his office, pacing. Soon Sadie called back.

"Jethro, I just wanted to say that I want to be friends. I don't know how to express myself; I'm sorry."

Of course, Jethro told her it was okay, but he felt troubled by how confused and erratic she sounded. Although Sadie was now making an amicable appeal, her tone of voice was heightened by the burst of energy she invested in her effort.

"Really, Jethro." She continued. "I just want to have fun. I want to be *free*, and I want a *new* life."

What a woman! Jethro sighed. *All she cares about is living on easy street. She scolds me for not calling her, when only days ago she demanded that I stop calling,* he thought with bitterness. *She's a nut.* The call ended not soon enough for Jethro.

Jethro stepped out of his office. Idalia was busy organizing a shuffle of papers in a thick file.

"Mr. Derecho waited for you," she said with a frown. "He finally left. He seemed really upset." Her tone of voice was flat.

Jethro looked at her blankly without answering. He had completely forgotten about Mr. Derecho and the hostage load of meat. This Sadie business was beginning to hurt his business.

The phone rang. It was Sadie yet again.

"Jethro, I need to talk to you. Will you have lunch with me tomorrow?"

"Sadie, my patience is growing really thin." Jethro huffed audibly. "Where do you want to have lunch?"

"At the Chinese restaurant; we can talk."

Jethro thought for a moment, and then agreed with reluctance.

CHAPTER 38

FIREWORKS AT THE CHINESE RESTAURANT

Jethro woke up early, eager to get on with it. He went to the office and managed to focus on his work but kept glancing at his watch. No sooner than the approach of lunchtime, he took off.

Arriving at the Chinese restaurant, Jethro spied Sadie's car already there. He felt relief, as he had half suspected, given Sadie's erratic behavior, that she might not keep the appointment. He found her waiting for him in the booth they had usually favored when all seemed well. He sat down in front of her.

"What's this all about? I'm getting really fed up," he flatly stated as a curt hello.

"Jethro, I want peace." Sadie looked coolly at him. "You're angry because of my friendship with Benny. Jethro we're just friends. You've made everything up in your head." She smiled maternally and, canting her head to one side, nodded a gentle dismissal of the notion.

"I'm making this all up in my head, am I?" Jethro slowly shook his head from side to side. "Then why the many falsehoods? Why all the deception? And why did you take his side at his shack the other day? I didn't make any of that up."

"I didn't lie." She answered calmly with a sober look. "I couldn't tell you about my friendship with Benny because you couldn't take it, just like you can't take it now."

Jethro tried to remain calm, but his anger was on the rise. *She knows exactly what to say*, he thought. *She's playing me. So, you want to play, huh?*

"Where did you go the night of the photo contest, after the contest was over?" Jethro pressed, although taking care to appear nonchalant by shoveling a mouthful of happy rice into his mouth upon the question, and then reaching for his icy mug of beer to wash it down.

"I went to dinner with Benny and Carla."

"Oh you did; whose car did you go in?" Jethro thought of Carla's *nalga*[1] on display. It was obvious that Sadie had not spoken to Carla, or if she had, Carla had not mentioned her being with him that night.

"I went in my own car," said Sadie. "Carla went with me."

Yeah sure, Jethro wanted to say. Instead Jethro asked, in between another forkful of comfort food, "Did Benny also go with you?"

"No, he went in his own car; he met us at Toños."

"Dinner at Toños, how nice." Jethro was amazed at how compliant she was being in answering all his questions, and at how well she lied.

"So, at what time did your party end; when'd you get home?"

"I'm not sure, it was eleven or twelve; I wasn't really paying attention."

Jethro took a big gulp of beer.

"Are you still seeing Benny?"

"No, Jethro, for your information, I'm not. I see him at the gym whenever he happens to be there when I go, but I'm not *seeing* him, okay?"

Now she was growing impatient, but ever the lawyer, Jethro continued with the line of questioning for as long as he could get away with it.

---

[1] Spanish slang for buttocks or ass.

"Does he still ask you out or make plans with you?"

"No, Jethro, he was *just a friend*; how many times do I have to tell you?"

Jethro studied her while thinking of the ridiculous things Carla had told him about Sadie and decided on a shift of gears.

"Look, Sadie, I know Benny is just your friend. In fact, I know everything. You should have just told me all along. I'm open-minded enough; I would have accepted you."

"What are you talking about?" Sadie frowned.

Jethro paused, took another swig of beer, and then set his eyes dead on Sadie's. It was time to lay it on her.

"Please don't ask me how I know, but I know you have a girlfriend."

"A girlfriend?" Asked Sadie, obviously puzzled. "I have a lot of girlfriends; what do you mean?"

"No, I mean a *girlfriend* girlfriend."

Sadie stared blankly at him.

"I know you're gay, Sadie, and you have a girlfriend."

"How do you know?" Sadie crossed her arms in front of her and sat back with a look of amusement.

"I'm not going to tell you how I know. I just know. I know Benny is gay, and he's your girlfriend."

Sadie wiped the smile off her face.

"Why didn't you simply tell me, Sadie? There was no need to take it out on me by throwing me out and lying to me and sneaking around and everything. You didn't have to destroy our home over it. I don't mind you having a girlfriend named Benny."

"Jethro, don't confuse my privacy with my wanting to be free. You can call it whatever you want; I don't feel any less trapped, as long as I am with you. I still want you out, and I'll be with whomever I want."

"I'm trying to be fair with you, Sadie, that's all."

Sadie seemed to relax a bit; however, her arms remained tightly clenched across her chest. Jethro read the guarded demeanor well, and understood it to mean that he had indeed hit upon a closeted secret of hers.

"How long has this been going on, Sadie?"

Sadie unfolded her arms and placed her hands on the table, interlacing her fingers. She met Jethro's eyes.

"Benny's not my *girlfriend*, Jethro."

"Oh, so she's your boyfriend?"

"Where are you getting all this from?"

"How come you never told me? Either Benny's a boy who's your girlfriend; or, Benny's a girl who's your boyfriend. Now which is it?"

"Jethro, I came here to try and make peace, but now you can forget it. I'm not going to tell you anything." Sadie snapped, her face reddening in color. "You see the world from your own, very narrow point of view. I mean, look how you've reacted to my friendship with Benny. You have completely freaked out, and *you* are the one who has ruined everything. If a situation doesn't fit into your neat little world, you can't handle it. You see everything in black and white, and the world happens to be more complicated than that. That's why I feel so trapped. I feel trapped by your closed mind."

Jethro sat there listening, taking mental note of her choice of words. Sadie appeared to have been coached by Carla. He regarded Sadie, sitting there, so sure of herself, so arrogant. Jethro was filled with loathing.

"Okay Sadie, so you can have Benny, as a girl or a boy. You come in many colors, don't you? Tell me, who or what are you going to do next?"

"I will do whatever I want; and I don't care what you think or say." She declared.

"What time did you leave the university the night of the photo contest?" He insisted.

"I left around nine." Sadie stammered, momentarily caught off guard by the quick change of topic.

"Why did you tell me you left in your own car? That was a lie; I saw your car parked at the university at around ten that night!"

"You were following me!" Sadie exploded. "You *bastard!* Is that it?"

"No, I wasn't following you. I just happened to pass by on my way home and I saw it there, so I know you lied. Now tell me, where did you go with Benny?"

"That's right, I left there with Benny." Sadie's brief moment off guard now having vanished, she seethed with venom. "We wanted to talk and so we went and had a nice, quiet dinner at Toños, and there we ran into Carla and a bunch of other girls. Benny left before we did. So I wasn't with him, okay?"

"When did you get home?" Jethro continued exploring the extent of her falsehoods well noting how protective she was of her adulterous behavior—admitting enough to cloak it in innocent garb yet concealing the cuckoldry underneath.

"That's none of your business, Jethro. Get used to it, it is over between us! And just so you'll know, it's your fault. Your chauvinistic ideas don't allow for simple friendships, so sometimes instead of having to deal with your macho bullshit, a simple lie serves to get rid of you easier."

"Oh, now I understand. Yes, I can see how you'd have to lie in order to deal with me. You're so reasonable."

"There are so many things you don't understand, Jethro, and I can't be the one to show them all to you and help you work through them. You have many issues, and I'm not your mother."

"No, of course not, Sadie," Jethro mocked. "I'm sorry. I don't know what gets into me," he offered. "Look, I want to be friends. We need to just work something out. We can't keep on like this. Will you have dinner with me on Sunday?"

"I'll be out of town." Sadie seemed caught off guard and as though she might have kept her mouth shut and would rather she had.

"Where are you going?" Jethro pounced.

"I'm going into Mexico, to Bustamante," she said merrily.

"Bustamante? What on earth for?" The seriousness of Jethro's demeanor contrasted sharply with her abrupt cheerfulness.

"I'm going with the bicycle club. We're going on a Valentine's Day biking trip. They go every year, and this year *I'm invited*." She stated with glee.

"Is this with Benny?"

"He'll be there."

"Are you going with him?" asked Jethro, now breathing shallowly as his anger grew.

"We're going together, but the group will be there. Here you go again, Jethro. Benny will be there, but I am not *with* him. I'm going to be with someone else, and it's going to be great. It's an overnight thing."

Jethro took in what she said and let it go. He did not want her to know where his focus was. She had just revealed travel plans into Mexico next weekend with Benny – or someone. This might provide a chance to tie down what he needed to fully protect himself and be prepared for matters ahead; and, to dictate the outcome—of course.

Jethro looked at his wristwatch, and, feigning sudden haste as though realizing he was late for an appointment, took a last gulp of beer and announced that he had to go.

Sadie calmly took a sip of tea as though she had all the time in the world, and, with a smile as pleasant as it was mean, handed Jethro the bill.

CHAPTER 39

PLANS FOR BUSTAMANTE

Jethro knew Bustamante, Mexico to be a small town in the northeastern part of the Mexican state of Nuevo Leon, about a hundred miles southwest of Laredo. Most of its four thousand inhabitants were folks of Tlaxcalan extraction. The town was surrounded by mountains of the Sierra Madre Oriental, and featured a canyon that was popular among hikers, as well as some famous caves with—*of course*, Jethro now realized as that photo at the art fair came to mind—ancient petroglyphs. The only other thing that Bustamante was known for was its local pastries filled with pecans and caramelized goat's milk. Biking trails, however, were not on Bustamante's list of tourist attractions, at least not to Jethro's knowledge, though he was now determined to make sure.

He had only a few days to work with. Certainly the group had to stay somewhere while there; a motel most probably. And Bustamante, being the small village that it was, couldn't have too many motels for travelers to choose from.

Jethro called an international directory and asked for information on accommodations in Bustamante, Nuevo Leon. According to the operator's data, there were only two such establishments and both were small, bed-and-breakfast-type inns: La Casita and El Mirador. Jethro jotted down their names and phone numbers. He decided to call La Casita first, and luck was with him. A nice, elderly-sounding lady answered the phone.

"Good morning, señora." Jethro said in greeting. "I understand that there is a biking group going to Bustamante this weekend for a riding excursion. Are you aware of this event?"

"No, señor, I am not aware of any bicycle event here in Bustamante." Typical of Mexican country-folk, the patron lady was extremely polite and sounded eager to please. "Bicycles? Nobody rides bicycles here, señor."

"Well, some friends of mine from Laredo are going there this weekend, and I wondered if any were staying with you there, because I might want to go, too."

"Well, we do have a few people staying here this weekend, and two *are* from Laredo."

"Two from Laredo; could you tell me who they are?"

"Oh yes, they've stayed with us before. They are a really nice couple from Laredo. Both of them are Americans (read: *gringos*), and both of them are blond."

"You don't say. That sounds like my friends." Jethro knew that in referring to the two Americans as "blond," the matron of the inn was referring to eye color, and not necessarily hair color.

"Yes, one of them is a tall man with very long blond hair, and the other is a small woman with very pretty brown hair, and with grey eyes, only her hair is shorter than the man's. They are the nicest people, and a lovely couple."

Jethro swallowed hard. "Will they be staying with you this weekend?"

"Yes, of course; they always stay with us."

Jethro paused at this, but then a thought popped into his mind.

"I think I know them; do they drive a red car?"

"Oh yes, they always come in a red jeep sort of vehicle.

Jethro stood silent for a moment. He reflected on how Manfredo had been so mistaken in his report that Sadie had been dropped off by a tall, thin blonde woman at three in the morning. And there was nothing gay about Sadie's activity that night. It *had* been Benny all along; only instead of having his hair in a ponytail, he had let it fall free as it was on that cold December afternoon when Jethro had barged into Benny's bungalow and found them there. *Why had he let his hair down?* Jethro wondered. *Women let their hair down when they ...*

"Señor?" The lady on the phone in Bustamante snapped Jethro out of his naked thoughts.

"Oh, yes...sorry. Do you have any more rooms available?"

"Yes, I have two more at the moment."

"Great, I'd like to have one of them, but I need to make sure I can go. May I call you back in a little while after I make sure of my plans?"

"Yes, of course. I will wait for your call."

The lady was nice indeed, Jethro thought. Little did she know how sharply her words had stung, and little did she suspect the sting that Jethro was arranging.

Jethro dialed Manfredo's number.

"I have a serious job for you. You and I are going to a little town in Mexico. There's a little bed-and-breakfast-type inn that you'll be staying in."

"I'm going to stay at a bed-and-breakfast with you?" Manfredo sounded dubious.

"No, you're going to stay at one place, and I'll be staying at another," Jethro explained. "I think my wife is going alone with her boyfriend in that little red SUV of his. You'll be staying where they'll be staying. I have a little plan, Manfredo. Why don't you come to my office in a couple of hours so that I can go over it with you?"

Manfredo complained at first of the lack of notice and admonished Jethro that he would have to rearrange his work schedule and cancel some weekend jobs he'd already been hired to do. Jethro understood this to mean that Manfredo's spy services for the weekend would cost him a premium. At any rate, Manfredo was game. Besides, he was embarrassed about having mistaken Benny for a woman and having given Jethro an inaccurate report.

Jethro called La Casita again to reserve a room. He then called El Mirador to reserve another. The attendant at El Mirador sounded drunk, it seemed to Jethro, and indicated in garbled words that El Mirador had *all* its rooms available, adding with enthusiasm that they'd be sure to clean one up just for him. Why, they'd even wash the sheets and provide a clean towel. After securing accommodations, Jethro thought he was probably the only customer El Mirador had had in years, given how surprised the innkeeper sounded at the prospect. He then grabbed his car keys. He didn't have much time.

"Idalia, I have to run a quick errand. Call me on my cell if anything comes up. I'll be back in about an hour or so."

"Where are you going?"

"I've gotta go get my firecrackers."

"Firecrackers?" Idalia shook her head slowly from side to side, utterly bewildered. "He's becoming stranger by the day," she muttered.

In a little over an hour, Jethro was back. And, not long afterwards, Idalia called out, "Jethro, Manfredo's here; do I show him in?"

"Yes, Idalia. Thank you."

Idalia narrowed her eyes at Jethro as she went toward the foyer.

Presently, Manfredo strode into Jethro's office. It had been a long time since Jethro had seen him, as they conducted most of their dealings over the phone. He had not changed. What he lacked in stature, being just over five feet tall, he made up in reputation. Manfredo had enjoyed a colorful career as an undercover narcotics agent as part of a federal task force in the war on drugs. He had been in several firefights. On two separate instances, while working undercover, he had been recognized as a narc by the drug dealers he was setting up for a sting. On one such occasion, the surprised smugglers lunged in attack, and Manfredo got skewered with a long filet knife. On the other, Manfredo scrambled over a fence as he beat a hasty retreat to safety while guns were blasting and bullets whizzed by. On both occasions, police backup teams, hiding nearby, came to the rescue in the nick of time. Jethro knew Manfredo as a man who could be counted on in a bad situation.

"A little town in Mexico; you were saying?" Manfredo grinned as he flopped into a chair in front of Jethro's desk.

"Bustamante, to be exact."

"You mean that little village by that canyon over there?" Manfredo's grin had vanished, and he was now grumpy at the idea. "It's barely civilized. It's full of Indians, and I don't feel much like doing any hiking."

"*Tlaxcalans*, Manfredo." Jethro corrected him impatiently. "And this won't be a hiking trip. Now listen closely."

Jethro explained the job: Manfredo would travel to Bustamante and stay at the motel where Benny and Sadie would be staying. There, he would simply observe and take photos if he could. The photos would be needed as evidence in the near future to protect Jethro's interests. In the meantime, Jethro would install himself at El Mirador—the only other motel in the village. Manfredo would keep in telephone contact—motel to motel—as the plan developed.

With that they were set. Jethro, came to terms with Manfredo as to fee and expense requirements, and they agreed to touch base on Friday before departure. After that, they would not hear from each other again until Manfredo called Jethro at El Mirador on Saturday with the job in progress and after Manfredo had the time to watch their targets and plot their moves.

"There is one more thing we're going to do, Manfredo." Jethro grabbed the small paper bag that lay on top of his desk and displayed its contents— the two giant firecrackers that looked like miniature sticks of T.N.T.

"What the hell are those—some kind of little bombs?" asked an amused Manfredo.

"These are serious fireworks that are really loud when they go off; about ten times louder than a regular Black Cat. They can blow your hand off. But we're gonna have some fun, and no one is going to get hurt..."

As Jethro explained, a wide grin grew on Manfredo's face.

CHAPTER 40

THE TRAP IS SET

So as to avoid being detected by his quarry, Jethro had rented a car at the airport in Nuevo Laredo. He then drove to the little village, entering on the north end of its single strip. It was late afternoon, and there, near the entrance of the hamlet, was La Casita—a quaint, white-stuccoed structure with a handsome red tiled roof. Its porch was populated by potted plants of many varieties, and drapes of fuchsia bougainvilleas adorned most of its walls. Off to one side, Jethro spotted the red SUV parked there by itself.

Jethro drove on past La Casita, peering about to see if he might catch a glimpse of Sadie and Benny, but not trying too hard. He couldn't afford to blow his cover and wanted to get out of sight fast.

El Mirador was located on the opposite end of the main street, about a mile from La Casita. Jethro checked into the small room that would be his hiding place for the next day. And a small room it was—it was more tiny than small. The walls were covered with decaying plaster that had fallen away in places, exposing ancient adobe bricks behind. *Charming*, thought Jethro. The room was bare except for a couple of chairs, a small table with a mirror hanging on the wall behind it, and, for a bed, a bare mattress flopped atop a couple of warehouse pallets. On the mattress lay a neatly folded blanket and towel—there were no sheets to be found and no pillow. For a shower, Jethro was treated to an adjacent room, or rather small vestibule, where a lone, copper tube hung draped over a wall, like a garden hose. Jethro turned the knob. The copper tube gurgled until a rather tepid stream of water flowed out. Jethro looked around for what else El Mirador provided for its guests. There was an outhouse in the back yard. *What this bitch hasn't put me through*, Jethro grumbled. The room had no phone, but Jethro let the innkeeper at the front desk know that he was expecting a call, which came in around eight in the evening.

Manfredo had arrived at La Casita early that same Saturday, just before the noon hour, and coincidently only moments before Benny and Sadie had arrived in the red Bronco. There was no bicycle group, Manfredo assured Jethro, and there weren't any bicycles. No, theirs was not any bicyclist group event; instead, it was just a plain ol' tryst.

"So it was the red Bronco after all," commented Jethro.

"The very same," said Manfredo. "I just didn't get a good enough look at it that night."

"So you see, and it wasn't a slim woman, either. It was him."

"Yeah, it was him," admitted Manfredo. "He's got that ponytail almost down to his ass, and that threw me off. I mean, with his hair down, from the back, he looks like a skinny chick."

"So what's next?"

"After they got here I waited a bit, and it wasn't long before they went on a hike into the canyon,"said Manfredo. "I followed them but I kept a good distance. They would have known something was up if they saw me there, hiking in that big canyon with no one else around. So I mostly waited here at the motel. It's almost dinnertime now. There's a dining room here where everyone sits down at the same table and eats like one big happy family. So I'll join in and watch what happens. After that there isn't anything to do around here, so I'll just settle back and watch."

"I'll be here," Jethro responded dryly.

"I don't know if I'll call you again tonight," Manfredo said. "But I'll come see you in the morning."

"We'll play this by ear, Manfredo," Jethro warned. "Just find us a window of opportunity."

"Don't worry, I'll be in touch," Manfredo assured him. "I won't miss them this time."

Jethro was awakened abruptly the next morning by a sudden knocking on his door that sounded urgent. It was Manfredo, who practically pushed his way into the room as soon as Jethro cracked the door open to see who it was.

"We'd better hurry, man," Manfredo exclaimed. "They've packed up the car and they're ready to get out of town, but they've gone on a morning hike before leaving. We have maybe an hour—hour and a half at most."

"Let's move." Jethro asserted as he reached for a duffle bag that was sitting on a chair next to the bed.

"Is that what you slept on?" Manfredo asked while looking at the lumpy mattress flopped on the warehouse pallets. He shook his head slowly in mock disapproval.

"Yeah, and so what?" Jethro answered dryly. "What happened last night?"

"The evening was simple enough. There was that family-style dinner I told you about. I sat there at the table along with Benny and Sadie," said Manfredo. "There was another random couple there, too, complete strangers." Manfredo paused and gave Jethro a look of scrutiny.

"Jethro, how thick do you want me to lay it on you, man, because they are definitely into it. Shall I spare your feelings?" His tone was laced with sarcasm as he looked about the room giving it further inspection.

"Just tell me what happened, damnit."

"Well, have a look at this." Manfredo produced a small digital camera. "I took a bunch of pictures, and they're saved here for you to look at. We can print them out once we get back to Laredo."

Jethro stood next to Manfredo as the private eye scrolled through a collection of photos he had taken. Some were of low quality, having been taken in poor lighting conditions or at odd angles. Others, however, were well done. There were some photos of Sadie and Benny hiking—two tiny figures walking along a skinny trail in an immense canyon. There were other pictures of them sitting on the porch in the evening, quite snuggled up, and engaged in a public display of affection. Another set of photos had them enter a room together, and then close the door behind them. The picture had been taken at night. A small light bulb hanging over the door provided enough light for ready recognition.

Photos taken the following morning showed Benny leaving the same bedroom early, with Sadie remaining behind. A short time later, Manfredo took a snapshot of Benny delivering a cup of coffee to Sadie; another showed her giving him a warm kiss in return; yet a third showed the door closed with Benny walking away, down the sidewalk, towards other rooms which were all enclosed around a small courtyard. The only way in and out of the courtyard was through the front entrance by the owner's home which led to the open areas outside and the parked cars.

"They rented separate rooms." Manfredo explained. "I guess there were some things they did not want to share."

"Well at least Sadie drew the line somewhere." Jethro remarked as he stopped and studied a certain photo taken at the dinner table.

The scene depicted Sadie leaning somewhat forward with head and shoulders over the table while her arms remained underneath. Her face looked as though in deep concentration. Jethro could not help but wonder what actions her hands were performing under the table. Opposite her, leaning against the wall with his head reclining all the way back, was Benny, who, with mouth slightly opened, seemed to be sighing in pleasure, and to Jethro, appeared as though reaching a climax.

"What the hell is this?" Jethro demanded.

"Oh, that's your wife giving Benny a foot massage under the table during dinner."

"A *foot massage?*"

"Yeah." Manfredo explained. "I guess they were tired from all that hiking during the day. Benny's feet must have ached."

Jethro looked at Manfredo in disbelief.

"You're wife sure is a sweetheart." Manfredo went on. "She invited Benny to put his foot on her lap. Benny obeyed, and she just rubbed away on those bony feet of his. I'm sure it felt good—just look at his face."

Jethro stared at the photo. *She never gave me any foot massages.*

"Yeah," Manfredo went on. "She made him feel a *whole* lot better. Right there at the table; I'm not kidding. Just look at the photo. I thought the guy was going to blow his wad. He was moaning like she was rubbing a different part of him—if you know what I mean. I almost told them to spare everyone else at the dinner table and just go to the room already."

"You didn't get any photos of them actually *doing it*, did you?" Jethro turned his gaze at the P.I.

"No, I couldn't," Manferdo explained. "They went into the room, closed the door and drew the curtain. There was no way for me to get a camera in there. But don't worry, I heard some things, and saw some things, and, with these photos, it all adds up Jethro. A judge or a jury will never believe that they were there as buddy pals."

"What sort of things did you see and hear?"

"Well, for example, take after dinner. There's nothing to do but sit around on the porch," Manfredo continued. "And that's what they did. They sat outside, drank a few beers, had a few laughs, and then they turned in to watch TV."

"La Casita has TVs in the rooms?" asked an incredulous Jethro.

"Yeah. The rooms have TVs over there, unlike this shithole you're in." Manfredo smirked.

"Yeah, well good for them," Jethro responded. "So what did they do, did they watch TV all night?"

"Yeah, you *wish*. I mean, the TV was on—you could see the light it makes through the closed curtains, and you could hear it. They *had* it on. But then I also heard a certain creaky-cranky noise with a rhythm to it that the bedsprings made," Manfredo deadpanned. "And Jethro, I don't think they were jumping on the bed. They *got* it on." Manfredo grinned while Jethro glared at him, not amused. "It adds up, boss."

Jethro looked away from Manfredo as he acknowledged the implications, and then looked again at his private eye.

"And so what happened this morning?" he asked as visions of his wife copulating with that hippie burned in his mind's eye.

"They were up early. Benny came out first to get some morning coffee for Sadie. You saw the photos. She gave him a really nice kiss for that little favor."

"Yeah, so what happened next?"

"Sometime later, they met at the breakfast table," continued Manfredo. "It was a lazy breakfast, you know. They served those pastries they make around here, and coffee. And they just snuggled there. It was *so* romantic. You know, they look happy together, Boss, I hate to say it."

"Well then don't say it, damnit." Jethro spat with disgust.

Manfredo smiled broadly, obviously enjoying seeing Jethro in such a pickle.

Jethro was sick of it.

"Okay, let's get on with it. Here, I'll take these." He said referring to the two firecrackers and a plastic lighter. "We're going to position ourselves to give them a little scare. And remember, they're fast fuses, so when you give me the signal,

I'll light them and throw them without hesitation. Okay? I don't wanna get my hand blown off. And here you'll need this." Jethro reached into the bag and retrieved a large, black automatic pistol.

"What the hell is that?" Manfredo exclaimed. "Hey, I understand you're pissed, but I'm not ready to get into any of this kind of shit, Jethro; this is a foreign country, you know!"

"*Relax*, it's a squirt gun."

"Oh." Manfredo frowned. "Well, it looks real."

"That's the idea." Jethro squirted a jet of water into the mirror and then one at Manfredo who ducked. Jethro next tossed a black ski mask over to Manfredo.

"Here, you'll also need this. I got one for me, too."

"Hey wait a minute, Jethro." Manfredo warned. "They might recognize you, mask or no mask. You could blow this."

"If we get the right opportunity, the firecrackers will scare the hell out of them so bad, they're not going to remember anything but the shock."

"So what do you want me to do? Rob them?" Manfredo asked.

"No, we're not going to rob them. We're just going to make them think you're shooting at them so they can crap in their pants and then we'll get the hell out of there. Now let's move."

They drove in their separate cars to La Casita and parked a distance away. They then sneaked cautiously closer, stopping at a certain spot by a wall alongside the motel where Manfredo had located a good vantage point. They hid behind some four-o-clock bougainvilleas that clung to the side of the wall and a few bushes of purple sage that spread out at its base.

"Is that the sidewalk that leads to the trail?" Jethro asked, gesturing to a path that pointed towards the canyon. "Is that where they'll be coming back through?"

"Yeah; that's where they went, and that's where they'll be coming back from. I'll go up it a ways to watch for them so we can be ready. You wait here."

Jethro crouched behind the purple sage as Manfredo hobbled away.

What seemed like a long ten minutes later, Manfredo came scurrying up the sidewalk as fast as he could.

"Jethro, they're not hiking!"

"What do you mean, not hiking?" Jethro demanded. "You said they had gone for a hike."

"They did, but I guess they cut it short—they're in their room!" Manfredo was breathless with excitement."

"In the *room*?"

"Yeah. After I saw no sign of them, and saw that their car is still here, all packed up and ready to go, I went into the courtyard where the rooms are just to check it out. I guess they wanted one more roll in the hay before leaving. They're in there!"

Jethro stared at Manfredo with incredulity.

CHAPTER 41

THE TRAP IS SPRUNG

Jethro could hear laughter coming from within the motel room. They had left the window open, but had drawn the curtains. He crept up to the window and crouched under it. Listening in, he caught part of their pillow talk.

"...that was great, baby." Benny was heaving. "It's too bad we can't stay longer. I really enjoy our hiking trips."

"Me, too." She cooed. "But we'll come back; you know how easy it is for us to get away."

"Yeah, but it's still dangerous." Benny said with some reservation. "That husband of yours is crazy; he behaves like he's gonna blow up at any minute."

"Oh, don't you worry about him." Sadie answered confidently. "If he tries anything stupid, I'll just call the cops on him again."

"Yeah, and they'll just let him go like they did before." Benny moped. "I just don't want any trouble."

"Oh, stop your whining." She sneared. "He'll be mincemeat by the time I get through with him."

"When are you going to finally divorce him?"

"Soon enough." She seemed impatient. "Why are *you* in such a hurry?"

"I'm just wondering that's all." He answered sounding somewhat aloof. "You sure like the idea of reducing him to nothing don't you?"

"It's not the idea of it, you moron," she spat. "I *like* doing it. Carla's right. You gotta destroy them; they deserve our violence!"

"Are you sure you'll get the house?"

"What?" She snapped. "Do you think I'm gonna let *him* keep it?"

"Come here, baby..." Mmm, mmmm, mmmmmmm

The kissing went on and Jethro could hear the sheets rustling. Moving quickly away from under the window sill, he beckoned Manfredo to join him over by some other bougainvilleas.

"Put on that ski mask, damnit." Jethro commanded angrily as he wriggled his head into his own mask. "When I give you the signal, poke your head through that open window like you're gonna climb in, and point that gun at them. Be sure you open the curtains wide."

"What do you want me to tell them?" Manfredo's adrenaline was beginning to rush.

"Tell 'em to stick 'em up."

"Jethro, nobody robs anybody through *a window*," Manfredo protested in a loud whisper. "This is *ridculous*!"

"I don't give a damn," ordered Jethro. "Just do it."

"What are *you* gonna do?"

"I'm gonna lob one of these firecrackers into the room. They'll think you shot at them."

"Okay, so they'll think I'm a killer. And then?"

"Hell, I don't know! Things will probably happen really fast after that," Jethro clamored. "So I don't know what will happen. Just be ready to haul ass."

Manfredo donned the ski mask, and both of them hustled over to the open window. Beyond the window, inside the room, they could hear Sadie and Benny continuing with their amorous exchange.

Jethro fished the cherry bombs and plastic lighter out of his pocket. Holding one of the tiny TNTs in his right hand, he flicked at the lighter until it produced a flame. Looking at Manfredo, he nodded quickly thus signaling the start of the action, and Manfredo wasted no time in springing into it.

Pushing the window pane wide open, Manfredo grabbed the curtain with his left hand, flung it to the side well out of the way, and, pushing half his body in, pointed the gun at the bedded couple yelling, "Stick 'em up" as he did so.

Simultaneously, Jethro had put the flame to the fuse which fizzled away with startling acceleration. With only a fraction of a second to accomplish his mission, Jethro threw the cherry bomb at the window, but in his excitement, missed the opening and struck Manfredo on the side of the head instead. Glancing off of Manfredo, the firecracker exploded with amazing force not far from where Manfredo held the toy pistol but close enough to his head to make him withdraw violently from the window in reaction. Gaping at Jethro in a quizzical daze, Manfredo reflexively pressed the squirt gun to his ear palm-wise as thought to lend it comfort, and a jet of water shot upwards towards the sky. But this happened in a split second, as in that gap between the recognition of the crash to come and the impact. Jethro barely had time to stare.

In that very same moment, a high pitched scream emitted by Sadie tore through the air, followed by a tumbling commotion in the room and a loud wail issuing from Benny. In almost the same instant, there were two loud bangs at the door as though one of the occupants, or both, were struggling to open it. Jethro readied himself with the lighter and the fuse.

"What are you doing?" Screamed Sadie from inside the room, followed by more commotion. "What *are yooou dooooiiiinggg*?!" She yelled.

The door to the room burst open to reveal Sadie, half-wrapped in a sheet and struggling to robe her body completely with it, meanwhile pushing backwards against Benny, who was behind her, and forcefully pushing Sadie towards the source of the violence which was also the only way out of the courtyard. Thus Benny was using Sadie as a human shield.

"What are you doing? What are *yooou doooiiinnggg?*" Sadie continued screaming in utter panic, as she resisted Benny by pushing backwards, her bare feet slipping on the ground. But Benny was the more determined of the two, and shoved her forward like a bulldozer pushing a mound of dirt towards the sidewalk, the bougainvilleas, the would-be bandits, and the path to the awaiting cars. He had one arm wrapped around the front of her shoulders, just below her neck. As Manfredo and Jethro jumped in their way, Sadie turned as white as the sheet she was wearing, her mouth gaping open in horror. Benny meanwhile, emitted a low pitched, guttural cry, "*Ahhh, ahhhh, ahhhhhh.*" But Jethro was well on the move.

Having brought the second firecracker up for firing, he was already in the act of lighting it as Benny had torn out of the room pushing Sadie in front of him. Putting the flame to the fuse, Jethro threw it as hard as he could toward the couple.

KABOOM! Went the blast and with it Benny hopped high. The one arm that was not holding Sadie had held a towel in front of him, covering his private parts. Now, with the blast, he shed the towel he might have wrapped around himself, and, with a shriek that begged for mercy and a cessation of all hostilities, he shoved Sadie violently forward at the bandits and bounded away like an antelope towards the cars, his exposed buttocks flapping freely in the wind.

Wildly, Benny sprinted for his red SUV and became airborne as he jumped in through the open passenger window. It happened so fast that Jethro, as he scurried out from his protective foliage, almost missed seeing Benny's stockinged feet diving through the window and into the car, and then hustle himself behind the wheel in such a frenzy it was as though he were fighting bees.

He didn't take his socks off?" Jethro marveled but not for long, because Sadie's screams had risen above the chorus of sound.

AMERICAN BITCH

While Manfredo had dashed away in reaction to the explosion of the second grenade, Sadie had recovered from the shove Benny gave her, and was now hurriedly trying to wrap the sheet around her while frantically running away from the source of danger, and chasing after Benny.

"Benneeeeeeeee...." She yelled as she chased after him. Losing her grip on the sheet as she hustled, it trailed behind her, leaving her half-exposed. Apparently confused by her sudden exposure in public, and trying to figure what to do next and where Benny had gone, she scattered back to gather the rest of the sheet, but then doubled back toward Benny who was too busy taking his leave. Instantly, he started the car and took off with car wheels spinning, gravel flying backwards, and giving rise to a dense cloud of dust while quickly disappearing from Jethro's line of sight behind the structure of La Casita.

As she scampered after Benny, a bit of Sadie's backside flashed in broad daylight, or as they say in Old Mexico, *andaba con las nalgas de fuera*. Still in the throes of the imbroglio, she ran after Benny, yelling for him to stop for her, but he didn't, he just kept going, and she got pelted with enough dust and gravel to make her cough, sputter, and choke. The last Jethro saw of Sadie, as he glanced back at the scene, over his shoulder, before tearing away to his getaway car in the distance, she was still tugging at the sheet as she was swallowed by a brown cloud of dust and debris.

"Manfredo, let's get outta here!" Jethro called out to his companion as he was about to make a run for it, but was stopped momentarily by an unplanned development and potential threat: the owner of La Casita, a plump, apron clad woman of elder years with grey hair done up in a bun, popped out of the little motel.

Coming to a sudden stop on the sidewalk as she encountered the two unknown, masked characters before her, she raised her hands to either side of her head and shrieked, "*Bandidos! Policia! Policia!*" Suddenly, a little girl and the tiniest Chihuahua dog

Jethro had ever seen emerged from the motel. While the little girl stood there, as though frozen on the sidewalk, the old woman continued with her yelling, "*Bandidos! Bandidos!*" The chihuahua, taking the motel matron's alarm as its cue, began barking wildly at the two would-be bandits, and appeared poised to attack.

Jethro, wondering whether the village of Bustamante could even have a police force, and being more concerned about the Chihuahua, wasted no time in dashing for his ride. The Chihuahua, sensing fear in its enemy's attempt to flee, attacked on instinct. Running as fast as a little dart, it latched onto Jethro's pants with its tiny, razor-sharp teeth, giving Jethro a sharp scissor-like pinch just behind the right knee.

"Uh!" Jethro shrieked.

Growling and shaking its head viciously from side to side, the Chihuahua was determined not to let go at any price. Jethro, feeling the nip as he dashed, looked down at his leg in disbelief at the diminutive beast growling and swinging from his leg.

Rushing up to his car, he grabbed the door handle, but as he tugged hurriedly on it, his fingers slipped off the latch and he fell backwards onto the ground. Scampering back up, he opened the car door but before climbing in, he pried the growling little beast off his leg. Holding it aloft in one hand while it twisted and squirmed, trying to bite, he managed to get in his car. The Chihuahua kicked and clawed, but Jethro's hold on the glorified rat was firm. Slamming the car door with his right hand while holding the dog aloft with his left, Jethro lowered the one-pound terror down the side of the car door and dropped it onto the ground as he sped away, headed for the border. The last thing he saw, in the rearview mirror, was the tiny chihuahua chasing after his car until it gave up except for its continued barking.

Manfredo had roared out of there at a high rate of speed, not waiting to see who would win between Jethro and the chihuahua. If there were any cops in Bustamante, Jethro and Manfredo would be long gone before they'd wake up from their *siesta* to try to figure out what happened.

And, everything that happened had happened really *fast* with startling results. Jethro had wanted to scare the pair, but this was far more than he had expected. *How about that*, he thought. *To save his own skin, the groovy hippie used her as a shield and then abandoned her in a foreign country. Hoo-fuckin'-ray!*

Jethro drove the rest of the afternoon in deep contemplation. *I wonder if she saw me,* he worried. *I'll be in big trouble if she did.* His ears would not stop ringing, and he could barely hear out of his left ear which had been closest to the second blast. As he drove, he rolled his pants leg up to reveal a small, bloody wound that the chihuahua had inflicted just below his right knee. *Damn that Chihuahua*, he cussed. *I may need a tetanus shot so that I don't get lock-jaw.*

It was not until after nightfall that he crossed the border into Laredo. Wondering whether Manfredo had made it home, he dialed.

"Did you make it ok?"

"Yeah," Manfredo laughed back. "I just got in. I'm here drinking a cold one at *El Poso*."

"Oh yeah? Do they still make those greasy hamburgers over there?"

"You bet, along with those soggy French-fries. I haven't eaten yet."

"Well I just drove in, and I'm starving. I'll see you in a bit."

Jethro opened the swinging doors at the entrance of *El Poso* and recognized Manfredo seated on a stool at the far end of the bar. Manfredo, on seeing Jethro at the entrance, raised his glass towards him, and beckoned him over.

"Well that was fun." Jethro proclaimed as he took a bar stool next to the P.I. and then called out to the bartender. "Hey barkeep, bring us a round, and how about a couple of burgers and fries?"

"I already ordered them, Jethro." Manfredo advised as he took a swig of beer.

"Oh, okay." Jethro took a gulp of beer as the frosty mug arrived. "You know, you make a great bandit."

"Yeah, sure." Manfredo smirked. "An incompetent one. No crook is going to rob any one through a window! That was the most ridiculous thing I've ever done."

"Yeah, but it worked like a charm." Jethro remarked as he took a long guzzle of cold beer. "I still can't believe what happened. I mean, he came out of there using her as a protective shield."

"Yeah, that was pretty damn bad." Manfredo agreed. "I've never seen anything like it."

"Can you imagine?" Jethro went on. "What if we had been real bandits, and you with a real gun willing to shoot them?"

"Well, there would have been a dead Sadie." Manfredo agreed. "Hey, how did you fend off that chihuahua? Man, I saw that thing go after you, and it brought you down!"

Jethro rolled his pants leg up to show Manfredo the battle wound.

"It was a fight to the death," Jethro assured the private eye. "But I prevailed."

Manfredo shook his head in dismay. "You'd better get a tetanus shot or you'll get lock-jaw."

"Yeah," muttered Jetrho. "I guess."

Just then, the hamburgers arrived, and they dug in.

"You know, Jethro," Manfredo muffled with a mouthful of cheese burger said, "as your wife was running after Benny, I got a good look at her ass, and I've got to tell you, she has a mighty fine ass."

"Yes, she does." Jethro agreed. "Yes she does indeed."

As he said this, Jethro stared at his somber reflection in the mirror, there among the bottles of liquor all lined up, behind the bar.

Monday morning after the adventure in Bustamante, Jethro called Sadie's home. Lupita answered and said that Sadie had gone somewhere for the weekend and had not come back. She expected her soon. *We'll see*, thought Jethro, and dialed Manfredo's number.

"What happened to your wife? Did she make it back?"

"She's hardly my wife anymore, Manfredo, but that's what we're gonna find out. She hasn't gotten back yet. I want to know when she gets home, and how. I don't know where her car is parked, but her luggage is in her boyfriend's Bronco. Whenever she does get back, she'll have to go to his house to get her stuff. I need you to stake out his house."

"I'm on my way." Manfredo was working overtime on this one, but clearly enjoying himself.

There was nothing more Jethro could do, so he sat there staring out his office window until it was almost time to go home. At last the phone rang.

"Well, you're lucky," Manfredo exclaimed, "I did a drive-by on Benny's house on Lover's Lane. Just as I got there, it looks like your wife had just gotten there, too. The back of her Suburban was open, and she was loading her luggage in it. That Benny dude was standing there, and your wife was yelling at him."

"I know what that's like."

"Yeah, it looked to me like they were fighting, only your wife was doing all the fighting and Benny was just standing there shaking his head, like with a nervous twitch or something. I drove by and overhead your wife calling him a fucking coward, and she was ranting about having to come home on a raunchy bus full of Indians with chickens and a goat, and how the old woman at La Casita had to buy her the bus ticket. Man, she was *really* pissed!"

"Thanks, Manfredo." Jethro enjoyed a laugh.

CHAPTER 43

A BLUE MOON IN MARCH

Mid-March rolled around, and Jethro's contact with Sadie had by then been reduced to no contact. Sadie did not look for Jethro, and Jethro did not look for her. In spite of everything, Jethro still felt sadness. He missed his wife; or rather, the idea of her as he had known her persisted in his mind, and that was who he missed. *That* Sadie, however, Jethro knew, was long gone. Only a ghost remained, living in that same body of hers, wearing that same face and living now only in Jethro's memory. *Did I really mean so little to her?* He continued to ask himself. *And was our marriage really something she despised so much as to purposely destroy it as she did?* In this regard, Jethro was at a complete loss. Whatever the cause—whether it was gross irresponsibility, a genuine hatred for him, a latent psychosis now realized, or merely a wild fling—the end result was the same: Jethro would soon be joining the multitudes of divorced people. At any rate, marriage was a definite no-no when married to an American bitch. Jethro thought of that moment in the elevator with Araceli, with the old couple standing between them...

It was time to get on with it.

Sadie had already visited with lawyers, or rather was seemingly trying to.

"I'm still talking to the legal assistant," she told Jethro. "They're screening the case." Jethro had not told her about his conversation with Porter. He understood Sadie's "screening the case" business to mean that Sadie was bluffing, and probably because she really did not want to risk having her recent activities scrutinized. Or maybe she was unsure of herself and really didn't know where she was going. Maybe her fling with Benedict the Coward was over—brought to a sudden end by a cherry bomb. *Whatever*, he thought.

Jethro, on the other hand, had already prepared a petition for divorce, which he would soon be filing, even at the expense of ignoring the old saw that a lawyer who represents himself had a fool for a client. Indeed, this was an operation Jethro had to perform for himself, fool heartedly or otherwise. He had prepared the petition according to form. But he worked hard to custom build the final order and decree. These he believed he would get Sadie to sign without a fight, especially since most of the property, including the house, all went to her. Jethro was not about to linger on any longer than he had to, and certainly not for the sake of furniture or things. The documents, however, included as much verbiage as possible, containing as much boilerplate language as he could muster so as to make the docs thick and laborious to read. Embedded deep within them, but spelled out in capital letters and highlighted in bold, Jethro included a clause stipulating that any indebtedness attendant to any asset followed the asset, and inured to the obligation of the recipient. Recitals followed making it clear that the parties fully understood the ramifications of the petition in its entirety, including the debt-follows-the-asset clause, and that they had been advised by independent legal counsel.

Jethro also considered the role that the photos Manfredo had taken might play if matters were contested. He thought, however, that a reference to them might work well to settle matters way beforehand. He doubted Sadie would want them publically aired.

He called Sadie and stated flatly, "Sadie, I've prepared the petition. Things will go much easier if you cooperate. If you choose not to cooperate, I'm going through with it anyway."

"Really?" questioned a rather subdued Sadie. "Why have you come around to this now?"

"It was a lot of things, but mainly it was your betrayal of me."

"*Betrayal* of you?" Sadie asked with feigned surprise. "Are you sure that that's what happened?"

"Yes, I'm sure."

"Really?" Sadie took on an exaggerated mocking tone. "Can you prove it?"

"Yes, as a matter of fact, I can."

"How? How can you?"

"You'll just have to wait and see; but I wouldn't push it if I were you."

Sadie seemed eager to know what Jethro knew. Much to Jethro's awareness, however, she denied nothing nor made any protestations of innocence. *A tacit admission*, he thought, but he didn't care as he used to.

Considering that the happenings in Bustamante and the delivery of the petition might have a cumulative effect, he decided that a face-to-face might be revealing. He called her, and she agreed to a visit. Arriving at her house, he knocked on the door.

"Come in." She called from inside. Jethro had expected that she would open the door as usual. But she hadn't. Wondering what he would encounter once inside, he turned the knob and pushed the door open.

He found Sadie with a dazed look, as though she had just woken up from a deep sleep and, not yet fully awake, did not recognize her immediate surroundings. Jethro handed her the papers which she held in her hands as though she were about to let them fall to the ground. She then sleepwalked over to a green chair that stood by a glass door leading to the veranda — a chair Jethro had never seen anyone sit in for as long as they had lived in that house. Conducting herself as though she were displaying proper manners at a society luncheon, she perched herself on the edge of the chair, her back upright in perfect posture, and with her feet and knees held appropriately together. With the awful papers now resting on her lap like a cup of tea on a saucer, she became increasingly docile and remained still, as though the papers might spill over for failure of rectitude.

Jethro scrutinized her. He was puzzled by her behavior, which appeared contrived. Just then, however, her posture melted from one of stiffness with excellent form to that of a sagging figure, now tired and worn. Slowly she lowered her head and began weeping in earnest, complaining, mid-sobs, about her present circumstances which, ironically, were the very circumstances she had fought for so viciously only two months before. How proud and haughty she had been. Now she looked like she was undergoing instantaneous withering, like a cursed fig tree.

Jethro felt a tinge of pity for her while she cried for what seemed a long while, never rising from the chair. She remained planted with feet held together, lips pressed white and arms sometimes crossed, the papers balanced on her lap. At last, she pushed her shoulders upwards, as though bracing herself for a blow — but not from Jethro. Instead, she seemed beaten by circumstance. What tug of war her emotions played inside of her Jethro could only guess at, given the clues of her demeanor; but soon she dispelled any speculation by giving utterance to the stuff of her turmoil.

"I want to be the petitioner in the pleadings instead of you." She demanded amid her sobs. "I want you to be the defendant."

Jethro would have none of it, saying, as he made for the door, "I hoped we could do this amicably, Sadie; a deputy will be coming by to serve you formally with the papers." He then walked calmly out of his former dwelling.

It was now the end of March and a blue moon sailed the night sky. A full eighty years had passed since the last blue moon. This one, though, was special to Jethro for reasons having nothing to do with any celestial event, for it was on this blue moon that he filed an original petition for divorce.

CHAPTER 44

MID-APRIL

Jethro drove to his former home on his way to gather some of his book collection. Expecting him, Sadie opened the door and stepped aside to allow him entrance. He thought she looked tired, haggard, and old—deflated somehow. Her condition did not stop her from going on at Jethro, however.

"You really are pathetic. You're terrible. I don't know how I lasted so many years with you; years of misery and torture. Everything that has happened is your fault. I never had anything to do with Benny, *never*; it was all in your head."

Jethro, with Bustamante on his mind, responded not at all as he gathered books and transported them to the trunk of his car. He could not resist looking at her, though—not to have any communication with her, but to gaze at her condition. The area around her eyes looked baggy and dark, her skin pallid and pasty. That fish eye looked like it was made out of glass. And she didn't look too happy at Jethro's taking the books, almost as though the consequences were sinking in.

"I have no regrets about anything," she went on, "and I am happy with my life. I am the source of my own happiness, and the source of my unhappiness was you. Now that you're gone, my life is great, and I love my new life."

"Good for you," responded Jethro dryly. "For once we're on the same page."

"No we're not," retorted she. "Your life is pathetic, and you're completely wrong about what you think happened. And for your information, you're not walking out of this so easily. I've been talking to Porter Swinefellow, and he agrees that you have been totally in the wrong and completely unfair. He promised me that he is going to get to the bottom of what you owe me, and he's going to get every nickel out of you that we can."

Jethro stopped and calmly turned to her. The words she had just spoken would have mortified him only weeks before, and not because of any guilty conscience or fear of being found out, but only because he was afraid of the prospect of divorce. Now those same words rang hollow, nothing more than a mere grasping at straws.

"Sadie, let's just get on with the divorce as painlessly as possible, shall we?" he said. "Don't push me because I will expose you."

"*Expose* me? You don't know anything, and you can't prove anything, and you are nothing; you're a nobody. What? What can you prove? What do you know?"

Jethro gazed at her. On her face was that cold sneer again; that arrogance with which she flaunted her pursuit of freedom. Thus she stood mockingly before him; her arms crossed in front of her chest.

"Well?" she insisted. "You're a stupid man, Jethro, and you don't know anything."

"Really," responded Jethro evenly. "Okay, let's do it your way. For starters, how about a nice foot massage under the table at *La Casita*?"

Her eyes, like Jiffy Pop on a hot stove, widened to the size of silver dollars, glazing over as her mind raced to the referenced scene, searching in vain for who had also been present that would allow Jethro to make such a pointed, knowing statement. Thus caught between surprise and puzzlement, Sadie began to stammer.

"Look, Jethro ... I ... uh ... I don't want to fight with you; I...I...I want to do this on a friendly basis. I won't cause you any trouble if you don't make trouble for me ..."

Jethro walked away, saying as he did so, "I'll be sending some papers over; you'll need to sign them."

He got in his car and drove away. Sadie remained at the gate, frozen like a pillar of salt, watching him until he was gone from sight. Only time would tell how effectively Sadie would climb out of the emotional ditch into which she had blundered. By then, however, Jethro would not be looking.

He picked up a phone and placed a call to Puebla, Mexico.

CHAPTER 45
FIN

Jethro met with Sadie for the second time in the past couple of weeks to finalize the terms of the divorce. In spite of all the acrimony, both wanted to conclude the matter with minimal problems or delays. Sadie, in particular, seemed in a hurry to be done with it. She didn't want to spend any more time on particulars than she had to. Jethro suspected this. He was well acquainted with her hasty tendencies, especially when it came to signing documents. He offered to explain their meaning, but she only wanted to know who kept the house.

"You're keeping the house, Sadie, and everything in it, and everything that goes with it."

"I really believe we can be good friends, Jethro. You see, I'm already there. I think we can get together periodically, maybe once a week…well, let's just say periodically, and, I don't know, we can have dinner, and we can have discussions, and, you know, just hang out."

Jethro said nothing to such overtures, which made him feel nothing but contempt for her. He thought it preposterous to suggest that they be chummy after all that had happened. Contemptuous feelings aside, words simply failed him. But then she changed subjects.

"Jethro, I think that as part of the settlement, I need a new car. Mine is already a couple of years old, and I think it would be a good idea to trade it in and buy a new one. I think that would be fair."

Of course, Sadie expected Jethro to pay for it. Jethro again said nothing and just gazed at her instead. How he detested her, now. The look Jethro gave her did its work: Sadie did not mention her desire for a new car again. Quickly she signed the papers.

Jethro nodded. Sadie would not realize until some time later that along with the house went the bills—taxes and the mortgage—bills she could not afford to pay. No, in the end, she would not be keeping the house. It would surely go to foreclosure. But that would be many months hence. For now, Sadie thought she had gotten the better end of the deal and was smiling in triumph.

She had agreed to both the final decree and the final order. There would be no contest; no protracted hearings; no public spectacle; and no antics from Porter Swinefellow for Jethro to contend with. Only Jethro would appear to swear to the contents of the pleadings and otherwise "prove up" the final decree.

It was a morning in May. Jethro knew the judge well, having appeared before him on many occasions, and the matter was conducted in the judge's chambers, away from the general public, with the court reporter present, however, in order to make a record. The judge swore Jethro in at about 10:40. He took Jethro through a line of questions that established on record the divorce and it requirements, and by 10:43 it was all over. The judge signed the decree, and Jethro turned to stroll out of the courtroom a bachelor.

"I hope you enjoy your single status," the Judge said as a parting remark. "But I understand it gets old."

Jethro stopped at the door.

"It won't get old," he responded. "It's a new beginning for me. I'm free now."

"Freedom means being able to be with your family and to watch your children grow," answered the judge.

"Yeah, right." Jethro nodded politely, realizing that with Sadie he had lost out: he had had the benefit of neither.

He then left the judge's chambers.

Outside he was met with a bright, sunny day. To his surprise, Sadie was standing by the courthouse entrance. She must have wanted to see him for one last time. Standing next to her were Carla and Shirley—for moral support, Jethro supposed. He waved to them as though dismissing them, and then turned away to look opposite them, toward the beautiful woman who now strolled toward him: Araceli. Jethro had been in almost daily contact with her after he filed the divorce. She had just flown in from Puebla the day before. Araceli walked up to him and embraced him. Jethro welcomed her warmth. He gazed joyfully into her honey-brown eyes as he had before. The world was now theirs.

"Let's be free together, Araceli."

As Araceli wrapped her right arm into Jethro's left, Jethro moved his arm around her slender waist and glanced back at the small tribe of rebels poised at the entrance to the courthouse. Sadie was wearing her mouth full of vinegar look. Carla and Shirley appeared in danger of having a fly buzz into their mouths, for both of them stood there with their mouths gaping in shock.

Bye bye, bitches, thought Jethro with a surge of elation. He squeezed Araceli and did a little salsa step, which she matched in perfect time.

FIN

CPSIA information can be obtained
at www.ICGtesting.com
Printed in the USA
FSOW01n0237061215
14024FS